POLAR NIGHT

By

Julie A. Flanders

Ink Smith Publishing
www.ink-smith.com

Polar Night

INK SMITH PUBLISHING
P.O BOX 1086
GLENDORA CA
WWW.INK-SMITH.COM

Julie A. Flanders

Dedicated with love to my father, Urban Flanders, who was a poet and a master storyteller.

PROLOGUE

He loved the cold.

Raw, icy, bone chilling cold. It reminded him of home. Of January. Of her.

Most couldn't tolerate the harsh Alaskan winters. But he wasn't like most. He didn't fear the cold. He embraced it.

He stared out at the barren white landscape in front of him, and brushed a strand of straight blond hair from his forehead. He shook the snowflakes from his long, gloved fingers, and put his hands back into the pockets of his black coat.

He loved the cold, yes, but he loved the night even more. His first winter in Alaska had convinced him to make the state his American home. He knew he had found the right place.

He lived for the night. And it was coming.

It was almost December, and the darkness was coming.

When it came, she would be his again. He felt a rush of anticipation as he turned to go back inside.

The darkness was almost here.

CHAPTER 1

ONE MONTH LATER

Danny Fitzpatrick rolled over in his bed and stared at the ceiling. He glanced towards his window and winced at the sunlight filtering through the blinds. Sunlight? What time was it, anyway?

Danny put a pillow over his face to block the sun, as his head was pounding too much for his eyes to handle the light. He tried to remember what day it was. December 22nd? 23rd? If the sun was up, it had to be close to noon. Which meant he was already very late for work.

"Too much to drink last night, Danny?"

Startled, Danny jumped and tossed the pillow aside at the sound of her voice. Caroline. He turned towards her, in spite of the fact that he knew she wasn't really there. She never would be again. One of these days, he'd drink enough alcohol to get that through his thick skull.

He sighed and heaved himself to a sitting position, tossing his legs over the side of the bed. The clock on his bedside table flashed 2:00. Had the power gone out over night? He couldn't remember if the electricity had been on when he'd stumbled into his apartment last night after helping to close down Abe's

Bar. Or was it the Blue Moose he had visited? Either way, it wouldn't be a surprise if his electricity had been out when he had finally managed to find his way home. The slightest wind seemed to knock his lights out on a regular basis.

Danny picked his cell up from the table, and checked the time. 12:30. So he was even later than he thought. He forced himself to his feet and walked to his kitchen, where he started a pot of coffee brewing and downed four extra-strength Excedrin capsules. Then, he headed for the bathroom and the hottest shower he could stand.

Five minutes later, he stepped out of the shower and toweled himself dry. Dropping the towel on the floor, he checked out his reflection in the mirror above his sink. He had dark circles under his hooded brown eyes, and he definitely needed a shave, but otherwise, he didn't look too bad for a 40 year old guy. His face was long and narrow and his pale skin reflected his Irish heritage, but, except for the fact that his nose was too thin and too pointed, he didn't have much to complain about when it came to his appearance.

He picked up the towel and rubbed it through his thick chestnut colored hair. His mother had always said his hair was the color of a thoroughbred. But Danny was sure no horse had ever had hair as unmanageable as his. No matter how hard he tried to plaster the hair to his head, it seemed strands of it were always sticking out at odd angles. He tossed the towel on the sink, and ran his hands through his hair, causing it to stick out even more, as he walked back to his bedroom. He didn't feel like taking the time to shave.

Danny stepped into his closet, hoping he had something clean to wear. He was in luck, as he found a pair of khaki pants and a white oxford shirt he had just picked up from the dry cleaner. He grabbed a blue pullover sweater from the top shelf of his closet, walked to his dresser to get some underwear and warm socks, and quickly got dressed.

As he walked to his living room, he tried to think of an excuse to tell the captain to explain why he wasn't reporting to work until after noon. He'd come up with some bullshit about a lead he was following up on this morning. But he knew it really didn't matter. No one cared what he was doing, as long as they could say he was working diligently on cold cases.

He poured himself a mug of coffee and looked in his cabinets for something to eat. He had a choice of strawberry Pop-Tarts, or blueberry Pop-Tarts. He chose blueberry, ate two cold, and finished his coffee. Pouring the rest of the pot in his thermos, he headed for the front door. Of course, he needed his parka, gloves, and head scarf before he ever set foot outside. It was December in Fairbanks after all, and the temperature was a frigid -2.

Before he could get into his silver Subaru Legacy, he had to unplug it from the socket on the outside wall of his apartment building. Unplugging a car was something he was still getting used to, but he had quickly learned that if he wanted his car to start during an Alaskan winter, he needed an engine block heater installed and plugged in every night. He had also been told that all-wheel drive was an absolute must, something he was already used to from driving in Chicago snow. After reading online that Subaru cars were popular in Alaska, he had quickly made his purchase. So far, the car had not disappointed him.

Except for the fact that he cursed himself every morning for not buying the auto-start feature when he sat with his teeth chattering as he waited for the heater to warm the car enough for him to drive without shivering. Why hadn't he doled out the extra money so he could start the car from inside his apartment? Even better, why had he ever moved here to this god-forsaken place? Chicago wasn't cold enough for him?

After concluding his daily rant to himself, he pulled out of his driveway on Slater Street and away from his apartment building, an unassuming fourplex with a white siding exterior. The landlord, who lived next to Danny's apartment, kept the place clean and the lot and walkway plowed, which was all

Danny cared about. He knew his landlord's name only because he wrote the man a check each month. While he would smile and say hello to his other two neighbors, he had no idea who they were and he liked it that way. He assumed they did too.

Danny passed Slaterville Park and remembered how he had intended to start jogging there or at nearby Griffin Park last summer. The park entrance and sidewalks were covered with snow now, but he'd found the greenery and flower gardens inviting when he'd driven past in the summer. He'd also liked the moose antler arch that marked the entrance to Griffin Park, and kept meaning to check out the rest of it. He'd known a daily walk or jog would have done him good. But he'd never ended up doing either.

Danny turned left on Church Street and made another left onto Illinois, which eventually turned into Cushman Street, the home of the Fairbanks Police Department. As he always did when driving in to work, he noticed the old Catholic Church on his left. Danny had heard that the church was on the National Registry of Historic Sites, and had been around since the founding of Fairbanks. Danny liked the building, but had been amazed last spring when he had driven by and realized the roof of the building was green. He'd assumed the roof was white; not realizing the white color was only because of the constant covering of snow during the long winter.

He crossed the Chena River and continued towards the police station, stopping at a red light at the corner of Second and Cushman. He noticed the marquee sign of the bank on the corner flashing the date and time. December 23rd. Two days away from his first Christmas in Alaska.

When he left Chicago for Fairbanks last February, he'd never expected to still be here at Christmas time. But then, he hadn't expected to be anywhere else, either. He'd tossed his detective's badge on his captain's desk and walked away from his job and his life. What was left of his life, anyway.

Danny had no children, no siblings, and his mother had died several years earlier. He had no idea if his father was also dead, as the last time he'd seen him was when the man left Chicago and moved to Atlanta to start a new family. For the majority of his adult life, Danny's family had been his colleagues in the Chicago police department. His life had revolved around that department and that job, before it had all collapsed around him in a split second filled with ear-piercing screams, unrelenting terror, and gushing blood.

He'd packed a bag and driven to O'Hare without a clear plan in mind. When he'd seen the listing for Fairbanks on the departures screen, he'd remembered that he'd always wanted to see Alaska. And he'd decided that there was no time like the present. It was hard to imagine a better place to get lost in than Alaska. He'd bought a one-way ticket and hadn't looked back.

It was all well and good that he'd wanted to explore the frozen tundra of the north. But he couldn't go too far without an income, something that hadn't really crossed his mind back in Chicago. He realized he didn't know how to be anything but a cop, so he'd put in an application with the Fairbanks Police Department. His big-city detective credentials had gotten him in the door, but his refusal to use his experience in homicide had relegated him to cold cases.

Cold cases had suited Danny just fine. He didn't have anyone breathing down his neck and he didn't have to worry about making prosecutors or politicians happy. He knew no one outside of the victims' families really gave a damn if he solved the cases. All that mattered was that the higher-ups had a warm body they could point to in order to assure grieving families and nosy reporters that no cases were ever forgotten, and one of their best detectives was looking at every possible angle, no matter how old the case. And, Danny couldn't help but feel a connection to the victims whose cases he studied. He saw them as lost souls, something he could relate to all too well. He wanted to solve their cases, in spite of the fact that his efforts were mostly futile.

So here Danny was, ten months later, an official resident of Alaska and of Fairbanks, the Golden Heart City. He'd yet to explore the frozen tundra, but it was still on his to-do list. For now, he'd mostly explored the bars and liquor stores of Fairbanks. He'd been happy to know that Alaska's reputation for high alcohol usage was not unfounded. He'd fit right in.

Danny turned onto 10th Avenue at the blue sign advertising the Fairbanks PD, pulled his car into the police station parking lot, and parked as close to the building as he could. The building was the nondescript taupe color that was so typical of municipal buildings in cities all over the country. Whoever had designed the place had tried to brighten things up with green trim on the windows, but the effects had been negligent, and the only word that came to mind when describing the building was drab. City Hall was right down the road, as was the bright red and glass building that housed the Fairbanks Fire Department.

He braced himself to go back out into the cold. Pulling the hood of his parka tight around his neck, he made a mad dash to the door of the station. He heard Tessa Washington's laughter as he barreled into the front corridor of the office, and pulled the hood of his parka off so that he could actually see her.

At barely 5'2", Tessa was much shorter than Danny's tall and lanky 6' frame, even with her long braids piled high on her head. She had unusually dark brown eyes, and her skin was the color of a mocha latte. Tessa was always impeccably dressed, regardless of the weather. This morning, she wore a navy and cream striped cardigan over a pale blue tailored shirt, with thick cream colored corduroys tucked in to waterproof Caribou boots. She was Danny's closest, or really only, friend on the force.

"You're not used to this cold yet, Danny?"

"How the hell would I be used to it? This is my first winter here, remember?"

11

"I just thought a Chicago boy wouldn't be such a wimp."

"And I thought a military lady would have better manners."

Tessa laughed and helped Danny out of the arms of his coat. She had been in the military police at nearby Eielsen Air Force Base, and had decided to stay on in Fairbanks once her military duty had ended. Like Danny, detective work was all she knew. Also like Danny, she was a loner. As she put it, walking in on her husband screwing her best friend while all were stationed on the same base had killed any interest she had in being social. She was very happy living alone in Fairbanks with her "baby," a gigantic Siberian Husky named Maya, after Tessa's favorite author, Maya Angelou.

"So are you just reporting for work now?" Tessa asked, as the two walked towards their cubicles in the far corner of the office. Tessa's was decorated with tinsel, a red bow, and a Merry Christmas banner. Danny's stood bare.

"Yeah. Kind of a late night last night," Danny said.

"A drunken night, you mean."

Danny shrugged. "You could say that."

He glanced towards Captain Meyer's office. "Is he looking for me?"

Tessa shook her head. "No. He's been in meetings all morning."

Danny nodded and sat down in his chair. "Good."

He looked at the bulletin board above Tessa's desk, and noticed a picture of a pretty blond woman in the center of the board. "Your latest case?" he asked.

"Yeah."

"Homicide?"

"No. Not yet, anyway. Missing persons."

Danny leaned back in his chair and put his feet on his desk. "How long has she been missing?"

"Two days now. That's why I got it."

"So what's the story?"

"She's a 28 year old Fairbanks resident, and was last seen on the morning of the 21st when she left her boyfriend's apartment and said she was going shopping. She can be seen on the security camera outside the store where her car was found, so she did go shopping. But she never showed up for her job that night, and nobody's seen her since."

"What was the job?"

"She was supposed to be taking Santa photos at the winter solstice celebration down at the Golden Heart Plaza. You know, the 21 Days of Solstice event?"

Danny nodded. "Yeah, I saw that advertised."

"Ms. Treibel's a freelance photographer and worked the event last year too. She had this year's celebration scheduled months ago. "

"So there were a lot of little kiddies who couldn't get their picture taken on Santa's lap?"

"Yeah. I guess it was a PR fiasco because the photos had been advertised all over the city, and they didn't have another photographer lined up."

"Safe to say missing this job was a big deal then."

"A very big deal. And apparently, Ms. Triebel here has always been very reliable."

Danny stared at the photograph of the missing woman. It had been taken outdoors, and her cheeks had the rosy glow that came with a chilly day. She had a cheerful smile and her straight blond hair fell to a clean line along her shoulders. Her face was angular, with high, prominent cheekbones and an aquiline nose. She was pretty, Danny thought, and he couldn't help but think there was something familiar about her.

"Ms. Triebel. What's her first name?"

"Maria."

"You got any suspects?"

"Not yet. Except the obvious, the boyfriend. I just got the case this morning though, so I haven't had much time to go over it."

Danny nodded and turned his attention to the stack of folders on his desk. "Let me know if you need any help with it. I know Barkowitz is on vacation this week."

"Yeah. Must be nice to have seniority."

Danny laughed. "You don't expect sympathy from me, do you? You know you're way more than one up on me. I'll be the low man on this totem pole forever."

"You will be if you keep sleeping in until noon."

"Don't you worry about my sleeping habits. You need to concentrate on finding Ms. Triebel."

Tessa stared at the photograph. "What do you think are the odds she's still alive?"

"Not great. But then, you never know. She might have wanted to disappear."

"No better place to do that than here."

"Those were my thoughts exactly when I came to your fair state."

"Yeah, but I'm sure you told folks back in Chicago where you were going."

Danny shook his head. "Tessa, sweetheart, I didn't have anyone to tell."

"That's a sad story."

"You don't know the half of it."

"You'll have to tell me over a few beers sometime. I know getting you drunk is the only way I'll ever get you to talk."

"It'd take a hell of a lot more than a few beers."

"A keg, then."

"That's more like it."

Tessa laughed and reached for her coat from the back of her chair. "Alright, I better leave you to your work, and get back to mine. I need to go pay a visit to

Ms. Triebel's boyfriend. A Mr. Nate Clancy."

"An Irish guy like me," Danny said.

"I guess so."

"With the name Clancy, I know so. I should go with you. See if he's from the old country. We could swap stories."

"You are so full of shit. I bet you've never set foot in Ireland."

Danny laughed. "True. But parts of Chicago are close enough, trust me."

"I can believe that. Your part anyway. A bunch of drunk Irish fools."

Danny chuckled again. "Didn't you say you were gonna let me get back to my work?"

"Yeah, I did." Tessa walked towards the front door. "See you later."

Danny turned back to his desk and started to page through the records of the case he had been going through the day before, but his eyes were drawn back to the photo of Maria Triebel. It was hard to imagine the pretty, smiling woman in the photograph choosing to disappear. But then, there was a time when those he knew would have said the same about him.

"Are you still with us, Ms. Triebel?" he whispered.

He stared at the photo, wondering why Maria Triebel seemed somehow familiar to him. Had he known someone who looked like her back in Chicago? He didn't think so. Suddenly, his mind flashed to a case he had looked at a few days before.

He booted up his computer, and impatiently brought up his files. He had been working on a case that had just passed its three year anniversary. The victim's family had refused to give up no matter how many years went by, and had been in touch with the department on a fairly regular basis.

Danny clicked on the name of Anna Alexander. A blond, smiling young woman who had disappeared from the campus of the University of Alaska, Fairbanks, three years ago this week.

It was clear now why Maria Triebel had struck a chord with him. She and Anna didn't look exactly alike, but there were enough similarities that it would have been easy to mistake them for sisters. Or at least cousins. He felt the hair on the back of his neck rise up and a prickle of energy he hadn't felt in nearly a year. His gut told him there was a connection between these two women. He could feel it.

Danny scrolled through the details of Anna Alexander's case. She had last been seen on December 21, 2009. The winter solstice. He heard Tessa's voice in his mind. "She was supposed to be taking Santa photos at the winter solstice celebration…"

Danny's energy went from a prickle to a straight out deluge.

CHAPTER 2

Maria Triebel rested her head against the chilly dirt wall behind her and hugged her knees to her chest in a futile attempt to stop trembling. She took slow, deep breaths in order to keep from hyperventilating, and forced herself to quit crying. She needed to think, and using all her energy crying wasn't going to help anything. Unfortunately, she had no idea what was going to help.

The place she was sitting in was so dark she was unable to see her own hands when she held them up to her face. She had felt around on the floor and walls around her, but had found nothing but hard, cold dirt. She had no idea how long she'd been here, or, for that matter, where "here" was. She remembered leaving the clothing store and heading towards her car, and bumping into a tall blond man as she turned into her row in the lot. He seemed familiar, and he had leaned towards her as if he wanted to ask a question, and then everything had gone dark.

The next thing she remembered was opening her eyes in this pitch black, deathly silent room. She had filled the silence with her screams until her throat was raw and too parched to scream further. No one had come to her aid.

Now, she tried to think logically. Even if she couldn't remember it, someone had put her in this place. So if there was a way in, there had to be a way out. She needed to stand up and find it. Even if she couldn't see, she could feel.

She stood up slowly, never lifting her back from the wall. She turned around, and put a shaking hand against the hard dirt. She'd just take it a step at a time, feeling the wall until she found the door. It had to be there.

She took two steps, and screamed when she heard a door open across the room. She turned towards the sound, still unable to see, and froze. She wanted to keep absolutely still, but her chattering teeth and trembling body betrayed her.

A light in the form of a lantern came into the room, and Maria could see it was held by the long fingers of an unusually tall man. A blond man. The man from the parking lot.

Maria screamed again.

He walked down stairs so steep they were more like a ladder and entered the room, carrying the lantern with him. He set the lantern down on the floor, illuminating the room, and leaned against the dirt wall opposite Maria. He put his hands in his pockets.

"You don't have to be afraid of me," he said.

Maria opened her mouth to respond, but found herself unable to speak.

"I want you to enjoy your time here."

Maria stared at him, incredulous at the sincerity in his voice. Her fear started to be replaced by anger.

"Who the hell are you?" she said, her voice raspy and weak. "I saw you in the parking lot…"

"That's right."

"What do you want with me? Where am I?"

"In a root cellar next to my home. And you're my guest for the next few months."

"The next few months? Are you fucking nuts?"

A disapproving scowl crossed the man's face. "I don't allow that kind of language in my home. I expect my guests to have manners."

"I'm not your guest, asshole. Fuck you."

Before Maria had time to think, the man was across the room and his hand was around Maria's neck. Her eyes widened as his face came within a centimeter of her own.

"I said, I don't allow that language in my home," he said, spitting out the words. "Do you understand?"

Maria nodded.

"Answer me!"

"Yes," Maria whispered. "I understand."

The man relaxed his grip, and seemed to almost fly back to the other side of the cellar. He was seated next to the lantern again before Maria could put her own hand to her now aching throat. She slid down the dirt, which felt as hard as stone, and sat back down on the cold floor.

He bent his knee and leaned back against the wall. For the first time, Maria noticed his feet were bare. He seemed oblivious to the cold temperature.

"Now that we have that out of the way," he said, his voice once again calm, "we can go back to discussing your stay here with me." He seemed to notice Maria's trembling for the first time. "Are you cold?"

She started to nod, then remembered his rage. "Yes," she said.

"Fine," he said. "I have warm clothes for you in my house. I imagine you must be hungry as well."

Maria was sure she'd vomit if she tried to eat. But her throat ached. "I'm thirsty," she said.

"Of course. I'll bring you some water. Do you like coffee?"

For the first time, Maria noticed his accent. It was slight, but sounded Eastern European. Or maybe Russian? "I do, yes," she said.

"Very well, then. We just need to finish discussing your stay, then I'll get you what you need."

"How about you tell me who you are?" Maria asked.

"I'm Aleksei."

"What do you want with me?"

"You'll find out soon enough. First, I have some ground rules for you."

"Ground rules?"

"Yes. For one, your name."

"What about my name?"

"I know you consider your name to be Maria Triebel. You live in Fairbanks and you work as a photographer. Your boyfriend is Nate Clancy."

Maria stared at him, her eyes again widening.

"But from now on, Maria Triebel no longer exists."

"What?"

"You heard me. You're not Maria Triebel. Your name is Natasha Koslova."

"I don't understand."

"I think I'm making myself very clear. There's nothing for you to understand, Natasha."

Maria shook her head and clenched her fists, trying her best to keep her voice calm. "Listen, I don't know who this Natasha is, but I'm not..."

"No, buts, Natasha."

"Stop calling me Natasha! What the hell is wrong with you?"

A cloud passed over Aleksei's face, leaving behind a scowl. "Do I need to remind you about your language?"

Maria swallowed hard. She could still feel his hands on her neck. "No. Sorry. Why are you calling me Natasha?"

"Because that's who you are. While you're here with me, anyway. I'll make everything perfect for you."

"Perfect? You kidnap me and bring me God knows where, lock me up in this pitch black cellar... That's perfect?"

"No, not yet. But it will be perfect for Natasha."

"So that's the deal? I pretend my name is Natasha and I get out of this…what did you call it?"

"A root cellar."

"What is that? Some kind of basement?"

"It's basically just a large hole in the ground."

"I'm assuming you have some nicer accommodations since you said this is your home."

Aleksei nodded. "Definitely. But they're for Natasha, not for Maria."

"I get it."

"Good. You understand now?"

Maria was silent.

"I bet I can guess what you're thinking," Aleksei said, a smirk creeping into his voice. "You're thinking, how dumb is this guy?"

Maria noticed the smirk, and tried to swallow her fear. "What do you mean? I don't think you're dumb."

"You're thinking, I'll play along, I'll be Natasha, and I'll make myself comfortable up in his house. Then the first chance I get, I'll run out the front door."

"I wasn't thinking that."

"Don't lie to me."

Maria stiffened her shoulders. "What if I was?"

Aleksei stared at her without responding.

"What would stop me from doing exactly what you said?" Maria asked.

"I would stop you."

She glanced down the length of his body looking for weapons, but saw none. "You know I'm not some pushover, right? I'm an athlete. I do cross-country skiing, I run in the summer. I don't know how you knocked me out to get me here, but I can fight you."

"No, you can't."

"You're so sure of that?"

"Completely. You may very well be an athlete. But I can assure you I'm a better one." Aleksei stood up and walked up the steep stairs. "I'll prove it to you."

He opened the door and let it hang open. Seeing nothing but snow outside the door, Maria shuddered. She really was in a hole in the ground.

"What's the trick?" she asked.

"No trick," Aleksei said. "I just intend to show you that you're wasting your time if you're plotting to run away from me."

He walked across the room, positioning himself so that Maria was between him and the wide open door.

"Go ahead," he said. "Give it your best shot."

Maria stared at the door, hesitant. She knew there had to be some kind of catch. But what did she have to lose? She knew how fast she could run. She took a deep breath, and sprinted towards the stairs.

In a whoosh, Aleksei was in front of her, blocking the door and filling it with his tall frame. He grinned. "Want to try again?" he asked.

"How did you..."

Maria couldn't finish, as Aleksei once again had his hands around her neck. He pushed her back across the room and shoved her against the wall with a speed that left her disoriented. She clawed at his hands and tried to break his grip, but it was like grasping a brick wall. He lifted her off the floor, and tossed her to the corner of the room, where her head hit the floor with a thud. She tried to lift herself up with her arms, but found Aleksei standing over her. He put his foot on her back and pushed her to the floor.

"Have I made my point?" he asked.

Maria tried to answer, but was unable to find her voice.

"I'll assume I have," Aleksei said. "I'll leave you here to think about my rules."

Maria knew he was moving back to the door, now walking at a normal speed. She needed to stop him, as she couldn't bear the dark again, but she couldn't make herself react. The glow of the lantern bounced off the walls and circled the room as he picked it up. The light disappeared, and Aleksei closed the door behind him. Maria heard him bolt the locks of the door into place, and was left with nothing but absolute silence.

She tried again to raise herself up. She knew where the stairs were now, she'd go to them and find a way to unlock the door. Her arms failed her once more, and she had a split-second to be grateful for the loss of consciousness as her head hit the hard dirt floor.

CHAPTER 3

Danny drummed his fingers on his steering wheel as he sat waiting at another red light. He glanced at Tessa, who was sitting in his passenger seat.

"Thanks for coming back here with me," he said.

"It's not a problem. Except that Mr. Clancy's gonna think I'm nuts for showing up at his office twice in one day. And I don't think he'll be too thrilled."

"I don't give a shit if he's thrilled or not. I wanna see if he reacts at all to being asked about Anna."

The light turned green and Danny pushed the accelerator a little too hard. He was edgy, and anxious to get to Clancy's office.

"I told you I don't think he's involved with Maria's disappearance. I believed he was telling me the truth."

"Yeah but that was before you knew about my discovery that Anna and Maria are connected."

"You haven't proven that. You know that, right? The fact that they look alike and they disappeared on the same day isn't quite enough."

"It's enough for me. I know they're connected." He turned right on Clancy's street, and began to look for a parking space near the office. "You think the winter solstice is just a coincidence? Come on."

"I'm not saying I'm not intrigued. I wouldn't be here with you if I wasn't.

But it is possible it's a coincidence. You know that as well as I do."

Danny parked the car and turned off the ignition, immediately sorry when the heat turned off along with it. He shivered and pulled his coat tighter around his neck, bracing himself to go back outside.

"What I know is that this is not a coincidence," he said. "You mean to tell me you never had gut feelings in all those years in the military PD?"

Tessa followed Danny up the sidewalk to the offices of Wilson and Clancy, attorneys at law. It was a small firm, with only the two partners, and she could see the receptionist watching her and Danny arrive. She wasn't surprised to see her pick up the phone, no doubt to let Clancy know the police were back.

"Of course I've had gut feelings. You can't arrest someone based on a gut feeling though."

Danny stopped as they got to the front door. "I'm aware of that. I also don't plan on arresting Mr. Clancy. I think you're right that he's not involved. But I just want to make sure."

He opened the door and held it open for Tessa, gesturing for her to walk through. "Ladies first," he said.

Tessa rolled her eyes. "First time I've known you to have manners."

"You bring out the best in me."

Tessa walked to the receptionist's desk and flashed her badge.

"I was here earlier today for Mr. Clancy," she said. "Detective Washington."

"Right, I remember." The receptionist glanced at Danny.

"And I'm Detective Fitzpatrick," he said. "Pleased to meet you."

"We need to speak with Mr. Clancy again," Tessa said. "If you'll let him know, please?"

The receptionist nodded. "Of course."

She picked up the phone again, and relayed the message. Within seconds, Nate Clancy entered the lobby. He was about Danny's height, with a medium build, and black hair peppered with strands of grey. His green eyes stood out on his drawn, pale face. He adjusted his cufflinks as he walked towards Danny and Tessa, his expression a mixture of anxiety and irritation.

"What can I do for you, Detectives?" he said.

"We need to ask you a few more questions," Tessa said. "This is Detective Fitzpatrick."

Danny extended his hand for Clancy to shake. "Sorry for troubling you, Mr. Clancy. Can we talk in your office?"

Clancy scowled, and instructed the receptionist to hold his calls. He gestured for Tessa and Danny to follow him back to his office. As they entered, he shut the door behind them.

"Do you have information on Maria?" he asked. "Some of our friends are planning a vigil for her tonight. I'd love to be able to share some good news with them."

"I'd love that too, but we don't have anything new at the moment," Danny said. "Except for the fact that I'm now involved in the case as well."

"Okay. What can I do for you?" Nate asked again.

"I understand you told Detective Washington earlier that you and Ms. Triebel weren't getting along too well lately."

Nate pulled a chair out from his office table and sat down, motioning for Danny and Tessa to do the same.

"I wouldn't put it that way," he said. "We were just getting close to breaking up."

"You were breaking up, but you wouldn't say you weren't getting along?"

"Not if you mean we were fighting all the time, we weren't. It was more just that we knew this wasn't going anywhere, and we'd been spending less and less time together." Nate ran his hand through his thick dark hair. "Look, I didn't do anything to Maria. I don't know where she is."

Danny smiled. "I didn't say you did, Mr. Clancy. I just want to get to the bottom of this."

"So do I."

"Good. We're on the same page." Danny paused. "You say you and Maria weren't fighting all the time. But you knew your relationship wasn't going anywhere."

"Right."

"Was there anything specific that made you feel that way? Anything strange going on with Maria, or something she did you didn't approve of?"

Nate shook his head. "No, nothing like that. Really we hadn't been spending that much time together since we went on a trip at Thanksgiving. We got on each other's nerves that weekend so since then we've just drifted apart somewhat."

"Where'd you go on this trip?"

"Prudhoe Bay."

Danny raised his eyebrows. "Prudhoe Bay?"

"Yeah. I know it's nuts, but Maria loves all that frozen tundra shit. She wanted to go to Deadhorse and the Arctic Circle. He paused and shook his head. "Look, I grew up in Fairbanks so I don't give a rat's ass about the tourist stuff. But Maria's from California, she didn't come to Alaska until she went to college. She's never gotten all the Wild Alaska bullshit out of her system, and she'd never been to the far north. So we went up there for the weekend and did the tourist crap."

"I take it you didn't enjoy the trip."

"Not really. I froze my ass off and looked at the Arctic Ocean. Went to some supposedly haunted psychiatric hospital and stayed in a crappy hotel. Not my idea of fun. But Maria loved it. She was fairly pissed at me on the way home."

Danny nodded. "Have to say I think I'd be in agreement with you. Sounds like hell to me."

"It was."

"Other than that, you haven't had any squabbles?"

"No, nothing. She stayed at my place the night before she disappeared."

"Right. And she told you about the photography job?"

"Yeah. She was excited about it. She loves the Solstice crap, too."

"Sounds like she's an enthusiastic person."

"She is. She loves just about everything. It doesn't take much to get her excited."

"I'm getting the feeling you're not that way."

Nate laughed. "I'm not, I admit it. At least not in the winter."

Danny leaned back in his chair. "So Maria's an adventurous type. You think she could have just decided to go off on a trip on her own, something that seemed fun to her?"

"No. Not without telling people. And she wouldn't have stood the Solstice people up. I'm telling you, she was thrilled to have that job. Plus, it's Christmas. Maria loves Christmas and she has a party planned for tomorrow night. She wouldn't just walk away from that."

Danny nodded. "I understand. Tell me, have you ever met a woman named Anna Alexander?"

Nate looked puzzled at the change in subject. "Anna Alexander?"

"Yeah. You know her?"

"I don't think so. Should I?"

"There's no should or shouldn't. I'm just asking if you do. Does that name ring any bells for you?"

Nate shook his head. "No. Why?"

Danny watched him, looking for the obvious signs of deception. There was nothing in Nate's body language to suggest he was anything but confused.

"No reason," Danny said. "Just trying to put some puzzle pieces together." Danny sat up straight and put his hands on his knees. "You've been very helpful. I appreciate you taking the time to talk with me when you'd already been so cooperative with Detective Washington."

"I don't have any reason not to be cooperative. I want to find Maria, too."

"I believe you do." Danny stood up and put his card on the table. "You'll call us if you think of anything more that might help?"

Nate stood up and walked Danny and Tessa to the door. "Of course I will."

Danny and Tessa headed for the lobby, zipping up their parkas and putting on their gloves as they walked.

"Will you let me know when you learn anything?" Nate asked. "I'm really worried."

"I know you are, Mr. Clancy," Tessa said. "We hope we'll have good news for you soon."

CHAPTER 4

Danny leaned back in his chair and put his feet up on his desk. He drummed his fingers on the metal surface as he turned the cases of Anna Alexander and Maria Treibel over in his mind. He was certain they were connected, but he hadn't found a damn thing in Anna's case file to tie her to Maria Treibel. And he and Tessa hadn't learned anything that gave them a single clue to Maria's disappearance.

He glanced around the now empty office. He was the only detective who remained, as everyone else was either out on a case, or gone for the Christmas holiday. He had volunteered to cover the Christmas shifts, figuring it was the least he could do. It wasn't like he had anyone to spend the holiday with anyway.

He put his feet back on the floor and ran his hand over the stubble that was well on the way to becoming a beard. He really needed to shave tomorrow. Right now though, he had other things on his mind.

He had already searched every file he could find on Anna Alexander, but he knew he was still missing something. He wanted to go back to the day or week she disappeared. Back to 2009.

Danny loved online newspapers, but there was no question their archives were severely lacking. If he wanted to see all that was going on in Fairbanks in December, 2009, he needed the print copies. He looked up at the clock on the wall. 5:00. There was still time to make it to the library.

A few minutes later, Danny was driving down Cushman Avenue, away from the police department, and towards Cowles Street and the public library. He didn't have to worry about his eyes adjusting to the sun now, as the sun had set more than two hours ago. Fairbanks was lucky to see four hours of daylight in December.

Danny pulled into the library parking lot, unsurprised to find it nearly empty. This was hardly a busy time for the library, as most people were busy preparing for Christmas. And most people weren't digging up ghosts.

Danny walked inside and headed for the reference desk, where he asked the librarian for the Fairbanks Daily News-Miner from December, 2009.

The librarian was a tall and slender woman with wavy golden hair that fell in a curtain to her shoulders. She had fair, almost translucent skin, and large blue eyes. Danny couldn't help but think that her eyes looked as tired as he felt. He noticed a nametag on her berry-colored sweater. Amanda Fiske.

"Did you need specific dates?" Amanda asked.

"I'd like to get the whole month if I can. But I especially want the 21st. Or whatever day was the winter solstice that year. Isn't it always the 21st or 22nd?"

Amanda nodded. "I can get you the whole month, just give me a minute."

"Thanks."

Danny watched as Amanda disappeared into the seemingly limitless back room that all libraries had. He sat down at one of the reading tables near her desk, and picked up a Time magazine someone had left on the table. Browsing through it, he tried to keep his mind from thinking about his own life in December, 2009. He didn't want to remember the warm living room decorated with red and green bows and garlands. He didn't want to remember the smells of cinnamon and chocolate and apple cider. He didn't want to remember the sound of Caroline's laughter as she tripped over the pile of gifts on the floor and almost knocked over their Christmas tree. He didn't want to remember anything at all.

CHAPTER 5

Amanda walked into the newspaper storage room and quickly found the 2009 editions. She pulled out the December papers, noticing her hand shaking as she did so. She stepped back from the shelf of papers, and took a deep breath. She had to calm down.

She told herself that she was probably making something out of nothing. There could be any number of reasons why a police detective would want to go through newspapers from three years earlier. She wished she hadn't even noticed the badge on his belt. If she hadn't, she wouldn't have thought twice about his request. People looked at old newspapers all the time. But she had seen the news coverage about another woman who had gone missing…

Amanda ran her fingers over the cross around her neck and admonished herself. She was acting ridiculous. When was she going to let this go? At some point, she had to put the incident in the past, and leave it there.

She clutched the cross again for good measure, picked up the stack of papers, and carried them out to Danny.

"Here you go," she said as she put the stack on the table Danny now occupied. "It's the whole month of December, but I put the week of the Solstice on top."

"Thanks," Danny said. "I appreciate it. How late are you open?"

"Until 7."

"Great. Gives me plenty of time."

Amanda nodded. "Let me know if you need anything else."

Danny watched as she returned to her desk and couldn't help but think that she seemed nervous and twitchy. Probably just his imagination. Or maybe she had noticed his badge. He knew by now that cops made a lot of people nervous.

He sighed and pushed a clump of hair out of his eyes. Damned if he didn't need a hair cut again. Hadn't he just been to the barber shop? He wondered why some men were so paranoid about going bald. He had enough hair for ten men and it drove him nuts.

Because this wasn't the time to bitch about his hair, he forced himself to focus on the newspapers in front of him. He started with Sunday's paper and skimmed through each day of the week. There were lots of stories about the winter solstice event and listings of holiday closings. In addition, there were several articles about a fight over the display of a Nativity scene outside of the county administration office and Danny was fairly certain he had read about this fight in the current week's news too. Apparently it was ongoing.

He continued through the pages, not finding anything he was looking for. But then, he didn't exactly know what he was looking for. Just...something. He was sure he'd know it when he saw it.

He stopped when he came to an article about the disappearance of a young woman named Anna Alexander. He recognized the photo of the smiling Anna very well. But except for the day of her disappearance, he didn't see anything that connected her to Maria Treibel. As he stared at the photo, he noticed someone standing over his shoulder. Startled, he jumped in his chair.

"Oh, I'm sorry!" Amanda said. "I didn't mean to startle you."

Danny rubbed his eyes. "It's okay. I guess I'm a little jumpy."

"I'm sorry," Amanda said again.

Danny turned to face her. Talk about jumpy. Amanda's eyes darted back and forth, and she had the demeanor of a frightened rabbit. Her hands twitched as she clutched the silver cross on her necklace. Danny resisted the urge to roll his eyes. He didn't have much patience for religious nuts.

"It's really okay," he said again.

"Did you find what you were looking for?"

"Not really. But then I don't actually know what I'm looking for, anyway."

"Can I help?"

Danny shook his head. "No, I need to figure this out on my own. But thank you."

"If you need any other papers…"

Danny stood up from his chair before she could complete her sentence. "No, really, I've looked at everything I wanted to here. I'll get out of your hair. Maybe you can close early and go get ready for Christmas."

Amanda smiled. "I'm afraid I can't do that."

"I guess not. But at least you don't have too much longer to work." Danny smiled. "Have a Merry Christmas."

"Thanks, you too."

Danny nodded and walked towards the exit. "Thanks for your help."

Amanda sat down in the chair he had just vacated, her hand still clutching her cross necklace. She looked down at the papers on the table, and stared at the photo of Anna Alexander smiling up at her.

She hadn't been making something out of nothing. She had been right. Now, she just had to decide what to do.

CHAPTER 6

Maria opened her eyes, groaned, and immediately shut them again. Unfortunately, closed eyes did nothing to stop the throbbing in her head. She wished she could return to unconsciousness.

She waited a few moments, or maybe it was hours. Her sense of time had disappeared along with her freedom. She had no idea how long she had been unconscious, or for that matter, how long it had been since the psychopath upstairs had captured her.

Her muscles tensed at the mere thought of him. Maria wondered what kind of drug he had given her to knock her out, and make her so disoriented she hadn't even been able to put up a fight against him. She had felt frozen in place as he dashed around the room at speeds that couldn't possibly have been real. She began to wonder if her encounter with him had been real at all. Had she been given some kind of hallucinogen?

Maria suddenly realized that something about the room was different than it had been the first time she had woken up on this dirt floor. It wasn't dark.

Ignoring her pounding head, she pushed herself into a sitting position, her arms barely holding her weight. She leaned back against the wall, and forced her eyes to focus. She wasn't imagining the light.

It was clear that the blond man had returned while Maria was unconscious. He had left a lantern on the floor, next to a plate of bread and a glass of water.

Maria's memories of her earlier encounter with him came flooding back. She knew it had been real, and that certainty chilled her to the core.

The lantern in the room now was tiny and its light paled in comparison to the huge lantern the blond had carried with him. The lantern lit only its own small area, causing shadows to dance on the wall behind it. The rest of the room was still pitch dark.

It dawned on Maria that she had no way of knowing what, or who, else was now in the room with her. For all she knew, she wasn't alone.

Maria steadied herself and slid along the wall to the lantern. She picked it up in her shaking hand, and shone the light across the room. She jumped when she saw something there.

Forcing herself to hold the lantern steady, Maria tried to make out what that something was. It looked like a ceramic vase, or a jar. Puzzled, Maria shifted the light closer to the vase. A wave of humiliation washed over her as she realized what the jar was. It was an old-fashioned chamber pot.

She put the lantern down as tears seeped from the corner of her eyes. Just how long did this psycho plan to keep her in this room? She glanced over at the water and bread, wondering if he had put more drugs into either of them. She knew she shouldn't touch anything he provided for her.

But she also knew that she couldn't deny the hunger pangs in her stomach. Or the pain of her parched, aching throat. And, she knew she was probably close to being dehydrated. If she ever wanted to be able to fight this son of a bitch, she had to get some nourishment.

Intent on making sure she didn't spill a drop of the water, she picked up the glass with both hands, and brought it to her cracked lips. She took a sip and immediately cringed at the increased pain in her throat. She wouldn't have believed that the simple act of swallowing could be so painful. The tears returned to her eyes, but she forced herself to take another sip. Eventually, the swallowing got easier.

When she was fairly sure she could manage it, Maria grabbed a slice of the bread. She took a small bite and felt immediate relief when she could swallow it. It was just plain white bread, but it was thick and it had substance. She finished the first piece, took a few more drinks of water, and grabbed the second slice of bread.

Maria took a deep breath when she finished eating and slid down the wall again, away from the water and the lantern. She was dying to finish the glass of water, but because she had no idea when she would get more, she wanted to save some for later. She needed to pace herself.

Ignoring the humiliating chamber pot across the room, she focused her attention on what her next move could be. Obviously, she couldn't do much of anything until the psycho came back. But when he did, she wanted to be ready.

While her head still throbbed and her face ached from the pain of being thrown on the unforgiving dirt floor, she felt more human now that she had been able to drink and eat. She felt more alive. She had every intention of staying that way.

Maria tried to motivate herself by thinking of difficult situations she had faced in the past. But nothing seemed to come to mind. At least, nothing that could possibly compare to this. What had she faced? A difficult course in college? Unemployment? It all seemed remote and silly now that she found herself alone in this dark, cold hole in the ground.

Regardless, this was what she had to face, and she would. She wrapped her arms around her knees and hugged her legs to her chest. Whenever that pyscho outside returned, she told herself, she would be ready for him. She wished she could make herself believe it.

CHAPTER 7

Aleksei lay in the center of his king-sized bed and dreamed of blood. He clutched at the thick black bedspread and recoiled from the sounds of gunfire in the distance. The gunfire came closer now, and was accompanied by screaming.

Men screaming for their mothers, for their wives, for God. Ear-piercing screams of unrelenting agony. He tried to block out the yelling, but it was impossible. The screams were so shrill they echoed through his skull, causing him to cover his ears with his frozen hands and beg for silence.

The hunger was even worse. Pangs of hunger threatened to take over his whole being. And the cold. Icy, bitter cold covered his body and left him shaking from head to toe. He longed for a real coat and gloves that were more than tatters on his fingers.

He couldn't have that, but he had her. She was there, next to him, her hand brushing his blond hair from his forehead. He was sure she was an angel.

Aleksei opened his eyes with a start and sat straight in bed. He cursed at the bedspread crumpled in his hands. He had never intended to rest now. He had work to do.

He got out of bed and quickly re-arranged his bedding and pillows. He hated an unkempt bed. He ran a brush through his hair, and straightened his black sweater and pants. He didn't need a mirror to know that he looked perfect. He always did. Satisfied that his bedroom was back to being presentable, he left the room and headed for his kitchen.

He didn't want to keep his guests waiting.

CHAPTER 8

The alarm blared to signal a new day and Danny reached over to hit the snooze button without opening his eyes. He was glad he had been sober enough last night when he got home to remember to set the alarm, as he couldn't afford another day of not heading into the office until noon. Although he wondered if anyone would notice either way.

He rolled over onto his back and opened his eyes to stare at his white ceiling. The whole apartment was painted in an institutional white shade that could have depressed even the happiest of souls. He had been meaning to hire a painter and brighten the place up a bit, but he'd never gotten around to it. Maybe next year.

He glanced at the calendar he had taped to wall next to his dresser. December 24th. Christmas Eve. He wondered if Maria Treibel was still alive to see the holiday. If she was, he was fairly certain she wasn't doing much celebrating.

And Danny wasn't going to be doing much celebrating either. He took a deep breath and rubbed the sleep out of his eyes, forcing himself to sit up and turn off the alarm clock before it assaulted his ear drums yet again. He needed to get to the office and get back to the Anna Alexander case.

Something about the case had been nagging him since he had been sitting at the bar at Abe's Grill the night before. He hadn't been able to pinpoint it, but something bouncing around the edges of his brain. He just needed to figure out what that something was.

He showered and finally took the time to shave, hoping to ward off being called on his appearance, which was starting to lean more towards homeless man than police detective. He filled his thermos with coffee and chose cherry Pop-tarts for his Christmas Eve breakfast, and bundled up before heading outside into the still dark morning. The sun would not rise for quite a few hours.

Danny drove to the office and headed for his desk as soon as he got inside. He saw Tessa already sitting at hers.

"What time do I have to get in here to beat you?" he asked.

Tessa turned to him and looked him up and down. "I'm glad you finally decided to clean up a little bit," she said. "The beard was a terrible choice for you."

Danny smirked. "Thanks for the fashion advice, I'll keep it in mind."

"Least I can do. You know how I love Tim Gunn."

"How are you at interior decorating?" Danny asked as he slid into his chair. "I need to do something about my apartment. It's depressing as hell."

"I thought that was how you wanted it."

Tessa was the only person in the department who had even been to Danny's apartment. In fact, except for the one-night stands he occasionally found at one of the bars he frequented, she was the only person besides him who had been there, period.

"Maybe I'm starting to change my mind."

"You know I'll help you. I've told you before that place needs a lot of work. It's no wonder you never want to get out of bed."

"I think we both know the alcohol is more to blame for me not wanting to get out of bed."

"Yeah, well, the fact that your home looks like a poorly-maintained prison can't help. Say the word and I'll come over and start working on it with you."

"Alright, maybe after the holidays." Danny booted up his laptop and waited for his programs to load. "So you're stuck here on Christmas Eve?"

Tessa nodded. "I didn't get anywhere yesterday on this Treibel case. Just trying to see if I missed anything."

"Can I help?"

"No thanks. I've gotten to everyone I can think of. Talked to the people at the store where Nate said she was going shopping, the folks running the Solstice event, her friends, called her family in California… I've basically talked to everyone Maria Treibel ever met, and I've got nothing."

"What about the car? Wasn't it found at the store lot?"

"Yeah, with the driver's side door open. The techs are going over it with a fine-tooth comb, but so far there's nothing."

"She just vanished into thin air then, right?"

"Looks like it."

Danny glanced at his laptop and brought up the case file he wanted. "Just like Anna Alexander."

"Yep. You get anything new on that?"

Danny shook his head. "No. It's bugging me the crap out of me though. I feel like I'm missing something but I don't know what it is."

Tessa stood up from her chair and grabbed her coat from the back of it. "Let me know if I can help. I'm heading back to the lot where we found the car so I can canvas the stores again.

"Good luck," Danny said, his eyes fixed on his laptop screen. He scrolled through the files, not finding anything of interest and feeling his frustrating growing, when suddenly his eyes stopped on a name. Amanda Fiske.

That was it. The librarian. He hadn't recognized her name when he read her name tag, but it had been poking at his memory ever since. She was listed as a witness on the case, although she hadn't actually seen anything, according to the files. She had come to the department to offer her services, but the original detective on the case, Ryan Cobman, had determined she had nothing of value to offer.

Danny scowled, wishing he could talk to Cobman, but he had been killed in an auto accident more than a year ago. Although Danny had never met the man, he felt like he knew him after going through so many of his cases. And Tessa spoke highly of him. He didn't strike Danny as the kind of detective who would blow off a witness in a case where he had next to nothing to go on.

From his scribbled notes, it seemed Cobman had thought Fiske was a kook who was wasting his time. Danny found that puzzling. He had noticed Fiske was jumpy and seemed high-strung, but he wouldn't have pegged her for a nut.

He brought up the library's web site, and was glad to see that they were open even though it was Christmas Eve. Danny was fairly confident Ms. Fiske would be manning the desk again. He got up quickly and headed for his car. He couldn't wait to talk to her.

CHAPTER 9

Danny walked into the library and headed straight for the reference desk. As he expected, he found Amanda Fiske there at the desk, her eyes focused on the computer screen in front of her.

"Ms. Fiske," Danny said. "I was hoping you'd be working again. You remember me?"

"Of course. You wanted the old newspapers."

"Right." Danny flashed his badge. "I didn't introduce myself last night. I'm Detective Danny Fitzpatrick."

Amanda nodded. "What can I do for you?"

"You knew I was a cop last night, didn't you?"

"I noticed your badge on your belt, yes. Why?"

"I'm wondering if that's why you were so jumpy."

"I hadn't realized I was jumpy." Amanda placed her hands on the desk in front of her, trying, and failing, to keep them from trembling.

"Is there a place we can talk privately, Ms. Fiske?"

"I'm the only librarian here today, I have to stay out here. Is there some kind of problem? What's this about? I don't understand."

Danny looked around the library and realized he and the librarian were the only people present. He'd keep an eye on the door, but for now there wouldn't be any harm in talking out in the open.

"Honestly," he said, "I don't understand what this is about either. I'm hoping you can clear that up for me."

Danny gestured to the table he had occupied the night before. "Can we at least sit down?"

Amanda nodded and came out from behind the desk, where she sat down across the table from Danny.

"What do you know about the disappearance of Anna Alexander in 2009?"

Amanda's hands immediately went to the cross around her neck. "I don't know anything about it."

"Then why were you staring over my shoulder last night when I was reading about her? And why did you go to the police station and volunteer yourself as a witness back when she disappeared?"

"I saw on the news that she had disappeared and I thought I might be able to help, that's all."

"Did you know her?"

"No."

"Then why did you think you could help?"

"Does it matter? The cop I talked to didn't think so."

"Well I do. Tell me."

"I just thought it might be connected to something that happened to me." Amanda let out a deep breath. "Some years ago I almost got abducted. When I heard about Anna I thought it might be the same guy."

"What made you think that? Where did this happen to you? Around here? Was it the same time as Anna disappeared?"

Amanda shook her head. "No. It was almost 10 years ago now. And I lived in Sitka then."

"Sitka? Then why would you think there could be a connection? Just randomly out of the blue you decided your near-abduction 10 years earlier was connected?"

"It was only 7 years then."

Danny scowled. "Why did you think there was a connection?"

"Because it was the same time of year. The winter solstice. And, she looked a lot like me."

Danny looked at her and realized she was correct. He hadn't paid enough attention the night before. But she did look similar to Anna Alexander, although obviously not as young and fresh-faced. But ten years earlier would have been a whole different story.

He sat back in his seat. "You do look like her."

"I was thinking about her because I saw that another woman went missing this week," Amanda said. "I was reading about her disappearance online when you came in asking for those 2009 papers. I just had a feeling it was connected."

"Why didn't you say anything to me?"

"Because it didn't exactly go well the last time I tried to talk to a cop in your department."

Danny thought back to Cobman's notes. "Right. That's one of the things I'm trying to understand. Why didn't he listen to you?"

"You'd have to ask him that."

"I can't. He's dead."

Amanda shifted in her seat. "Well, I'm sorry then."

"Don't be, I never even met the guy. I want to know why he didn't listen to you."

"And I told you I don't know."

"What was your story? Tell me what you told him."

"That I was almost abducted in Sitka. A man grabbed me when I was leaving work late on the afternoon of the Solstice. It was already dark then and no one was round. He grabbed me near my car and put his hand over my mouth so I couldn't scream."

"What did he look like? Did you get a look at him?"

Amanda nodded. "He was very tall. I mean, unusually so."

"Like some kind of giant?"

"No, no. But maybe 6'5" or so. He was just big, and intimidating."

"What else? Did you get a look at his hair? Eyes?"

"He was blond. And his features were handsome. But his eyes were strange. They were blue, but so dark they looked almost purple or black." Amanda closed her eyes and rubbed her fingers on her forehead. "I still see them. Have you ever seen a corpse?"

"Why do you ask?"

"Because that's what his eyes looked like. The eyes of a corpse. They just seemed dead. You know what I mean?"

"I'm been a cop for most of my life. I've seen plenty of corpses."

He left it at that, forcing himself to not think of the corpse that haunted his every moment.

"There was no soul behind his eyes," Amanda said.

Danny nodded. "If it was dark, how'd you get such a good look at him?"

"Because we were standing under the light in the parking lot."

"Alright," Danny said. "Can you excuse me for just a minute?"

Danny pulled his phone from his pocket and typed a quick text to Tessa. "Ask if anyone saw a tall good looking blond man with blue eyes. Will explain later."

He smiled at Amanda. "Sorry about that. So what happened? How did you get away from him?"

"I don't really know. I was struggling but couldn't get him off me. He turned me away from him and pulled me towards him with his arm around my neck. I thought he was going to strangle me." Amanda glanced around the library. "But then something must have startled him and he just let me go. Before I knew it, he had disappeared." She stared straight at Danny as if she was daring him to challenge her.

"So something startled him so much he let you go, but you have no idea what that was."

"Right. Maybe I just blocked it out, I don't know…"

Danny leaned back in his chair again. "You're lying to me."

"I'm not!"

"Then you're not telling me the whole story."

"Yes I am."

"Did you tell the police in Sitka about this near abduction?"

"I did."

"And?"

"And they didn't believe me. They dismissed it."

"So the police in Sitka dismissed your report. And Detective Cobman here in Fairbanks thought you were a kook…"

Amanda rolled her eyes. "Oh, that's nice to know."

Danny held up his hand. "Sorry, poor choice of words. But really, what the hell difference does it make? You already know he didn't believe you."

"Fine."

"So do you understand why this isn't making a damn bit of sense to me? Based on what you just told me, there's no reason in the world why all of these cops would have given you the brush-off. What aren't you telling me?"

"I'm telling you what I know. I can't help it if it doesn't make sense to you." Amanda pushed her hair out of her eyes. "This is why I didn't say anything to you last night. There's no point."

"There is a point if you know something that could help us find Maria Treibel."

"That's the woman who just went missing?"

"Right. Who also happens to look a hell of a lot like you."

Amanda crossed her arms across her chest. "I've told you what I know. I can't help you."

Danny drummed his fingers on the desk and stared at Amanda. He was going to find out what she was hiding, he had no doubt of that. He wasn't about to let this go.

He heard a noise and turned towards the front door in time to see a woman and two children entering the library. It looked like he would have to wait to question Amanda more.

Danny stood up from the table. "Alright, you're off the hook for now. But I'm coming back when you get off."

"You can't. I have plans for Christmas Eve."

"Then you're gonna have to tell me what I want to know quickly. I'm coming back."

Danny walked out of the library before Amanda had a chance to protest.

CHAPTER 10

Aleksei smiled as he heard the sound of his guests chattering as they finished their breakfast. They would be on their way again soon and he was certain they had been pleased with their stay. He loved satisfied customers. They could only lead to more.

He walked into the dining area of his Snow Creek Arctic resort and waved to the family he had shown around the supposedly haunted Snow Creek Asylum for the Criminally Insane the night before.

"Good morning," Aleksei said. "I trust you enjoyed your breakfast?"

"Morning, Mr. Nechayev," a blond, slightly plump woman replied. She took a final bite of what had once been a stack of pancakes. "Everything was fabulous."

Aleksei turned on the charm with what he knew was his most disarming smile. "Now didn't I tell you all to call me Aleksei? Please. We're all friends here, right Mrs. Bailey?"

The woman blushed slightly, and swallowed her pancakes. "Of course we are. And you know I'm Christine."

"Right. Such a lovely name." Aleksei turned to the two teenagers sitting at the table with their mother. "What about you two? What do you think of Snow Creek?"

"It's awesome," the boy, who was the younger of the two, replied. "I can't wait to tell everyone at school about the ghosts. The pics I took on my phone are perfect."

"I told you we'd see ghosts, Jacob," Aleksei said. He noticed Jacob's sister didn't look quite as happy. "Is something wrong, Katie?"

Katie shook her head. "No, nothing."

Cristine took a sip of coffee and smiled at her daughter, before turning back to Aleksei. "Katie had a little trouble sleeping. I think the ghosts scared her."

"They did not. I told you I wasn't scared, Mom."

"Right, you did. Sorry."

The girl rolled her eyes and stared down at the table with the sullen expression perfected by teenage girls. Aleksei chuckled and watched her. She was blond like her mother, but much more attractive. Tall and slender, she moved with the grace of a ballerina. Aleksei had watched Katie closely while giving the family their tour the night before. She reminded him of Natasha.

According to Christine, Katie was 17, although as Katie was quick to remind her mother, she would be turning 18 in a month. So she was a little younger than Natasha. But she had a maturity to her features and to her manner that made up for any deficiencies in age. She was a beautiful girl.

He forced his eyes away from Katie and turned his attention back to her mother. "Where is Mr. Bailey this morning?"

"Oh, he finished eating before the rest of us, so he went back to the room to finish packing."

Aleksei nodded. "So you'll be heading up to Deadhorse soon?"

"Yep, our coach leaves in a bit. We're all ready for our Christmas in the Arctic."

"Sounds wonderful."

The family got up from the table.

"Speaking of," Cristine said, "we better get busy packing ourselves." She stopped and shook Aleksei's hand. "Thank you again for the tour. We had a wonderful time."

"I'm so glad. Please, tell all your friends about us up here in Coldfoot."

"You know we will."

Aleksei's friendly face turned to a smirk as he watched the family depart. If he wanted to, he could get rid of the whole lot of them and no one would ever be the wiser. Well, except perhaps for their driver. But he could easily get rid of him, too. Lucky for all of them, that wasn't on his agenda.

What was on his agenda was maintaining the impeccable reputation of the Snow Creek Arctic Asylum for the Criminally Insane. It wasn't just his cover. It also made him a good deal of money.

The Asylum was one of Alaska's dirty secrets. In the years before mental health care became available, the Alaskan authorities had transported all of those deemed insane to the Asylum in Coldfoot, where they were warehoused in conditions much worse than those found in any zoo. As treatments for mental illness came into the mainstream, the Asylum was closed, and later turned over to the oil companies to provide residence halls for pipeline workers. The problem came when the pipeline workers refused to stay in the rooms. They insisted the entire building was haunted.

Aleksei bought the old building when the town of Coldfoot started to thrive as the last truck stop along the Dalton Highway. He quickly realized that the pipeline workers had been correct. The building was haunted. After the cruelty that had been perpetrated on the inmates of Snow Creek, that was to be expected. But it was all the better as far as he was concerned.

He refurnished the asylum, knocking down the walls between cells and turning blocks of cells into hotel rooms, and attached a bungalow that functioned as his own living quarters. Finally, he had turned the asylum kitchen and staff dining area into a restaurant. Once he started offering overnight tours of the "haunted" asylum, and advertising encounters with the ghosts of the mentally ill patients, business took off. Now, tourist trips to Prudhoe Bay always included a stop in Coldfoot and an opportunity for a tour of Snow Creek.

Aleksei had hired a cook and hospitality staff for the accommodations and a caretaker to run the establishment during the summer months when Aleksei traveled. He couldn't tolerate the long summer days in Alaska and sought refuge in the southern hemisphere, where he could find winter even in the heart of the North American summer. The snow covered mountains of the Australian state of Victoria were always a favorite destination, especially considering their proximity to Melbourne. There was something to be said for the nightlife in a big city.

Aleksei and his staff all got along fine by ignoring each other most of the time. Aleksei had always made it clear he was a man who liked his privacy. And one of the reasons he loved Alaska so much was that those who made the Arctic their home nearly always felt exactly the same way.

He picked up the Baileys' dishes from their table and carried them to the kitchen for his staff to clean later. There was no hurry, as the Baileys would be Snow Creek's last guests until the spring. He stayed open for Christmas, as he could always count on tourists wanting a Christmas trip package, but the Snow Creek would now close its doors until March.

The weather was too harsh for tourist activity in the dead of winter. And this suited Aleksei just fine. December was always the start of his time. His, and his Natasha's.

He glanced around the kitchen and thought of Maria Treibel, safely locked away in the root cellar next to the Asylum. Had some of the screams the Baileys heard last night been hers? There was always a chance. But, that was the beauty of a haunted building. Screams could always be explained, couldn't they?

He smiled at the thought of Maria. When she got cleaned up, he knew how beautiful she would be. And how much like Natasha. He felt a stirring in his groin at the thought. He needed to make sure the Baileys were indeed on their way to Deadhorse, and his staff had finished their jobs and left Snow Creek for the long winter. Everyone would be gone.

He'd be alone, except for Maria. And Maria would be his.

CHAPTER 11

As promised, Danny drove back to the library at 4:45, fifteen minutes before Amanda Fiske was set to close for the holiday. He pulled into the parking lot, which was empty save for a grey VW Mountaineer that he assumed belonged to Fiske. A light snow had been falling all afternoon and Danny's tires slid in the untreated lot.

He got out of the car and walked to the entrance, his boots crunching in the snow. He walked inside and shook the snow from his collar and hood as he stamped his boots on the carpet. His entrance was not unnoticed by Amanda Fiske, who watched him from behind the reference desk.

"I told you I had plans for Christmas Eve," she said.

"And I told you I was coming back," Danny said.

He walked to the same table they had used earlier, removed his coat, and draped it over the back of his chair before he sat down.

"So I'll be waiting here when you get done closing up," he said.

Amanda pursed her lips and remained silent as she continued her closing duties. As she had not had a customer in several hours, it didn't take her long to finish. She locked the front door and came to sit down next to Danny, making no attempt to hide her irritation.

"Obviously you're hell bent on harassing me," she said. "But I want you to know I'm not happy about it."

"Duly noted. Believe it or not, lots of folks aren't happy to talk with me. Kind of comes with the territory." Danny leaned back, lifting the front legs of the chair off the ground. "It doesn't bother me at all."

Amanda pushed a strand of blond hair behind her ear and stared across the table at Danny. "So what do you want me to say? I already told you what I know and you made it clear that wasn't good enough. So you're gonna have to tell me what you want me to say."

"I want you to say what happened to you when you were almost abducted."

"I did."

"You gave me the Cliff's Notes. I want the whole story."

Amanda looked down at the table and continued to fiddle with her hair. Danny could see her hands trembling.

"I'm honestly not here to upset you," he said.

"You're not? You have a funny way of showing it."

"I just want to know what happened to these women. And I think you do, too. That's why you went to Detective Cobman when Anna went missing."

Amanda rolled her eyes. "Right. And as you so graciously reminded me, he thought I was a kook."

"Whatever he thought, I'm not him. And believe me, there are a hell of a lot of people who would call me a kook."

Amanda sighed and leaned back in her chair. She crossed her arms across her chest, and clutched the cross around her neck with her fingers.

"You're big on that cross necklace, aren't you?" Danny asked.

"What? Why do you ask?"

"Because you're always clutching at it or playing with it."

"Nervous habit."

"Yeah, I've got some nervous habits, too. Or one, anyway. I drink alcohol."

Amanda lips spread into a thin smile. "That's probably a better cure for calming the nerves."

Danny nodded. "Sometimes."

For what felt like an eternity, the two sat in silence, with no sound in the room but the ticking of the clock on the library wall.

"This cross is what saved my life that day," Amanda said, her voice barely above a whisper.

Danny sat up and folded his hands in front of him on the table. "How so?"

"I just happened to have it around my neck. My aunt gave it to me and I thought it was pretty, even though I wasn't even religious. But I wore it that day, and now I've worn it every day since."

"How did it save your life?" Danny asked again.

"Because it scared him. Or burned him somehow."

"Burned him?"

Amanda nodded. "He's not human."

Danny suddenly understood the late Detective Cobman's reaction much better.

"He's not human," he said, repeating Amanda's words. "So what is he?"

"I'm not certain, but I think he's a vampire. That's why the cross burned him."

"Oh, Jesus."

"It's the truth!"

Danny forced himself to keep from rolling his eyes. "Of course it is."

"I knew you wouldn't believe me."

"Well I'm sorry, but you have to admit it's a little far-fetched." He glanced around the rows of books lining the walls. "Don't tell me, you read Twilight? Ann Rice novels, maybe?"

"You don't believe it's possible."

"That some guy's a vampire? No, I don't."

"I didn't either. But when I was trying to get away from him I looked at him and somehow I just knew he wasn't a person. Something told me to grab the cross and push it against his face and it worked. He screamed and leaped away from me."

Danny sighed and rubbed his eyes. He couldn't believe he had waited all day for this.

"It was like it totally shocked him," Amanda continued. "He was holding onto his cheek and staring at me like he couldn't believe it. I started screaming, and ran away from him as fast as I could. Some customers from a gas station across the street heard me screaming and came towards me, asking if they could help. I guess that scared him off, because when I got over to the gas station I looked back towards the lot and he was gone. There was no sign of him anywhere."

Danny nodded. "So what happened then?"

"I asked the people in the gas station to call the police. I was just screaming and crying, I don't know exactly what happened next, but the police came pretty quickly."

"And when they did, what did you tell them?"

"That I'd almost been kidnapped by a monster. I told them that he wasn't human, he might have been a vampire…"

"How'd they react to that?"

"First they asked me if I'd been drinking. When I couldn't calm down, they ended up sending me for a psych evaluation."

"I'm not surprised."

Amanda frowned and slumped in her chair. "You don't believe me either, do you?"

"I believe something may have happened to you, or that you were traumatized by something. I don't know what but..."

"You think I'm crazy?"

"You tell me you were nearly abducted by a vampire, what the hell am I supposed to think?"

Amanda looked away. "I knew I shouldn't have told you. You're no different than those other cops."

"If by that you mean I don't believe in vampires or werewolves or things that go bump in the night, then yes, you're right. I'm no different."

"It's so arrogant."

"What is? Living in reality?"

"Thinking you can be so sure what reality is. Scoffing at anything that doesn't fit your own experiences. Vampire legends have been around for centuries."

"Legends being the key word."

"I told you, I used to feel the same way. But now I know better." Amanda stared across the table at him. "There are all kinds of evil out there."

Danny blew out a deep breath and started to get up from his chair. "On that we agree. Believe me, Ms. Fiske, I know all about evil."

"So that's it? You harass me until I tell you my story and then you just walk away and totally dismiss what I've said?"

Danny nodded. "That about covers it, yeah." He held up his hand as Amanda opened her mouth to protest. "I'm sorry I took up your time. Enjoy your holiday."

He shook his head as he walked out of the library and headed for his car. Now he'd heard everything.

The temperature seemed to have dropped 20 degrees in the time he'd been inside and the snow was falling at a much heavier clip. Danny zipped up his parka and pulled on his gloves and cursed to himself as he cleaned the snow from his windshield.

He should have realized there was a good reason his predecessor had considered Amanda Fiske a kook. Maybe he'd lost his touch. He had been so sure he finally had a lead that would break the Alexander case for him and maybe find Maria Treibel too. Instead, he had a nut spinning tales about vampires. He could almost hear his former colleagues laughing at him.

Danny got into his car and slid into the driver's seat. He turned on the radio, and immediately switched it off when he heard the opening notes of "Have Yourself a Merry Little Christmas." Merry Christmas, indeed.

He looked up and down the street at the now closed stores, their fronts decorated with wreaths and bows and mistletoe. He heard the bells of the nearby Catholic church playing "Silent Night." An appropriate song choice, as the snow continued to fall and muffle what little sound remained on the nearly deserted street.

Danny shivered and turned up the heat. All of the stores might be closed, but he knew Abe's would still be open. It better be, anyway. He wanted nothing more than a drink.

CHAPTER 12

Aleksei opened the door of his cellar and peered inside, where he saw Maria curled up in the fetal position in the corner of the room. He was fairly certain she was awake, but he was curious to see if she would acknowledge him. He climbed down the stairs without speaking and set the tray he carried on the floor next to the now empty plate he had left earlier.

The room had been dark when he entered, as the batteries of the small lantern he had left for Maria had obviously died. She must have let them run on high. He'd have to teach her how to conserve her resources.

Aleksei sat on his haunches and balanced himself against the wall. He rocked back and forth on the balls of his feet.

"I know you're awake," he said. "I'm wondering how long you're going to ignore me."

Maria made no response.

Aleksei clasped his hands together in front of him and cracked his knuckles. "I would think," he said, "that you wouldn't be so quick to forget our lesson on manners. Ignoring someone who is talking to you is most certainly bad manners."

A shiver went down Maria's spine and her muscles tensed. The throbbing pain in her face and neck was a constant reminder of her captor's opinion of her manners. She knew he had no plans to leave her alone. She had to respond.

"What do you want?" she asked, her voice barely audible.

"Look at me when I'm talking to you."

Maria froze.

"Sit up and look at me!"

Maria pushed herself into a sitting position and gently rested her aching head against the wall. She looked across the room at Aleksei and immediately began to shake.

"Why are you shaking? Are you afraid of me?"

"Yes."

"There's no need to be." Aleksei gestured towards the tray he had placed on the floor. "I brought you food, and a pot of coffee. Also some more water."

Maria glanced over at the tray of food. "Thank you," she mumbled.

"You're welcome. And, I'm so glad you're remembering your manners." He sat down on the floor and bent his knees in front of him. "Aren't you wondering why I brought you a special tray?"

"Why did you?"

"It's Christmas Eve. I thought you should have something to celebrate that. See, I even brought a red coffee mug and a green plate." He smiled, as if proud of his thoughtfulness.

Maria felt tears streaming down her face again. She had forgotten it was Christmas. Forgotten all about the party she was planning for Christmas Eve.

She wondered what Nate was doing now. And her parents. Had they come to Alaska after she had gone missing? They must be worried sick..

"You could at least say thank you," Aleksei said, interrupting her thoughts.

"I thought I did," Maria said.

"Well, Merry Christmas to you." Aleksei gestured towards the food. "Go ahead, help yourself."

Maria slid over to the tray and grabbed a piece of bread. She steadied her hand and poured a small amount of coffee into the large red mug. She sat back against the wall and took a sip, savoring the warm liquid.

"Is it good?" Aleksei asked.

"Yes."

"Good."

He watched her eat and drink, remaining silent until she had finished the chunk of bread and reached for another piece.

Maria drank the last of her coffee and put down the mug. "So this is how you celebrate Christmas?" she asked. "Locking up women in your house?"

"Well, kind of," Aleksei said. "It is a tradition for me. But this is Christmas for you, not for me. My Christmas is different."

"What do you mean?"

"In my home country, Christmas is in January. That's when the Orthodox Christmas is celebrated."

"What's your home country?"

"Russia."

Maria nodded. So she had been right about the accent.

"We have a big celebration to bring in each New Year," Aleksei said. "We give presents on December 31, and celebrate all through the night and the following day. Then, we have the Orthodox Christmas a week later."

"Why are you telling me this?"

"Because you and I are going to celebrate next week. The Russian way."

"What??"

"We're going to celebrate. We'll go upstairs and you'll stay in my home. We'll have it all to ourselves. And we'll celebrate the New Year."

"And what if I don't feel like celebrating?"

"That will be a shame for you."

"Why? Because I'll have to stay down in this room if I don't?"

"No. It's more serious than that."

Maria felt a chill run up her spine. "What do you mean?"

"I'll explain it to you. See, this is a tradition for me, bringing a woman to my home for the holidays. Since New Year's is our most important holiday in Russia, it's important for me to celebrate it with my guest. It's like having a touch of home. A Russian New Year, with my Russian princess."

"I'm not Russian."

"Not right now, because you haven't listened to what I told you yet. But you will be. You'll be my Natasha. We'll celebrate."

"And if I don't?"

"If you don't, I'll kill you."

Aleksei watched as Maria's already pale face turned as white as an Arctic hare. He smiled. "I figured I might as well just give it to you straight."

Maria opened her mouth to speak, but no sound came out.

"If you were an actress," Aleksei said, "I would tell you to consider the holiday as your audition. The most important audition you've ever gone on."

Maria finally managed to find her voice. "What am I auditioning for?"

"To see whether you're fit to stay here and share my winter with me. You see, I like to bring my guest here on the Solstice, with the intention of keeping her with me for the winter. But the winter is special for me, and I don't want to have it ruined by an uncooperative guest. So, if you don't pass your audition, I've still got plenty of time to find someone else."

"You mean, kidnap someone else?"

"Well, if you want to look at it that way."

Maria had never felt so cold. She clutched her knees to her chest and tried to keep from shaking. "So what am I supposed to do to pass your audition?"

"Just be Natasha. That's all I want."

"How can I be her when I have no idea who she even is?"

"I can guide you. And I chose you because you already resemble her. Once you get cleaned up and dressed appropriately, you'll be beautiful, just like she was."

"Why don't you just have her here with you? Why do you need me or some other woman?"

"I wish I didn't need you. But I can't have Natasha without you. She's gone." Aleksei looked down at the floor. "She's been gone for years. Decades."

"Decades? How old are you?"

Aleksei stood up and brushed his black pants with his hands. "It doesn't matter. I need to go." He glanced towards the tray again. "I think I've spelled out the situation for you. You know your choices. For now, you might as well just enjoy your Christmas dinner."

He climbed up the stairs and was gone without another word. Maria heard the door of the root cellar slam shut behind him.

She looked down at the food and felt her stomach convulsing. If she'd thought about it rationally, she would have known all along he planned to kill her. But now that he had spelled it out, he had left no doubt. She jumped up and ran to the chamber pot across the room. She barely made it to the pot before she vomited.

CHAPTER 13

Danny walked out of the bar and stumbled down the empty street, trying to remember where he had left his car. He looked up and down the street, but found no car in sight. Puzzling. Hadn't he driven here when he'd left the library?

He shrugged and decided he'd worry about it tomorrow. Home wasn't that far away. And he was drunk enough that the cold didn't bother him. He noticed flyers hanging on every telephone pole he passed, and saw Maria Treibel's smiling face staring back at him. He remembered Nate Clancy mentioning a vigil, and assumed Maria's friends had posted flyers around the town as part of the event. He wished he could say he thought they would do any good, but he knew the efforts were futile.

He walked past the Catholic church, where the bells were playing Christmas music once again. What time was it, anyway? Wasn't it a little late for church bells?

He had his answer a few seconds later, when churchgoers began filing out of the Christmas Eve Midnight Mass. They were all dressed in their best, in spite of the cold, and they held hands and clutched arms as they made their way to their cars and headed home for Christmas.

Danny had vague memories of going to Midnight Mass with his mother at St. Patrick's church in Chicago. He loved when the mass was over and he could run to the car. He couldn't wait to go home and go to bed, as he knew Christmas would be there when he woke up.

He pulled up the neck of his parka and trudged through the snow-covered sidewalks, wishing he had thought to wear his boots. He felt like the boy who couldn't wait to get home again. But not because it was Christmas. Because the cold was sobering him up. He was glad he'd had the foresight to go to the liquor store and stock up before everything closed for the holiday.

Finally, he turned onto his street and walked up the sidewalk to his apartment. He fumbled with his keys and managed to unlock his door. He got inside and tossed his coat and gloves on the floor and kicked off his soaking wet boots.

He considered starting on one of the bottles in his cabinet but felt too light-headed to open the cabinet door. He just needed to lie down for a minute. He headed to his bedroom and collapsed onto the bed. He was out before his head touched the pillow.

CHAPTER 14

Danny woke up to the sound of more church bells. He groaned. Christmas morning church bells, now. He needed a drink.

He forced himself out of bed and stumbled to his kitchen, where he pulled a bottle of scotch from the cabinet. He didn't bother to get a glass and took a long swig from the bottle. He padded to his living room and slumped onto the couch with the bottle in hand. He looked out the window at the heavy snow falling and blowing in the wind.

"Merry Christmas, Danny."

He turned towards the sound of Caroline's voice.

"You're not here," he said. "Leave me the hell alone."

"What's happened to you?"

Danny shook his head and took another drink. "Like you don't know."

"Know what?"

"Are you really going to act like you don't know?" Danny yelled at the empty room. "Give me a fucking break, would you?"

He leaned his head back on the couch. What had happened to him? She really needed to ask? He scoffed and closed his eyes.

He could still hear the asshole taunting him. There in the bedroom he shared with Caroline. He could see him, his hand around her neck as she knelt on the floor next to the bed. The knife touching her throat…

"Leave her out of this, Jackson," Danny said. "I'm the one you're pissed at."

"You got that right. So why would I leave her out of it?"

"She had nothing to do with this!"

"Yeah, I'm aware of that. But she's the way to get to you, isn't she? To hit you where it hurts? Surely even you can figure that out."

Danny's hand started to shake as he stared at the knife at Caroline's throat. He couldn't have that. He needed a clear shot.

"Just get the knife away from her. Please."

Jackson chuckled. "Please? You're seriously saying please to me? Oh, okay, well, now that you asked nicely, sure I'll let her go." He laughed again. "Give me a fucking break, Fitzpatrick."

Caroline stared at Danny, tears streaming down her cheeks. "Danny…"

Danny tightened his grip on his gun. No shaking now. He could put a bullet right through Jackson's head.

He squeezed the trigger just as the knife slid across Caroline's neck, and her pale skin erupted in a sea of red. The champagne colored walls of their bedroom were instantly splattered with Caroline's blood. Danny heard himself screaming as the sound of the gun echoed in his ears, and the blood pumped out of Caroline's neck.

"Caroline!"

Danny sat up straight on his couch, startled. He looked around him, at first not recognizing the sparse furnishings of his dreary Alaskan apartment.

There was no blood on the walls.

He grabbed for the bottle of scotch, finding it empty, and slowly forced himself to his feet. He needed another bottle in order to forget that he had been too late.

He had fired the gun too late.

CHAPTER 15

Danny's eyelids fluttered as he slowly came to consciousness, a state he immediately regretted. He was spread out flat on his stomach, one arm hanging off the side of his disheveled bed. He was still wearing the clothes he had worn to meet with Amanda Fiske, and had no idea how much time had passed since that meeting.

He glanced at the clock on his nightstand. 1:00. He briefly wondered if that was AM or PM, then realized the sun filtering through his window blinds meant it had to be afternoon. So it was 1:00 on what he assumed was Christmas Day. But, for all he knew, that day had come and gone while he was too drunk to notice.

He slowly raised himself to a sitting position, keeping his throbbing head as still as possible. There were no voices to accompany him this morning. Or afternoon, to be more accurate. There was no Caroline. He wasn't sure if that was a good or a bad thing.

Setting his feet on the floor, he forced himself out of bed and stumbled down the hall to his kitchen. He turned on the light and squinted from the glare. The bright kitchen light was too much for his eyes to handle. Danny made a pot of coffee as quickly as he could and walked into his dark living room, where he collapsed on his couch. He briefly noticed his boots on the floor next to him and figured he must have kicked them off after he got home. Had it been last night?

He still couldn't remember.

Danny rubbed his eyes and tried to will himself back to a state of sobriety. It wasn't going to work without coffee.

Grateful to hear the beeping that indicated his coffee was done brewing, he got up and headed back to the kitchen. This time, the light wasn't quite as hard to take. He grabbed his biggest mug and filled it with coffee, then headed back to the couch.

He drank the hot coffee and breathed a sigh of relief. It wasn't going to work immediately, but at least he was on track to feeling like a human being again. If he could keep this mug down, he'd try to find some breakfast.

Danny rested his head on the back of the couch and tried again to focus. He turned on his television and was greeted with a Christmas parade from Hawaii. Hula dancers wearing Santa hats in addition to their traditional leis and grass skirts smiled at him through the television as they danced to a curiously Hawaiian version of "Jingle Bells." So it was still Christmas Day.

Suddenly remembering he was on call for the department, he grabbed his cell phone. Fortunately, he had no messages. Apparently Fairbanks criminals also took a break for the holiday.

Danny took another gulp of coffee and tried to remember what he had been doing before going off on his latest bender. Amanda Fiske popped into his head and he groaned. How could he have forgotten the vampire lady?

He finished his coffee and sat up, resting his elbows on his knees and cradling his face in his hands. He was back to square one on Anna Alexander now that his big lead had turned out to be a crazy woman, so he had to figure out what he could do. He wasn't willing to concede that he had nothing on Anna, or on the recently disappeared Maria Treibel.

He needed to go talk to Anna's parents. He'd never actually met them, but he'd talked to them briefly on the phone when he first took over Anna's case.

The Alexanders had called in to the department to check on what, if any, progress had been made on finding out what had happened to their daughter

Mostly, Danny had relied on the case notes left by his predecessor to get up to speed. According to the records, Anna's parents had been a dead end and, by all accounts, they were simply terrified, grieving parents who wanted answers about their only daughter. Danny wanted to give them those answers, but he'd have to figure them out for himself, first.

He wondered if he could talk with the Alexanders today. Would they be angry if he turned up on Christmas? A light bulb went off in his head as he mentally scanned the case notes about Anna and her family. The Alexanders were Jewish, so odds were good they wouldn't care at all if a detective showed up at their door on Christmas.

Danny headed back to the kitchen and poured a second mug of coffee. He grabbed the last of his blueberry Pop-Tarts and ate one cold while he waited for the other to toast. He could feel his energy returning. For whatever reason, he had a good feeling about meeting the Alexanders. His gut told him the visit was going to be worthwhile.

He just needed to get cleaned up and make himself presentable. He finished the last of his coffee and headed for his bathroom and a steaming hot shower.

CHAPTER 16

An hour later, after more coffee and several Excedrin tablets, Danny pulled into the Alexander's driveway, glad he had remembered to call them and ask if they would be willing to talk to him before he had left his place. He was actually surprised he had been able to concentrate enough to make the call and relieved that the coffee combined with the shower had clearly had the desired sobering effect.

Danny trudged through the snow-covered sidewalk to the front door, anxious to get inside and out of the still falling snow. He wondered if the snow would stop falling before March. Danny had been sure the Alaskan winters wouldn't bother him, as Chicagoans knew all about cold and snow. But he was now sure that this had been a naive assumption.

A man Danny assumed was Ted Alexander opened the front door to the house as Danny stepped onto the porch.

"Detective Fitzpatrick?" he asked.

Danny nodded. "Mr. Alexander, I assume?"

"Right. Call me Ted, please." He opened the door and stepped aside to give Danny room. "Come on in and get out of the cold."

"Thank you," Danny said, stomping his boots on the floor mat. "This has to be the coldest day of the year."

Ted raised an eyebrow. "You new to Alaska?"

74

"Why do you ask?"

"Because this isn't even all that cold. Wait until January."

Danny shivered at the thought. "I was sure growing up in Chicago would prepare me for this."

Ted took Danny's parka and hung it up in the narrow hall closet. "You're more prepared than I was. I grew up in Florida."

Ted led Danny into a small living area, where a petite woman with short silvery-blond hair stood up to greet him.

"Detective, this is my wife, Marilyn."

Danny shook the woman's small hand. "Mrs. Alexander."

"I want to say it's good to meet you, Detective, but in these circumstances…"

"Believe me, I understand. Social niceties usually don't matter too much in my line of work."

Marilyn nodded and gestured to an olive colored armchair. "Please, have a seat."

She sat back down on the matching olive sofa and folded her hands in her lap. Ted rubbed his hand through his curly black hair and sat beside her.

"So you're working on my daughter's case now," he said, his voice instantly strained.

"I am. I've been following up on my predecessor's work."

"I don't mean this as a knock on him," Ted said. "But I doubt there's much for you to follow up on. He never found anything."

"I know," Danny said. "But I guess I want to start at the beginning with you. Try to see if I can dig up something that could have been missed."

Marilyn clutched her hands more tightly together. "I don't know what we can tell you that we didn't already say."

"Probably nothing," Danny said. "But I've got a new angle I'm working on, another missing woman case. I'm hoping something will tie in that wouldn't have made sense before."

"Another girl's gone missing now?" Ted asked.

"Yeah. A few days ago."

"This is when Anna disappeared."

"I know. That's why I'm trying to see if I can find a connection."

Both Alexanders seemed to perk up, however slightly. "What do you want to know?" Marilyn asked.

"Was there anything unusual that happened before Anna disappeared? Did she meet anyone new? A new job, maybe?"

Ted shook his head. "No. Not that we were aware of, anyway."

"What about the winter solstice celebration that year? Was Anna involved in it?"

"You mean did she work there?"

"Any involvement, really. Work, volunteer…"

"No, she wasn't working anywhere at the time because she was busy with her studies."

"What about the studies? Did she mention anything new at college?"

Marilyn shook her head. "No. But you would be better off talking to her friends. They knew more about what she was doing at college than we did."

Danny nodded. "I've no doubt of that. That's the way it works at that age, isn't it?"

"Most definitely."

Danny sat forward in the plush armchair, his elbows on his knees. "Could I take a look at her things? I know it's been a while but…"

"We still have all of Anna's things," Marilyn said, interrupting Danny. "You're more than welcome to look at anything you think might help."

Marilyn stood up from the couch and motioned for Danny to follow her.

"Let me just show you her room."

Danny got up from his chair and followed Marilyn, feeling a twinge of guilt that his request to search Anna's belongings may have given her mother a false sense of hope. It was impossible to miss the sense of eagerness in her voice and on her face as she led him to her daughter's room.

"We haven't changed anything," Marilyn said as she turned on the overhead light in the room she hoped would one day welcome her daughter back to it. "All of her things are here."

"Anna lived with you while she was in school, didn't she?" Danny asked, searching his memory for the details of Anna's case. "She didn't live on campus?"

"That's right. She lived here with us to save money."

Danny glanced around the room at the double-bed with a navy blue comforter and an assortment of blue and white pillows and a large mahogany desk filled with books and writing utensils. A laptop lay closed on top of the desk, and Danny knew from the case notes that his predecessor had involved the department's computer forensic experts to go over every detail of the laptops' contents, to no avail. Above the desk, Anna had hung a UAF Nanooks banner, proudly displaying the school's traditional blue and gold colors.

"Anna is an athlete," Marilyn said from behind him. "She runs cross-country."

Danny wondered if Marilyn would ever be able to refer to her daughter in the past tense. He knew all too well how difficult that was.

"Do you mind if I look through her desk, Mrs. Alexander?"

"Of course not. As I said, you're more than welcome to look at anything. I'll leave you to it."

Danny sat down on the Nanook cushion that lined the desk chair, and grabbed a pair of latex gloves out of his coat pocket. Regardless of how old this potential evidence was, the last thing he wanted to do was spoil it.

Rifling through the top drawer of the desk, Danny found what he supposed was normal for any college age girl. Her cell phone, which was almost certainly her prized possession and had been searched by the same forensics team that had searched her laptop, photos of a smiling Anna with friends, ticket stubs from movies and concerts, and various pens and colored pencils all fought for space in the drawer. Danny found nothing of interest.

He moved on to one of the side drawers and came upon notebooks with scribbled class notes mixed in with high school yearbooks and a few dog-eared paperbacks. It was apparent that Anna had not been a particularly organized person. Danny liked that about her. He opened another drawer and found a brown leather journal tied closed with a long strand of multi-colored yarn.

Danny picked up the journal and gingerly removed the yarn. He opened the pages to reveal Anna's flowery penmanship, full of exaggerated loops and crossbars. He didn't remember anything in Cobman's notes about a diary, but perhaps that was because he hadn't believed it contained anything noteworthy. That was something Danny would need to decide for himself.

He skimmed through the pages of Anna's writings, reading about her cross country exploits and decision to try out for the swim team in the upcoming spring. He read about a former boyfriend she wished she hadn't broken up with, and a professor who regularly put her to sleep. He was feeling a bit drowsy himself until he turned another page and a folded brochure fell out of the journal onto the carpet.

Danny reached down and picked it up. The brochure was for the Snow Creek resort in Coldfoot, Alaska. Danny hadn't heard of Coldfoot, but in his experience every town in the state deserved that name. He went back to Anna's journal and read the page where the brochure had been tucked away.

Monday, December 1, 2009

Our Thanksgiving weekend in the Arctic was so much fun. I'm so glad I let Sara talk me in to going. What a crazy experience! We stayed at a haunted asylum and the guy who runs the place was so fucking hot. It was creepy as all hell but I'd go back in a minute just to see more of him. From there we went to Prudhoe Bay and...

Danny stopped reading as his meeting with Nate Clancy flickered in his mind. Clancy had mentioned a trip he and Maria had taken to Prudhoe Bay over the Thanksgiving weekend. Could it really be a coincidence that Anna had taken the same trip a few weeks before she disappeared? He didn't need to read more of Anna's recollections to find out. He didn't believe in those kinds of coincidences.

As he'd been a detective long enough to know to never go to any sort of crime scene without being prepared, he pulled the evidence bag he had brought with him out of his pocked, and placed the journal and brochure inside it. He quickly perused the rest of the drawer but felt certain he'd already found the link he'd been looking for when he decided to visit the Alexander house.

Danny removed his gloves and walked out of the bedroom to rejoin the Alexanders.

"I need to bring this journal and brochure back to the station," he said to Ted and Marilyn, who had risen from the couch the second Danny walked back into the living room.

"Why?" Ted asked. "What have you found?"

"I'm not sure," Danny said, truthfully. "But I need to find out more about a trip your daughter took the Thanksgiving before she disappeared. Apparently she went up to the Arctic with friends. Do you remember this?"

"Of course," Marilyn said. "Anna had wanted to go to Prudhoe Bay and see the Arctic Ocean for ages. They also went to an old asylum in Coldfoot. Anna loved it there."

"That was the Snow Creek, right?" Danny asked.

"Right. Why do you ask? Do you think someone on that trip had something to do with all this?"

"I can't say, Mrs. Alexander. I'm sorry," Danny said. "But it's something I'm going to look into more."

He walked to the door and grabbed his parka from the coat closet. "I need to get going," he said.

"But what's going on?" Ted asked. "You can't just walk out now without telling us anything."

"I don't know if there's anything to tell you. I'll be back in touch as soon as I know something though, one way or the other. I promise."

"What the hell's going on?"

Danny zipped up his parka and stepped outside. "I hope I'll have an answer for you soon. Thank you."

He ignored Ted's repeated questions and got back into his car as quickly as possible. His pulse quickened as he started up his car and drove away from the Alexander home. He couldn't wait to talk to Nate Clancy.

CHAPTER 17

"It's no coincidence these two both went up to the Arctic before they disappeared, Tessa," Danny said into his phone.

"I'm not disagreeing with you. I'll meet you at Clancy's."

Danny turned the corner of Hampton Street and dropped the phone as his car started to fishtail in the snow. He straightened the vehicle, then grabbed his phone from the floor.

"You still there?"

"Yeah."

"Sorry, I dropped my phone."

"Why don't you just put it on speaker?"

"Because I hate that damn echo." Danny cradled the phone on his shoulder and used both hands to steer his car through the snowy streets. "Anyway, you don't have to meet me. It's Christmas."

"I'm aware of that. But this is my case. You shouldn't have to handle it on your own."

"There's not a hell of a lot to handle right now. All I want to know is where Clancy and Maria went up there in the Arctic. There's no reason for you to have your holiday screwed up."

It was obvious Tessa didn't take much convincing. "Are you sure you don't mind? And you'll get back with me as soon as you talk to Clancy?"

"What, are you worried I'm going to steal your case?"

"No, no, it's not that…"

Danny interrupted. "Kidding. I'll get back to you, I promise. And no, I don't mind."

He tossed the phone onto his passenger seat, and focused on driving. If he wasn't careful, he'd end up in a ditch before he ever got anywhere near Nate Clancy.

Relieved when he finally got to Clancy's house, he parked his car and once again trudged through a snow-covered sidewalk. His already cold feet turned freezing, and wet. He really needed a better pair of boots.

Just as Ted Alexander had, Nate opened his front door before Danny had a chance to ring the bell.

"Detective Fitzpatrick," he said. "What are you doing here?"

"What are you, psychic? How'd you know I was out here?"

"I was walking past my front window and saw you get out of your car. What is it? Have you found Maria?"

Danny shook his head. "Wish I could say I have, but no. I just need to ask you some more questions."

"On Christmas Day?"

"Criminals don't take holidays."

Nate's face turned red. "I know, I'm sorry. It's just that I was about to leave for my parents' house…"

Danny held up his hand. "I won't take up too much of your time." He shivered as a gust of wind blew across the porch. "But can I please come inside? I'm freezing my ass off out here."

Nate held the door open and stepped aside to give Danny room. "Of course. Please, come in."

He walked ahead, and led Danny into his sparse but stylish living room. He motioned for Danny to have a seat on his black leather couch. "Make yourself comfortable," he said.

Danny sat down and slid out of his parka while Nate took a seat on a black recliner. He didn't recline, but instead sat forward in his chair, his posture tense.

"What questions do you have?" Nate asked.

"I need to know exactly where you and Maria went when you visited Prudhoe Bay last month."

"You mean, our hotel? That's easy. There's only one there."

"What is it?"

"The Reindeer Inn."

Danny resisted the urge to roll his eyes at the name. "Alright, what else did you do there? What about restaurants? Tourist attractions?"

"The tourist attraction is going to the Arctic Ocean, and seeing the oilfields. That's it, honestly."

"Restaurants?"

"The Reindeer Restaurant is connected to the Inn. We ate there."

"So you went all the way up there to see the ocean and some oil drills?"

"I told you I wasn't thrilled about the trip."

"What about Coldfoot? Did you go to Coldfoot? A place called Snow Creek?"

Nate nodded. "That's where the tours stop on their way to Prudhoe Bay. We stayed overnight there. That's the old psychiatric hospital I told you about. It's a tourist attraction now, that's where we stayed. The asylum is a hotel now and there's a restaurant there, too. We went on the haunted tour with the guy that owns the place. I think his name was Alex, or Alexi, something like that."

Danny remembered Anna's excited ramblings about the "hot" owner of the asylum.

"Was he good looking?" he asked.

Nate shrugged. "I didn't exactly notice. But Maria thought he was. She teased me about it, said since I was being such a grump that maybe she'd just dump me for the Snow Creek guy."

"Did she have a lot of interaction with him?"

"Not really. He just took us on the tour of the place."

Danny put his hands on his knees and stood up, anxious to get going and find out more about this asylum and its caretaker. He knew he was on the trail of something now, he could feel it. And it wasn't going to end with a crazy woman and a vampire tale.

"Thank you; this is just what I needed."

Nate stood up next to him. "You think that guy or somebody else up there in the Arctic had something to do with Maria going missing?"

"I don't know, and I couldn't tell you even if I did."

"Will you let me know if you find anything out about her?"

He was talking to Danny's back, as Danny had pulled on his parka and walked to the front door before Nate could finish his question.

"You know I will. Merry Christmas to you."

Danny returned to his car and felt a surge of adrenalin that was even better than coffee for curing his hangover. He couldn't wait to call Tessa and share the news. And most of all, he couldn't wait to take his own trip up to Coldfoot and Prudhoe Bay.

CHAPTER 18

"*Danny, you can't go up* there by yourself," Tessa said.

"I'm not going by myself. Do you think I'm crazy? I'm meeting Sergeant Yazzie at the airport. He's the lucky stiff who gets to be my back-up." Danny struggled to hold his phone, drive, and look at his directions to the airport all at the same time. He thought back to the day he bought his Subaru after deciding to stay in Fairbanks. Why the hell hadn't he bought the model that had the built-in gps?

"But it's dark. You should wait until tomorrow."

"It's dark almost 24/7 in this god-forsaken place. I could be going at two in the afternoon and it would still be dark. What the hell difference does it make?"

"I'll come with you too."

"No, no, no. I don't want you walking out in the middle of your Christmas party. I already told you, I'm fine with doing this."

"But…"

"I'm not talking about it anymore," Danny said. "I'm almost to the airport and I still need to call Judge Shriver and get my warrant approved. On top of all that, I have to figure out where to find my charter."

"This seems dangerous. What about the snow?"

"I checked with the pilot when I made the arrangements. He said Coldfoot is fine. We're not going to Prudhoe Bay today because he doesn't think he can land in the weather up there right now. But I don't really care because I know it's the Coldfoot place we're interested in."

Danny pulled around the back of the airport and found the Arctic Charters hanger.

"I'm here now," he said. "I'll call you when I get back to Fairbanks."

"Call me from Coldfoot if you learn anything interesting."

"Demanding, aren't we?"

"Well I just.."

"I'm kidding," Danny said. "If I have a signal, I'll call you. Hell, I'll call you during the ride up if it would make you feel better to hear my voice."

"That would mean the world to me. In fact, it would make my whole Christmas."

Danny chuckled and ended the call. He paused and searched his contacts for the number of Judge Anthony Shriver. He knew Shriver wouldn't be thrilled about having his holiday interrupted, but Danny couldn't have cared less. Life was tough like that sometimes. He leaned back against his headrest, noticing Teriaq Yazzie pulling up beside him in his battered black pick-up truck. He gestured for Yazzie that he would be with him in a minute and waited for Judge Shriver to answer his phone.

CHAPTER 19

A few hours later, Danny was on the ground in Coldfoot, grateful to have Teriaq Yazzie as company. With the exception of Tessa, Danny hadn't bothered to get to know anyone in the Fairbanks police well, but he still liked what little he knew about Yazzie. The man seemed to abhor idle chitchat and was typically quite reserved, a quality Danny very much appreciated. What's more, Yazzie encouraged the non-native members of the department to call him Terry instead of his Inuit name Teriaq. Something else Danny greatly appreciated, as it had taken no time in Alaska at all for him to discover that he was hopeless when it came to pronouncing the words of the native tribes.

Danny and Terry shivered as they made their way from the hanger to their waiting driver. Danny knew he shouldn't have been surprised, but the temperature was so low it made Fairbanks seem warm. And, he had to wonder what the conditions must be in Prudhoe Bay if his pilot had considered them unsafe, but had no issue with landing in Coldfoot. Danny's hands still ached from gripping the passenger seat as the plane landed in what he would call a blizzard.

The pilot had seemed completely unfazed, and so did their driver, Doug Matheson. Matheson had agreed to drive him to the Snow Creek asylum in his 4X4 Ford truck. Danny was glad to see the truck had studded snow tires when he got inside. He may not be used to Alaska but, as a Chicagoan, he still knew what it took to drive in heavy snow.

"It won't take us long to get to Snow Creek," Matheson said, as Danny settled in next to him and Terry took the truck's rear seat. "It doesn't take long to get anywhere in Coldfoot. You go too long and you're out of here and on your way to Prudhoe Bay."

"I gathered that from looking at the map," Danny said. "Not much of a town."

"Not a town at all, really. Used to be a gold mining camp, did you know that?"

Terry likely did, but he stared straight ahead out the front window without responding, all but ignoring Matheson's chatter.

"No," Danny said.

"Yeah, that's how it got its start. The miners gave Coldfoot its name, for obvious reasons."

"How'd you end up here?"

"I used to drive through here all the time on the Highway, I was a trucker. Got sick of driving and decided to stick around here. I like living in the middle of nowhere."

Danny nodded. "I can see the advantages."

Matheson chuckled and pulled up next to a building that looked more like a military prison than a tourist attraction. Danny noticed the sign in the front.

"This is Snow Creek?" he asked.

"The one and only," Matheson said. "You heard all the ghost stories about this place?"

"I heard it's supposed to be haunted."

"Yeah. Aleksei milks that for all it's worth."

"Aleksei?"

"Guy who owns Snow Creek. He's the one that renovated it and re-opened it. Before that, this place had been empty for decades."

Danny remembered Nate Clancy mentioning a guy he thought was named Alex. "So this Aleksei gives tours of the asylum, right?"

"Right. Big tourist thing. People love it."

"He's the one we need to talk to." Danny started to get out of the car, and paused. He glanced towards Matheson. "You sure you don't mind waiting out here? It's freezing."

Matheson shook his head. "I don't mind at all. I'll keep the heater running if you guys take too long." He held up a paperback. "And I've got a book to read. So take all the time you need."

Danny nodded and slipped on the snowshoes that Terry had brought for him. Danny never would have thought of the shoes himself, and he really had no idea how to walk in them, but he assumed he'd figure it out. It couldn't be that hard.

"Thanks," he said to Matheson as he got out of the car and shut the door. Terry had already exited the rear and was gliding across the snow as gracefully as if he was on skis.

Danny's progress was much more plodding, but eventually he got the hang of his shoes and headed towards the Snow Creek entrance. Noticing a small bungalow that had been added on to the original building, Danny wondered if their arrival had already been noted by the bungalow's inhabitant. There was a light on, and Danny thought he saw a face in the window.

Relieved to find the Snow Creek door open, the two cops walked inside to the lobby. It was dark, and no one seemed to be working at the front desk. Terry saw a buzzer attached to the desk, and pressed it.

Within seconds, a tall blond man appeared and turned on the lobby lights.

"Can I help you?" he asked.

"I hope so," Danny said. "You the owner of this place?"

"I am. But if you want to book a tour or a room, we're closed for the winter season."

"No problem. We're not interested in staying here. We just need to talk to you."

"Talk to me? Why?"

Danny held up his badge. "I'm Detective Danny Fitzpatrick, Fairbanks PD. And this is Sergeant Yazzie."

The blond man nodded. "What can I do for you?"

"We're investigating the disappearance of a young woman from Fairbanks."

"What does that have to do with me?"

"How about telling me who you are? I feel kind of strange talking when I don't even know your name."

"I'm Aleksei Nechayev. Why do you want to know?"

"The woman I'm looking for, she and her boyfriend came up here a few weeks ago and toured your place." Danny took out a photo of Maria and showed it to Aleksei. "You remember her?"

Aleksei stared at the photo. "Possibly. We're always very busy in the weeks before we close, and we get so many people in and out that it's hard to keep track." Aleksei shrugged his shoulders. "I do think I remember this woman, but I can't say for sure."

"Do you keep a record of your guests?"

"Of course. Would you like to see it?"

"Yeah. That would be great."

Aleksei slid behind the desk and produced a large leather bound book. "I like having an old-fashioned guest book for our guests to sign. It adds to the atmosphere of the place."

"I can imagine." Danny pulled the book around to him, and thumbed through the pages until he got to Thanksgiving weekend. Sure enough, he found the names he expected.

"Here she is," he said, pointing to Maria's name. "And her companion, Nate Clancy."

Aleksei looked at the names and pretended to search his mind. He shrugged again. "Obviously they were here, but the names really don't ring any bells." He leaned backwards against the wall behind the desk. "I can tell you though that from here they likely went to Prudhoe Bay. That's how the tours work."

"Yeah, that's what I've been told." Danny stared at Maria's crisp handwriting, and drummed his fingers on the desk.

"What is it you're hoping to find here, Detective? How can I help you?"

Danny flipped through the rest of the book. The last entries were in 2011. He looked up from the book and stared at Aleksei. "What about your older records?" he asked. "Where are your listings of guests who were here before 2011?"

"We don't keep the books, but we have records of our guests on computer files. Why?"

Danny could have sworn he saw Aleksei flinch. But maybe that was just wishful thinking.

"I'd like to see your files from 2009."

"May I ask why?"

Aleksei's voice sounded the same. Maybe he hadn't flinched.

Before Danny could answer him, Aleksei spoke again.

"Was this..." he glanced down at the book and re-read the name. "Ms. Treibel here in 2009 as well?"

"I'm not sure," Danny said. "I'd be interested in finding out."

Aleksei booted up the desk computer and waited for the programs to load. "I can show you our database," he said. "It will just take me a minute."

"I don't mind waiting."

Danny glanced around the lobby while he waited for Aleksei's database to load. He knew very well how long a computer could take to actually get going. It had been too dark to notice much in the lobby when he arrived, but now he could see that Aleksei liked having an old-fashioned touch to everything here. Tacky brochures lined the desk, all promising fabulous Arctic adventures and polar bear sightings, but none looked as if they had been touched in decades. The whole lobby looked like that of a roadside hotel in the 1950s. The huge stuffed Arctic Owl that hung over the doorway behind the desk merely added to the creepiness factor. Danny expected Norman Bates to enter from the back room at any minute.

"Here you go," Aleksei said. "2009. Are you interested in a particular month?"

"November."

Danny looked for another flinch, but didn't see any. Aleksei clicked the mouse and stepped back from the computer to make room for Danny.

Danny stared at the screen and scrolled down the list of names. It took only a second to find Anna Alexander. He highlighted her name and hoped for some kind of a reaction from Aleksei. He didn't get any.

"I don't see Ms. Treibel's name there," Aleksei said.

"No, I don't either." Danny paused. "But I do see Anna Alexander's name. Anna also went missing not long after she stayed here at your lovely home."

Now, Aleksei flinched. "I can't say I remember Miss Alexander."

"Of course you don't. But regardless, we're going to have to take a look around this place."

"Okay. But first I'd like to know what this is about," Aleksei said, his voice sharp.

"I've told you what it's about. Two missing women named Maria Treibel and Anna Alexander. And before you ask, we've got a warrant."

Aleksei cleared his throat and regained his composure. "Not a problem." He opened the door of the lobby and held it for Danny and Terry. "Help yourselves, gentlemen. Or, I'd be happy to give you our tour."

Danny held up his hands. "No, we don't need the tour. We're fine on our own. I'd suggest you stay here."

Aleksei glared at him, and forced his mouth into a smile. "Suit yourself."

Danny and Terry left the lobby and found themselves in an empty hallway, with rooms lining the walls on each side.

"You know anything about this place?" Danny asked.

"Only that it's supposed to be haunted. Supposedly, people have heard crying and screaming, doors slamming, disembodied voices, that sort of thing."

"Nice."

"I wouldn't be surprised if it's true. By all accounts, they didn't exactly treat prisoners well up here."

"It was an insane asylum, right?"

Terry nodded. "Yeah. For the criminally insane. I think they just dumped people here when they didn't know what else to do with them."

Danny shook his head. "Why the hell would anyone want to stay here as a vacation?"

"Novelty I guess. Hoping to see ghosts or hear scary noises."

As if on cue, Danny heard the sound of a door slamming in the distance. Startled, he jumped and turned to Terry.

"Did you hear that?"

"Yeah."

"So I'm not crazy?"

Terry shook his head. "If you are, so am I."

Danny instinctively put his hand on his gun, noticing Terry had done the same. They moved down the hallway, entering each room as they passed and checking every closet and restroom they found.

Aleksei had furnished the old asylum cells to resemble hotel rooms, and each was decorated in a rustic Alaskan theme. Thick quilts covered the beds, and the walls were lined with photos of the frozen Arctic landscape, complete with polar bears, arctic foxes, and fluffy snow-white rabbits. The rooms were chilly, and Danny could hear the howl of the wind outside. It was the only sound besides Danny and Terry's footsteps, as none of the rooms showed any signs of life.

The only thing they found of interest in any of the rooms was a closet full of women's clothing. Long velvet dresses, button-up blouses, thick flowing capes and long full skirts were meticulously hung on padded hangers. Pointy-toed boots and velvet slippers were lined up on the floor. Danny thought the clothes looked old-fashioned, and they reminded him of clothing you'd expect to find in a costume shop.

"What do you think of this?" he asked.

"Can't imagine," Terry said. "Maybe they have some kind of costume drama here sometimes."

"No men's clothes, though. Or children's."

Terry shrugged his shoulders. "No clue."

"We'll have to ask Nechayev what he's doing with these clothes."

"Maybe he likes to dress in drag."

Danny fingered through the dresses and skirts. "You saw how tall he is. None of these clothes would fit him."

They left the room and came to the end of the hall, where they entered a large circular room with picture windows lining the walls. The hardwood floor was bare, and the room was empty of furniture.

"What is this, some kind of solarium?"

"I think it was a day room," Terry said. "I've read about these kinds of asylums. They used to tie people to chairs and sit them in here for the day. Let them get some sun I guess."

Danny and Terry both jumped as they heard a woman's voice coming from the corridor they had just vacated. They ran back to the hall and through each room, searching for the woman they had heard yell. They found nothing.

"This place is giving me the fucking creeps," Danny said.

"You and me both."

"Let's hurry up and get through the rest of it. He's gotta be hiding Maria here somewhere."

They went back through the day room and searched the kitchen and dining area, where they found nothing out of the ordinary. As they continued their search, they came to the attached bungalow which had to be Aleksei's living quarters. Danny felt his pulse quicken. Instinct told him this was what they were looking for.

But his instinct was wrong. They searched Aleksei's living room, study, bedroom, guest room, and bathroom and found nothing of interest. A fire roared in the study and it was clear that Aleksei had been sitting in an old-fashioned leather arm chair in front of it and enjoying a glass of vodka when Danny and Terry had interrupted him. The half-empty glass sat on a coaster on the end table next to the chair, with a copy of the St. Petersburg Times folded haphazardly next to it.

"There's nothing here," Danny said. "What are we missing?"

"I think we've seen everything."

"But where the hell is she?"

"I don't think she's here, Detective."

Danny shook his head. "I was so god-damn sure."

They left Aleksei's bungalow and Danny jumped again as they heard the sound of another slamming door.

"Holy shit this place is something else," he said.

"I'm ready to get out of here," Terry said.

Danny nodded and the two walked briskly back toward the lobby, where they found Aleksei waiting for them.

"I trust you didn't find anything of interest, gentlemen?" he asked.

"Why do you have a closet full of old-fashioned women's clothes?" Danny asked, forcing himself to ignore Aleksei's smug demeanor.

"We put on a play here sometimes in the summer. Try to recreate the asylum days. Those are some of our costumes."

"Those clothes didn't look like anything anyone would be wearing at an asylum."

Aleksei shrugged. "We make do with what we can."

"Do you only have women in this play?"

"Excuse me?"

"There weren't any costumes for men."

"Oh, well my cook has those. He's away for the winter season though."

Danny knew Aleksei was lying, and he was certain if he researched Snow Creek he'd find that a play had never once been held at the resort. But as he hadn't found a thing to back up any of his suspicions, he had no choice but to let it go. For now, at least.

"I guess we've seen everything we need to see here then," Danny said. He couldn't deny he was anxious to get away from this creepy place and its equally creepy owner.

Danny forced himself to hold his hand out for Aleksei to shake. He flinched when he felt Aleksei's strong, ice cold grip.

"Cold hands," Danny said.

"So I've been told. A hazard of living in the Arctic, I guess."

Danny stared at Aleksei, looking into his dark blue eyes, and felt a spine-tingling chill pass over him. He pulled his hand away, startled at the terror that had momentarily overwhelmed him. What the hell was wrong with him? He'd dealt with plenty of psychos before. But there was something different about this guy. Something really off.

"Let me know if you need anything else from me," Aleksei said, his voice cordial. "You can always call. Fairbanks isn't exactly a short trip from here."

"Thanks," Danny said. "We'll be in touch if we have any other questions."

"I hope you find that woman."

Aleksei watched Danny and Terry walk back to their waiting truck, and noticed they were walking much more quickly now than when they had arrived. They moved like men in a hurry now.

Aleksei waved at Doug Matheson, and shut the door behind him. He had to admit, this had been unexpected. He'd dealt with nosy cops before, but not any that seemed to know about two of his guests. He knew the Irish detective had highlighted Anna's name on purpose.

Aleksei locked up the lobby and headed back towards his living quarters. He wasn't really worried, as the cops had found nothing and would probably be out of his hair now. Most likely, Fitzpatrick was merely some stiff who had stumbled on the fact that Anna and Maria had both been to Snow Creek. Beyond that, he had nothing to go on. Aleksei knew he had covered his tracks. He always did.

Still, if this cop kept sniffing around he'd have to do something. He wouldn't have his winter ruined. If the cop came back, he'd get rid of him. That wouldn't be a problem.

Aleksei knew exactly how to get rid of people.

CHAPTER 20

"I'm telling you, there's something wrong with this guy," Danny said.

He had called Tessa from the Coldfoot hanger while he was waiting for the pilot to prep the plane.

"What's wrong with him?"

"I don't know. But something sure as hell is. He gave me the fucking creeps. Gave Terry the creeps too. The whole place, Tessa. It's like a god-damn haunted house."

"Isn't that what it's supposed to be?"

"Yeah but you don't expect those things to really be haunted, do you? I didn't think we'd be hearing all kinds of shit while we were looking around. I thought I was going fucking nuts."

"But you didn't find anything?"

"No. God-dammit, I didn't find a damn thing. Except that Anna and Maria were both there, but we already knew that. And we found a closet full of costumes that were fucking strange, but he had a cover story for them." Danny sighed. "I kept trying to get a reaction from the guy, but he didn't miss a beat. He was like a damn robot, saying all the right things, showing concern, insisting he didn't know anything about Maria's disappearance.."

"Isn't it possible that he really doesn't know anything?"

"Sure it's possible. I told you I didn't find shit. But I know there's something there. I'm telling you…"

"I know," Tessa said, interrupting him. "There's something off about him. I believe you. I just don't know what we can do, Danny."

Danny shook his head. He wasn't lying when he said he had been freaked out by the hallway lined with cells and the strange noises echoing around the building. He had no trouble believing there were ghosts there. And he already spent more than enough time with ghosts. Had he just imagined Aleksei's strangeness?

"Just get home now," Tessa said in her best mothering voice. "You need to get out of there."

"I will. I'll call you tomorrow."

The pilot called to Danny and Terry that the plane was ready and the two of them quickly boarded. They both agreed they were anxious to leave this barren place behind.

As the plane took off and flew through the snow, Danny couldn't stop thinking about Aleksei Nechayev, his deathly cold hands, and his cobalt blue eyes with their unflinching gaze. Danny had been around more rapists, murderers, kidnappers, and general human garbage than he could count, and none of them had ever given him the chills. None of them had caused him to feel a rush of terror that took him completely by surprise and floored him.

He leaned his head back on the seat and tried to figure out what was so different about Nechayev. Unbidden, his mind drifted back to Amanda Fiske. She had described her attacker as unusually tall and blond, with dark blue eyes that were filled with evil.

Danny frowned, remembering how his mother used to warn him that drinking too much alcohol would addle the brain. Maybe he had finally done it and his brain was addled. What else could explain where his mind was now going?

Addled brain or not, he couldn't deny what was now suddenly so obvious. Amanda Fiske may be crazy, but her description of her attacker had been spot on.

She had described Aleksei Nechayev.

CHAPTER 21

Aleksei settled into his leather armchair and sipped his glass of vodka. He didn't want to admit it, but the Irish detective had left his nerves on edge. He knew he could deal with him if needed, but he didn't want it to come to that. He was angry that his winter had been disturbed and his home had been violated. His plans were important to him and they didn't include dealing with a nosy cop.

He was angry at himself that he had probably showed too much of the real Aleksei to Danny Fitzpatrick. He hadn't been able to resist giving the jackass a glimpse of the monster inside him when he shook his hand. He'd wanted to frighten the man and he knew he had succeeded. But when he thought about it now, he knew he had let his anger at Fitzpatrick's intrusion get the better of him. After so many years of perfecting his human cover, he never should have allowed that kind of a slip. It had been fun to give the detective a scare, but it had also been stupid, and he'd probably managed to pique Fitzpartick's interest even more.

He put his feet up on the ottoman in front of him and rested his head on the back of his chair. He considered visiting his guest, but he wasn't ready for her yet. It wasn't time. The cop's interference made keeping to his schedule even more important. He needed to stick with what he could control.

The reminder that his guest was totally under his control brought a small smile to his lips. There was no reason his winter couldn't still go on as planned. The cop was nothing more than an irritating fly who needed to be swatted away.

He needed to forget about the cop for tonight. And about his guest. And, about everything here in December, 2012. He wanted another December. The most important one of his very long life.

He took another sip of vodka, and closed his eyes. In his mind, the present had already drifted away. In his mind, he was back in a decidedly different December.

It was 1916, and Aleksei felt nothing but cold and pain. He had no idea where he was, or how long he had been there. The last thing he remembered was being stationed at the front outside Petrograd. The sound of cannon fire was overwhelming and then suddenly everything had gone quiet. And dark.

He was lying on a cot now and staring at a flimsy grey ceiling that seemed to be flapping in the wind. Was it a tent? He had no idea. But whatever it was, it didn't provide any warmth for the freezing room. He tried to sit up and find a blanket, but he was unable to move a muscle. The pain was simply too much.

As if by magic, she appeared next to his cot, holding a threadbare blanket in her arms. She unrolled the blanket and spread it over his shaking body.

"This was the best one I could find for you," she said. "I know you're terribly cold."

He opened his mouth to say thank you, but no sound came from his lips. Instead, a searing pain filled his throat.

"You don't have to speak," the woman said. She sat down on the cot next to him and produced a canteen from her apron. "Here, take a bit of water."

She held the canteen to his lips, and he winced as the water touched his parched throat. It was painful to swallow, but the water brought relief. He tried to take more, but she pulled the canteen away from him.

"I can't give you too much right now," she said. "This is all we have. I need

to conserve it."

Aleksei blinked and stared up at the woman, who remained on the side of his cot. She had long yellow hair pulled back from her face, and wore a dirty white apron over her blue dress. She clasped a tattered fur cape around her shoulders in an attempt to stay warm. In spite of her thin, drawn face and the circles under her blue eyes, Aleksei was sure she was the most beautiful woman he'd ever seen. She was an angel.

"I'm Natasha," she said. "I'm your nurse. Do you know where you are?"

Aleksei shook his head no.

"You're in the field hospital in Petrograd. You were wounded at the front but we're caring for you now." She patted his hand. "You'll be alright. Try to relax now. Расслабьтесь"

Aleksei lifted his head from his pillow and glanced around the room. There were more cots than he could count, jammed together and filled with fellow soldiers. Some moaned in agony, others were so still and silent Aleksei wondered if they were still alive.

"You'll be alright," Natasha said again as she pulled the blanket around his shoulders. "If I can find another blanket, I'll bring it to you."

Aleksei tried again to respond, but was interrupted by a scream and a commotion from across the room. A man yelled in pain, and knocked over a table filled with medical instruments. Natasha jumped up from her cot.

"I have to help that poor thing," she said. She patted Aleksei's hand again. "I'll be back to check on you."

He watched her walk from his cot and wanted to yell for her not to go, to come back, to stay with him. Outside of the pain and the cold and the hunger, he felt something far worse. He felt fear. He knew Natasha's insistence that he would be alright was just her attempt to comfort him. He knew it wasn't true. He was going to die and he knew it. And he was afraid.

Polar Night

He didn't want to die alone.

CHAPTER 22

Danny headed for Rex's Tavern, an age-old bar which was conveniently located right down the street from the police station, as soon as he and Terry landed back in Fairbanks. Still edgy from his trip to what he now believed really was a haunted asylum, he wasn't ready to be alone in his dreary apartment.

He parked his car and headed inside Rex's, immediately grateful for the warmth of the place, and the welcome noise of country & western music coming from the old jukebox in the corner of the room. Everything about Rex's was cheap and tacky, from the sticky wood-paneled bar to the tables and chairs made of logs to the fake moose head wearing a straw hat on the wall behind the bar. The only thing of quality in the whole place was the alcohol that Rex poured with an expert hand.

Danny walked to the bar and perched on his favorite stool, looking around as he waited for Rex to finish with another customer. He was surprised to see most of the tables full. Apparently lots of people in Fairbanks weren't in the Christmas spirit. Or perhaps they had just had enough of the family togetherness by this time on Christmas night.

"What can I get you, Detective?" Rex asked as he placed a small square napkin on the bar in front of Danny.

"Scotch," Danny said. "And you might as well plan on keeping them coming."

"Rough holiday?" Rex asked.

"A strange one. I've been working so I wouldn't call it a holiday anyway."

Rex nodded. "I can relate."

"I didn't expect you to have such a crowd here," Danny said.

"I always do on Christmas. Holidays make lots of people want to drink."

Danny chuckled. "True enough."

He watched as Rex headed to the other end of the bar to pour another beer for a woman Danny was fairly sure he recognized. He had probably seen her in here before. Everything about her demeanor suggested she was a regular. Briefly, Danny wondered if he had ever slept with her. He was ashamed to admit it, but it was hard to say one way or the other.

He realized that except for Tessa, Rex was the only person Danny had formed any kind of relationship with since he'd come to Fairbanks. He chided himself for being so pathetic. His only friend was a bartender who looked as old and haggard as the bar he owned. But Danny couldn't deny it was just the way he wanted it. No entanglements, no responsibilities. And above all, no attachments.

As Rex returned to fill up his scotch, Danny retraced the steps of his day in his mind, unable to stop thinking of the tall, ice-cold Russian he was certain was hiding something in his Arctic wasteland. It suddenly occurred to Danny that Rex's last name was Chistiakov, a Russian name if ever he'd heard one. If he remembered correctly, Rex had come to Fairbanks from the deeply Russian city of Sitka.

"Rex," he said. "Didn't you tell me you came here from Sitka?"

"I did," Rex answered. "What of it?"

"That's Russian, right?"

"Used to be. It was the capital when Alaska was a Russian colony."

"Your folks Russian?"

Rex put down the glass he was wiping clean. "Yeah. They came to Sitka from Russia. Why the questions?"

"I'm just curious. I met a Russian tonight and it got me thinking." Danny took a sip of his scotch. "You don't know the guy who runs Snow Creek up in Coldfoot by any chance, do you? Name of Nechayev?"

"You think I know every Russian in the state??"

"No, no. I just wondered. I know you know most of what goes on around here."

Rex nodded. "I've heard of that place up there, but I don't know who runs it. Supposedly it's haunted."

"Yeah. After being there I think it's safe to say it is."

"Is that where you were today?"

"It is."

"You've gotta be nuts. Who the hell goes up there this time of the year?"

"Not many people, I can tell you that."

Rex chuckled. "So, you saw some ghosts up there, huh?"

"More like heard them."

"Are you shitting me?"

"I'm not. It was the creepiest damn place I've ever been in my life."

Rex couldn't hide his laughter. "Well I don't doubt it on a night like this. Christ Danny, what the hell sent you up there?"

"Just working on a case."

"Hmm," Rex said. "So the stories about that place are true then?"

"I don't know all the stories, but I'd guess they probably are."

"Well I shouldn't doubt it. You get up in the Arctic, there's no telling what's up there."

Danny's ears perked up. "You've heard stories of weird things up there?"

"Nothing specific, really. My folks just loved all those tall tales and legends, that's all."

"Legends about what?"

"Oh just supernatural shit. They heard it growing up from my grandparents and they loved sharing the stories with me."

"You ever hear anything about vampires?" Danny asked.

"What on earth makes you ask that?"

"Just curious."

"Well now that you mention it, yeah. Those legends were big in Russia and Eastern Europe in my grandparents' time. The undead and all that. People coming up out of their graves and slinking around in the night." Rex paused as if searching his memory for long-forgotten tales. "I remember my mother telling me stories about vampires who were the sons of witches."

He glanced at Danny, who was smirking over his glass of scotch. "You'll notice, I said witches, not bitches."

"Probably one and the same."

Rex chuckled. "I guess so. Anyway the Russians believed that to kill the vampires, you had to nail their bodies to the insides of coffins or else burn them so there was nothing left but dust." He poured another glass of scotch for Danny and shook his head. "I'll tell you what, my mother scared the hell out of me with those tales."

"I guess so. Not exactly Cinderella."

"No. Fairy tales were a lot different back in those days."

"You think they were true? The legends, I mean, not the fairy tales."

"Danny, how much scotch have you had? Did you get a head start before you came here?"

"Why?"

"What the hell are you thinking, asking about these old folk tales?"

"I told you, I'm curious."

"Well, I never thought about them being true. But at the same time, I figure something must have been going on in those times to make people come up with the stories in the first place. I've lived long enough now that I don't think anything would shock me."

Rex nodded towards the door of the bar and the windows. "You see the Northern Lights out there tonight?"

"No, I didn't notice," Danny said, puzzled by the change of subject. "Why?"

"Just look at them. All those lights dancing all over our night sky. Nobody really knows what they are. I know they give some explanation about the sun particles and all that but that doesn't really explain it. Not the magic of actually seeing it, anyway."

"So?"

"So it's just an example to me that sometimes there are things you can't explain and that don't go by the rules we think we know. Who knows what caused people to come up with all those old legends, but I wouldn't automatically discount anything in this crazy ass world of ours. Those tales were probably all bullshit, but at the same time, who the hell knows?"

Danny nodded. "True enough. After being up there in the Arctic tonight I'm not sure I can discount anything."

"I'd suggest you go home and sleep off whatever you've got going on in that head of yours. It's obvious this trip up there did a number on you."

"I think you're right. I need to sleep it off." Danny noticed the woman at the other end of the bar trying to get Rex's attention. "And, I think my friend down there wants a refill," he said. "It's on me."

Danny opened his wallet and left money on the bar for Rex before downing the last of his scotch and leaving the tavern.

Chapter 23

He walked outside and was immediately confronted with the spectacular Aurora Borealis, more commonly known as the Northern Lights. He wondered how he had managed to not even notice the lights before heading into the Tavern. Had he really become so numb that he wasn't even moved by a spectacle such as this?

Rex was right, of course. The lights were spectacular. A curtain of red, yellow, and green lights blanketed the sky. No fireworks display could ever hope to compete with this phenomenon that was as natural as the air and the sea.

Danny had read some articles about the Northern Lights when he had first moved to Alaska, in a series that had been featured in the Fairbanks Daily News Miner. He had chuckled when reading about the old Eskimo belief that the Lights were spirits playing ball in the sky, or the dead carrying torches to guide the newly deceased into the afterlife. The Point Barrow Eskimos had considered the lights evil, and carried knives at all times for protection and to keep the lights at bay. Still other tribes considered the lights an omen of war or pestilence.

When Danny looked at the lights now and watched the dancing ribbons of red and green, he didn't chuckle. It was easy to see how the lights had inspired both awe and fear. And who was he to scoff at anything at this point? After what he had heard up in Snow Creek, and considering the fact that he was

110

actually entertaining the idea that Aleksei Nechayev was something other than human, he no longer felt he was qualified to judge anyone.

He got into his car and drove away from the tavern, the lights display illuminating his rear-view mirror and casting a glow over the interior of his car. He had told Rex he was going to sleep, but he had no intention of doing so. No amount of scotch would put him to sleep now. There was too much he needed to learn.

CHAPTER 24

Danny plugged his car back into the socket outside his apartment and walked inside, immediately grateful for the heat of his living room. He struggled out of his boots, parka, and mittens, and tossed them all on the floor next to his coat closet. He knew he should hang the parka and mittens up as they were wet with snow, but he couldn't be bothered. He was anxious to get to work.

Danny had never cared much about sleep when he got wrapped up in a case. He winced when he thought of Caroline fussing over his sleeping habits back when they were first together. She had given up soon enough, and eventually had no problem at all with going to bed on her own while Danny typed away on his laptop. He pushed the memory aside now, thinking that he'd stop working on this or any case within two seconds if he had the opportunity to curl up next to Caroline in bed just one more time.

He ran a hand through his mop of brown hair and grabbed his Macbook from his kitchen table. This was one of the few items Danny had not skimped on when setting up house here in Fairbanks. He loved computers, and he refused to buy crap. He had left his old Macbook behind in Chicago, unable to bear the traces of Caroline that he knew he would find all over it. A new hard drive had been as necessary as a new address and a new city.

Danny plopped down onto his sofa and stretched his legs out, settling the computer on his lap. He booted it up and quickly went to the site everyone went

112

to for any information they needed, regardless of how obscure or bizarre it might be. He knew he could find what he wanted on Google.

He typed in vampires, and was immediately deluged with sites about the Twilight franchise, television shows Buffy the Vampire Slayer and True Blood, and Anne Rice's famous vampire novels. None of this was even close to what he needed, but he should have known a search on vampires would turn up fictional creations. After all, wasn't that what they were? Fictional creations?

Danny got off the couch and headed for his kitchen, where he grabbed a six-pack of beer out of the refrigerator. It was going to be a long night, and he needed refreshments. He plopped back down on the couch and turned his attention back to his Macbook. He stared at the screen, thinking of his earlier conversation with Rex about folktales and legends in Russia and Europe. Okay, he thought. Might as well start there.

Danny's fingers clicked over his keyboard, and he was soon reading stories of Russian vampires called Upierczi. Apparently, the Upierczi became vampires by murder or suicide and the only way to permanently kill their undead selves was to drown them in salt water. In addition, legend had it that a Russian man traveling at night came upon a vampire heading back to his grave after he had killed two village boys. The man asked the vampire how he could resurrect the boys, and the vampire gave the man a section of his burial shroud and instructed him to burn the shroud in a pot of coals. The boys' bodies were to be left in the room with the pot, and they would be revived by breathing in the smoke of the burning shroud. Sure enough, the man insisted the boys had in fact been revived. Danny couldn't help but notice no one but the man who told the story had ever seen the vampire in the first place, and no one else had ever seen the boys' supposedly dead bodies.

He rolled his eyes and leaned back on his sofa, taking a long swig of beer as he stared at his ceiling. This still wasn't what he needed. These were nothing but ghost stories told by children around camp fires. Whatever Aleksei Nechayev was, Danny knew without a doubt that he was real.

Danny sat up again and typed more terms into the Google search bar. He paged through various websites, finishing one beer and starting on another, before he finally landed on something that caught his interest.

It was the story of Le vicomte de Montargy, a nobleman in eighteenth-century France who had managed to survive the chaos of the French Revolution. Montargy started murdering his employees following the revolution, in order to avenge the deaths of his noble brethren at the guillotines. The murder spree led to his assassination and, not long after his death, numerous young children died unexpectedly. All were found with bite wounds. For more than 70 years after his death, Montargy was suspected in the ongoing deaths of children in the area. The people in the area insisted Montargy was "undead," or a vampire.

Danny felt the hair on the back of his neck tingle as he read about the vicomte and his bloody killing spree. The information in English was limited but, thanks to Caroline and her French roots, Danny's knowledge of the French language was adequate. Caroline's parents had moved to the US from France before she was born, and Caroline had learned to speak French and English interchangeably when she was growing up. She hadn't passed this skill on to him, but he knew enough of the language to get by. He could read it even if he had never managed to speak it correctly. He typed in a few French search terms, and found a goldmine of information on the infamous Montargy.

At some point, Montargy's grandson decided to put an end to the rumors and find out the truth about his grandfather. He and town officials opened the family tomb, and found the decayed bodies of the Montargy family. But one body in the tomb was not the least bit decayed. The body of the vicomte appeared intact, his skin fresh and his hair and fingernails immaculate. The terrified and bewildered grandson drove a thorn into his grandfather's heart and had the body cremated. The child murders ceased.

Danny leaned back on the couch and finished his beer. Could this have really happened? Was Montargy an earlier version of his own Aleksei? He opened another beer and jumped when he heard her voice.

"What are you up so late reading about, Danny?"

"You're not here, Caroline."

"I'm not?"

"No. It's just the French. It reminded me too much of you."

Danny cursed himself for going to the French websites and reading so much in his dead wife's family language. He felt his throat closing up. He could hear Caroline coming up behind him at home while he worked and feel her wrapping her hands around his waist. She'd rest her head on his shoulder and look at his mess of notes and documents.

"What are you working on, mon coeur?"

Danny choked back tears. My heart. The pet name Caroline had called him for as long as he could remember. She had always laughed at his complete inability to pronounce it correctly. His mind drifted back in time.

"What are you working on, mon coeur?"

Danny reached his hand up and stroked Caroline's cheek.

"Just this damn case I've been stuck on."

"You should come to bed. It's late."

"I know but I'm almost done."

Caroline kissed his cheek and ran her hand up his chest.

"I worry about you when you get like this, you know. I can't help it. You don't eat, you're hardly sleeping..."

"I'll be fine as soon as I get this sorted out."

Caroline stood up and kissed the top of Danny's head.

"Alright then. I'm going to bed. Good night."

Danny grabbed her hand and held it to his lips.

"Good night, babe. I love you."

"Love you too, chéri." She grinned at him as she headed for their bedroom.
"Wake me up when you come to bed."

Danny grinned back. "I already planned to."

The sound of howling wind battering his windows brought Danny back to the present and his empty apartment. He stood up and paced the room, forcing himself to focus his mind where it needed to be. On Alaska and Aleksei Nechayev and vampires.

He sat back down and read a bit more about the intriguing vicomte de Montargy, learning that his infamy continued to persist to this day. He even had his own online fan club, and people who claimed to be both descendants of the vicomte and vampires themselves.

Danny thought they all sounded like lunatics, but he couldn't deny that the original story of Montargy interested him. After what he had encountered in Coldfoot, he wasn't above believing it was true.

He'd had enough of French though and quickly returned to English websites. Not that they wouldn't remind him of Caroline too. He had realized quite a while ago that virtually everything reminded him of Caroline. He didn't see that changing any time soon.

As Danny continued his research, he was surprised to read of vampire sightings and stories in more recent times. In 2002, reports of vampire attacks swept through the African country of Malawi, and mobs accused the government of colluding with vampires. In the mid-1990s, vampiric entities called chupacabras, or "blood suckers" were frequently reported in Mexico and Puerto Rico. In 2004, relatives of a Romanian man feared he had become a vampire and dug up his corpse so they could burn it. In the early 1970s, vampire hunters flocked to Highgate Cemetery in London after reports that a vampire frequented the place. The reports were said to be rumors started by the local press, but many continued to believe in the existence of the "Highgate Vampire."

Danny felt both comforted and horrified by the various reports. On one hand, he couldn't believe he was actually reading them and considering the possibility that they were true. But on the other hand, he was glad that he wasn't the only one who had apparently encountered a creature that couldn't be explained by ordinary means. He felt some sort of kinship to the various people involved in the tales.

And he also felt like a drunk lunatic. He glanced at his clock and groaned at the time. 3:00 in the morning. Captain Jack Meyer would be blustering about the office and wondering where Danny was in just a few short hours.

He rubbed his eyes and got up from the couch, figuring he might as well hit the sack and get at least a few hours of sleep. He'd finished the six-pack anyway and he'd had enough of vampire tales for one night.

He stumbled to his bed, kicked off his shoes and stripped down to his boxers, throwing his clothes on a chair next to his bed. He burrowed under his heavy blankets and fell asleep as soon as his head touched his pillow. He dreamed of Caroline.

CHAPTER 25

To his own surprise, Danny managed to stumble into his office by 8:00 am, after his usual breakfast of coffee, Pop-Tarts, and Excedrin. He couldn't stop thinking about the Frenchman Montargy and the other vampire sightings he had spent most of the night reading about. A few hours of sleep and the dawn of a new day, in spite of the fact that the sun would not show its face for hours yet, had convinced Danny that everything he had read about the supposed undead had been a bunch of crap. So why couldn't he get it out of his head that Aleksei Nechayev could be another in a long line of undead beings roaming the earth?

Maybe it was the hangover or the residual effects of his trip to the haunted Arctic asylum. Whatever the reason, Danny couldn't deny it that he was seriously starting to believe that Aleksei really was a vampire. Or at least some sort of creature that defied explanation. He couldn't shake the feeling he had gotten when he shook Aleksei's hand and looked into his eyes. Whatever Nechayev was, it wasn't like anything he had ever encountered before. And he wouldn't have thought that was possible.

At any rate, he was glad the night was over now, and he would soon be greeted with daylight and the return of human companionship. He'd had enough of ghosts. He was also relieved to see December 26th on the calendar. It was a pleasure to have Christmas over for another year.

Danny was more than ready to work. If there was one benefit to his trip to Coldfoot, it was that the meeting with Nechayev had renewed his determination to get to the bottom of this case. It had been a long time since Danny had wanted to attack a case with this much vigor.

He might not have any evidence on Aleksei Nechayev now, but that would change. He just needed to know where to look. If Nechayev didn't keep his victims at Snow Creek, he must have another place where he took them. Danny also needed to find out who else Nechayev had kidnapped, and likely murdered, over the years. He was certain there were lots more unsolved cases, and lots more missing women. He just had to find them.

He started searching through the Alaska property records, certain Aleksei must own more property besides the Snow Creek resort. To his frustration, he came up empty-handed. He racked his brain for anything he and Terry could have missed on their visit to Snow Creek, but was sure they had covered everything. If Aleksei didn't have Maria Treibel there, and he didn't own more land where he could be holding her, there had to be an abandoned place somewhere that he claimed as his own. Or perhaps he had purchased property under another name?

Danny sighed and rubbed his hands through his hair as he leaned back in his desk chair and stared outside at the light traffic going by on Cushman Street. Most people were at home sleeping off their Christmas celebrations and the street was nearly empty of passers-by. He was getting nowhere fast with his real estate search. Maybe he'd have better luck looking for more victims.

Danny was sure that he would find connected cases all over Alaska, and realized he should not have originally limited his search to just Fairbanks. He also knew that Nechayev could easily have ventured in to Canada to find his prey. Or to the Northwestern US. Danny needed more tools and a broader scope, and he knew just where to find it.

For the first time since he had moved to Alaska, Danny took out his phone and called Chicago. He briefly wondered what time it was there, and was momentarily confused about whether he was ahead of Chicago time or behind, but then decided he didn't give a damn anyway. He didn't want to waste any more time, and this had to start now.

"Hello, this is Agent John Fisher."

Danny was relieved to hear his old friend's voice.

"Hello, Agent Fisher. This is Danny Fitzpatrick."

He wasn't surprised to hear nothing but silence on the other end of the line.

"Fitzpatrick?" John finally said. "Are you kidding me?"

"Not at all."

"What the fuck? Where are you?"

"I'm in Alaska. I work in Fairbanks now."

"Alaska? Are you kidding me?"

"Still not kidding you."

"Why haven't you called anyone? I haven't heard from you since…"

He stopped talking in mid-sentence, illustrating exactly why Danny hadn't called anyone. He couldn't bear the awkward silences and the "how are you doing?" mumblings he knew he would get after Caroline's death.

Danny cleared his throat. "I know. It's been a long time. I'm sorry. I just needed to get out of Chicago."

"I understand," John said, in a voice that made it clear he didn't. "So what's up now? What can I do for you?"

"I was hoping you'd ask that. I need access to your databases."

"What? Are you…" he stopped himself again.

"You were going to ask me if I'm kidding you again, right? Once more, I'm not."

"You got me. But if you're not kidding me, then you must be fucking nuts."

"I won't dispute that. But I still need the access. I'm working on a case involving missing women. I don't have the tools up here to do an extensive search. I need to be able to look outside of Fairbanks, outside of Alaska, and possibly outside the country. Canada, at least. I need the FBI, John."

"So you want my credentials to log in?"

"Yes."

"No way. You really are nuts. You think I don't need my job? I'd get fired for this in a heartbeat. Forget it."

Danny sighed. He had expected this response, but he figured there couldn't be any harm in trying. "Alright then. How about you go through your system for me. I'll give you the search criteria."

John was silent, obviously trying to decide how to answer.

"Oh, come on," Danny said. "Don't try to act like you're too busy. You think I don't know the FBI slows down at Christmas, too? I bet you're sitting in a half-empty office right now, aren't you? And, you're pissed you're stuck at work, am I right?"

"Not far off."

"Well then, what have you got to lose? You do my search for me, and send me everything you can find. I'll do all the work going through the files and finding the women that match my case."

John paused again, and Danny could visualize him leaning back in his chair and drumming his fingers on his desk. "Alright," he finally said. "Tell me what you need."

Danny gave John the details on Anna and Maria, and the search criteria he was looking for.

"How far back do you want me to go?" John asked.

Danny thought of Amanda Fiske and her crazy ideas. Did he really want to go there? He shook his head. Fuck it. "Go back as far as you can, nothing's too old. Just give me everything you can find."

"So you want old cases? You think you're dealing with some kind of a copy cat?"

"Possibly." Danny left it at that. He could only imagine John's reaction if he said he might be dealing with a vampire.

"Alright," John said. "I'll send you what I can find, shouldn't take long. One condition, though."

"What is it?"

"I want to know how this case ends up. And if you make some huge arrest, I want in on it."

Danny rolled his eyes. "I'll give you credit, don't worry."

"It's good to hear from you, Fitzpatrick."

"Thanks. Good talking to you, too." Danny spoke mechanically, hoping John couldn't tell he didn't mean a word he was saying.

He gave John his contact information and thanked him again for his help. He hung up the phone and returned to staring out the window. There was nothing to do now but sit and wait.

CHAPTER 26

Danny didn't have to wait long before a report from John Fisher appeared in his inbox. He clicked on the e-mail, and immediately began to download the attached files. Within minutes, the files were printed out and waiting for him.

He grabbed the papers from the printer and walked back to his cubicle, where he slid into his chair and propped his feet up on the desk. He was glad to see that Fisher had been considerate enough to arrange the files chronologically. Or at least, his database had been. Fisher likely had nothing to do with it.

Danny read through the first report in his stack. Rachel McKenzie went missing in December of 2011. A 25 year old blond woman, she was last seen leaving the doctor's office where she worked in Ketchikan, Alaska.

He paged through the reports.

December, 2010, Allison Saunders, 28 and blond, went missing in Juneau. Last seen leaving her law office.

December, 2007, Kristen Barrowman. Barrowman was a 23 year old blond who had disappeared in Anchorage. She was reported missing on December 23, and the last anyone could remember seeing her had been on the 21st. The Solstice.

December, 2005, Angela Marshall. Last seen at a shopping mall in Seattle, Washington. She was tall and thin, with striking long blond hair. She'd disappeared on the winter solstice. No body was ever found and the case was never solved.

December, 2002. Beautiful, blond-haired Erin Rothman disappeared from the town of Crescent City, California, about 20 miles south of the Oregon border.

December, 2001. Rebecca Scoggins. Disappeared in Prince George, British Columbia.

December, 1998. Bailey Simmons, last seen in Ketchikan, Alaska.

December, 1995. Samantha Sharapova. Disappeared in Vancouver, British Columbia.

Danny leaned back in his chair and stared at the ceiling over his desk. So many women, in so many different jurisdictions. No bodies had ever been found, and the cases had all quickly gone cold. It was the norm with missing person cases. Cops could never be sure if the person hadn't simply disappeared on purpose, so when there was no sign of foul play, it was easy to let the cases slide. Danny was sure his killer knew that. More specifically, he was sure Aleksei Nechayev knew that.

But what had he done with all the bodies? Danny thought back to his visit to Coldfoot. How hard would it be to hide bodies in a landscape as barren as that? Danny couldn't imagine a better place for a murderer to take up residence.

He put his feet on the floor and leaned over the papers on his desk, rifling through them to find older files. He didn't want to admit why he was doing it.

December, 1965. Betty O'Neill. A soldier's daughter living at Fort Wainwright. She was only 18, blond, and beautiful, and had never been seen again after she left home to attend the winter solstice celebration in downtown Fairbanks. Danny felt his jaw clench.

December, 1950. Anna Maria Thiessen. Another military kid, this time living at Elmendorf Air Force Base in Anchorage. Another blond 18 year old.

Danny put the papers down as he felt his stomach turning. He wondered when Nechayev had graduated to adult women instead of 18 year old kids. If he went back farther into the past, would he find even younger girls?

He browsed through a few more reports and got his answer.

December, 1930. A 16 year old girl named Elena Dobrynin had disappeared in Sitka, Alaska. Had this been Nechayev's first victim?

Danny tossed the pages onto his desk and leaned back in his chair, rubbing his eyes. What the hell was he doing here? How could Nechayev have kidnapped someone in 1950, let alone 1930? Danny had just met the guy and he sure as hell wasn't anything close to a senior citizen.

So why had he even looked at the old files? Was he looking for a copycat, as Fisher assumed? Or was he finally as crazy as Amanda Fiske? He needed to stop staring at these files of ghosts and talk to someone rational.

As if on cue, Tessa walked in and headed for her desk. Danny turned to her and smiled.

"Hey there," he said. "I thought you were still off today?"

Tessa shrugged. "I had the day off, but I wanted to get back with you on the Treibel case."

"You got something new on it?"

"I don't have anything on it. Trail's completely cold."

"That's no surprise. That's what happened with Anna Alexander, too."

"I know. I guess I was just hoping we could turn up something from your visit to Coldfoot last night."

"I wish we could. But I don't have anything more I can tell you than what I did last night. Terry and I searched that whole god-forsaken place and found nothing. The guy's off, and he creeped us both out, but I don't have anything tangible on him. Unless you want to arrest him based on my gut instinct."

Tessa frowned and rubbed her eyes.

"Mind you, my instinct is probably more reliable than most of the evidence we find. I'm always right."

Tessa laughed. "Yeah, I already knew that. Even in the short time we've known each other, it's obvious."

"It is?"

"Oh sure, honey. I tell everyone in the department that. You need something, go to Danny. That boy is never wrong."

Danny chuckled. "Joke all you want, but in this case, I really am right. Nechayev is guilty, whether I can prove it or not."

"Even so, it doesn't help our case. Or bring us any closer to finding Maria Treibel."

"He's got her up in that frozen hellhole somewhere, I know it. We just need something else to go on."

Tessa looked at the stack of papers on Danny's desk. "Is that what you've got there? Something else we could go on?"

"Maybe. I contacted an old friend in the FBI and had him send me records of missing women that matched our criteria. He sent me a hell of a list."

Tessa reached for the stack and flipped through the pages. "Interesting," she said. "All the way back to 2002 or 2001? If this is our guy he's been busy for a while."

"Why stop there? Didn't you see the rest?"

"I guess I just assumed..." Tessa stopped. "You met this guy last night. How old is he?"

"Not old. I don't know. Maybe 25. He looks young. Might be 30."

"25 or 30? And you think he was doing this before 2000? You think a kid could pull this kind of thing off?"

Danny tapped his foot on the floor. How much did he want to tell Tessa? Not much, he decided. "Maybe he had someone he was working with, somebody who taught him the ropes."

"You mean like a family member? A father-son kidnap team?"

"Could be."

"Or do you think he's copying someone else now?"

"That crossed my mind. He discovered these old crimes somehow and he's a copycat."

Tessa stared at Danny. "But you don't really think so."

Danny shrugged. "I don't know what I think. Except for the fact that Nechayev's a psycho. That, I don't just think. I know it."

Tessa glanced through more pages. "1930? What the hell are you up to, Danny?"

"I just asked my friend for reports of missing women. I didn't put any limit on him and asked for everything he could find."

"What's the point of going through cases from the 1930s? Or the 50s? You think Nechayev had a grandfather involved too?"

Danny sighed. "I told you, I don't know what I think."

"Bullshit. You've got something on your mind."

Danny ran his hand through his hair and across the stubble that had returned to his face. As much as he liked Tessa, he simply couldn't share his conversation with Amanda Fiske and subsequent suspicions. She'd think he should be committed and he wouldn't even be able to argue the point.

"I'm not lying to you, Tessa. I honestly don't know what the hell I'm thinking here. I just know we have to put the screws to Nechayev."

"How do you think we should do that?"

"I don't know. We can't exactly have a stake-out at his place, can we? The only way to be inconspicuous up there would be to be buried in snow."

Tessa booted up her computer. "I'll go back over everything I've got on Maria. See if I can link Nechayev to her some other way."

Danny nodded and re-arranged his stack of FBI files. He put them in a folder and got up from his desk.

"You going somewhere?" Tessa asked.

"Yeah. I need to talk to someone."

"Who?"

"No one you know. Just someone I think might have an idea about all this."

"Okay. If I find anything new here I'll call you."

"Great. Here's hoping."

Danny walked out of the office and back out into the never-ending snow. He pulled his hat and hood closer around his head, and wrapped a scarf around his face. He couldn't possibly tell Tessa where he was going, as he couldn't really believe it himself. But he couldn't deny it. He wanted to talk to Amanda Fiske.

CHAPTER 27

Maria shuddered as she heard the door to the root cellar open. She pulled her blanket closer around her face, not wanting to look at Aleksei as he descended the stairs. His lantern cast flickers of light around the walls of the cellar.

He stopped at the bottom of the stairs. "Let's not play this game again, okay? I know perfectly well you're not sleeping. Get up."

Maria sat up and pushed strands of blood-crusted, matted hair out of her eyes. She squinted at the light, as her own lantern had run out hours earlier and she had been in pitch black darkness ever since.

"How was your Christmas dinner?" Aleksei asked.

"Fine. Thank you."

Aleksei nodded. "Glad to see you're remembering your manners." He looked Maria up and down, scowling at her disheveled and generally filthy appearance. "God, you're a mess."

"You can thank yourself for that."

Aleksei smirked. "Be careful. I just congratulated you on your manners. Don't make me take that back."

Maria stared to reply but swallowed her words. She knew she wouldn't be able to handle another lesson in manners at this point.

"Now listen," Aleksei said, with his voice the brisk tone of a businessman calling a meeting. "When I said get up, I meant get up. This is a big day for you.

Stand up. Now."

Maria took a deep breath and forced herself to her feet. Immediately dizzy, she clutched at the dirt wall for balance, and nearly fell as her knees buckled beneath her.

As he had before, Aleksei moved across the cellar too quickly to be seen. He grabbed her arm and steadied her before she fell back to the hard mud of the cellar floor.

"Don't worry, I've got you," he said, holding her arm with a strength she had never felt before. Although he was trying to help her stand and walk, Maria felt as if he might break her arm in two.

He pulled her across the cellar towards the stairs, and pushed her in front of him.

"Go ahead," he said. "Get out of here."

Maria stumbled up the stairs and was hit square in the face with a mixture of ice pellets and wet snowflakes, and a blast of Arctic air. She cried out and fell face first into the snow.

Aleksei slammed the root cellar door behind them. He grabbed Maria by the arm and pulled her off the ground as if she was a rag doll. "Just hurry up and get inside where it's warm."

He quickly pushed Maria through the doorway of his home, where she again fell forward, this time onto a ceramic tile floor. Maria burst into tears and curled into the fetal position, pulling her legs around her chest and cradling herself.

Aleksei glared at her and sat down in a nearby chair. "For God's sake, get up," he said.

Maria glanced around and saw the bottoms of a stove and the cabinet of a sink, and the legs of a table and chairs. This was a kitchen. This monster's kitchen.

"I said get up!" Aleksei yelled.

When Maria didn't move quickly enough for him, he grabbed her again, jerking her arm and pulling her onto the chair next to his. "You better start doing what I say," he said. "Do I have to remind you what I told you about my substitute? My backup plan? If you want to live through the winter, you're going to need to do a lot better than this."

Maria bit her lip and tried to stop the sobs that were wracking her body. "I'm freezing," she said.

"I've no doubt you are. You're the idiot who left your blanket down in the cellar. Did I tell you to leave it there?"

"I didn't know what we were doing."

Aleksei held up his hand. "Please, I don't want to hear excuses for your stupidity. You didn't know it would be cold outside in Alaska in December?" He shook his head. "Maybe I really do need to fall back on my other plan."

"No, please," Maria cried. "I'm just not thinking straight. I'm sorry."

Aleksei waved his hand as if dismissing her. "Forget it. We'll just move forward."

Maria stared at him, noticing his perfectly hemmed and pressed black pants and grey t-shirt. The shirt was short-sleeved and, for the first time since he had come down to the root cellar, Maria noticed he was bare foot. Who walks in the snow with bare feet?

"How come you're not cold?" she asked, unable to stop herself.

"Because I'm not," Aleksei answered. "I like the cold. It doesn't bother me."

"But how is that possible?"

"Never mind how. What business is it of yours? And if you must know, remember that I'm Russian. I grew up cold." He shook his head again. "You American girls are such wimps. Natasha wouldn't have fussed about a little cold and snow."

Maria flashed back to his words about her "audition" to be his mysterious

Natasha. She forced herself to stop shivering. "I'm fine. The cold is fine."

Aleksei jumped up from his chair with a quickness that startled her. "Let's move on. I want you to be comfortable and I don't want you in my kitchen in such a filthy state. It's unseemly."

He grabbed her arm again and pulled her from the kitchen. "You need to get cleaned up."

Maria could barely make our her surroundings as Aleksei pulled her down a carpeted hallway and shoved her into a large bathroom with a small space heater in the corner. She nearly cried from joy at the blast of heat on her frozen legs.

"As you can see, I have everything you need here," Aleksei said. He gestured around the bathroom. "Towels, soap, shampoo, hair dryer, and a warm robe and slippers to change into when you are finished."

Maria nodded. "Thank you."

"Take as long as you need," Aleksei said. "I'm not in a hurry. But I expect you to be clean and presentable when you come out. I won't have a disgusting whore at my dinner table."

Maria nodded again.

Aleksei turned on the shower and Maria watched as the steam quickly filled the tub. He pulled the curtain closed and grabbed the bathroom door.

"I'll give you your privacy," he said. "Knock on the door when you're finished."

With that, he left the bathroom and closed the door behind him. Maria heard a key turn in the door, and realized there was no knob on her side. She was locked in.

She should have expected it, but she shuddered nonetheless. She pulled the shower curtain aside and was disappointed, but not surprised, to find that the bathroom had no window. There was no way out of this room except to do exactly as the monster had said. She would have to knock for him to let her out.

The enormity of her situation hit her again, and the walls of the bathroom seemed to close in on her. Even the much welcome heat now felt suffocating. She wondered if she could turn the heater off, or if that would offend him. She didn't want to risk it.

Forcing herself to focus on the fact that she could at least get clean, she stripped herself of her filthy clothes and piled them on the floor. Part of her didn't want to give them up, as they were the only connection she had to her real life. But she knew without a doubt that she would never be wearing them again.

She stepped into the shower and let the hot water rush over her swollen, bruised face. She wondered if he was standing right on the other side of the door, listening for anything that might piss him off. Grabbing a wash towel, she leaned against the wall underneath the shower head and stuffed the towel into her mouth to muffle the sound of her sobs.

CHAPTER 28

Danny barely noticed his car slipping on the snowy roads as he once again made his way from the police station to the public library. He was fixated on the list John Fisher had sent him and on the names of all those young women. What had happened to them? Were there more?

He pulled into the library parking lot and let out a deep breath as he turned off the ignition and stared at the brick building in front of him. Was he really going to pursue this vampire craziness? He shoved his keys in his pocket and answered his own question by getting out of the car and walked towards the library.

Yes, he was.

He walked inside and saw Amanda Fiske at her usual spot behind the reference desk. He briefly wondered if the woman ever took a day off. Then he realized she could easily wonder the same thing about him.

"Ms. Fiske," he said.

Amanda looked up from her computer and frowned as her hand went to the cross around her neck. "What do you want, Detective?"

"I want to talk to you."

"We've talked enough."

"No, we haven't."

Amanda got up from her stool and slammed her hands on the desk. Her

134

cheeks turned a fiery red. "Yes, we have. I can't even believe you're harassing me again."

Danny held up his hands. "I'm not harassing you. I just want to talk to you."

"One and the same."

"You didn't think that on Christmas Eve."

"That's right I didn't. At least not until you decided I was a kook."

"Hey, that wasn't me. That was my predecessor."

Amanda rolled her eyes. "Just leave me alone, will you? I told you my story and you didn't believe me. I don't have anything else to say to you."

Danny took off his gloves and hat and set them on Amanda's desk. "Listen," he said. "I'm sorry, I really am. And, I admit, I didn't believe you."

"Then why are you back here again?"

"Because the situation's changed. Or at least, the way I'm looking at it has changed."

Amanda raised an eyebrow. "What do you mean?"

"I met someone last night who scared the shit out of me. And he was the spitting image of the guy you described as your attacker."

"You mean the vampire I described?"

Danny tried to keep from making a face. Jesus, what was he doing? "Yeah, whatever. I still don't know if I believe the whole vampire thing."

"How did you meet him? Where is he?"

"I can't tell you the details about the case. But I can't get him out of my mind. I think he's the one who tried to abduct you."

"Then I want to see him. I want to testify and get him arrested."

"That's not going to be so easy given your history. No one's going to believe you if you come out again saying you were attacked by a vampire."

Amanda's cheeks flared red again. "Then what's the point of this? What the hell do you want?"

"I'm not even sure. I just want to talk to you. I can't explain it and to tell you the truth, I think I'm fucking crazy myself. But I can't shake it. You're the key to this, I know it." He shook his head and scoffed. "Oh, fuck it. I believe you, okay? I met this psychopath and I believe you. I don't think he's human. I don't know what the fuck he is, and I'm really not ready to start talking about vampires, but I know there's something wrong with this guy."

Amanda sat back down in her chair. "You felt it too, didn't you? That he's a monster. You knew it."

Danny let out a breath. "Yeah, I felt it. But that's part of the problem; I've met plenty of monsters before. Christ, I used to spend most of my time going after monsters." He rubbed his eyes and dropped into the chair next to the desk. "I'll tell you what it was. I was a homicide detective in Chicago for more than ten years. I've seen every kind of psychopath you can imagine, and then some. And never once did I get a chill down my spine when I looked one of them in the eyes."

"Obviously you did last night?"

"Yeah, I did."

"I told you about his eyes. There's nothing there but evil."

"I'm right there with you on that. Trouble is, I can't arrest someone because they've got evil eyes."

Amanda came around from behind the desk and sat down next to Danny.

Danny seemed to barely notice her presence. "You know, I don't have a career anymore to speak of. I mean, Jesus, how much worse could it get than cold cases in Fairbanks, Alaska? So it really doesn't matter to me what this does to my career. But do you know what's gonna happen if I start telling my superiors I know who's kidnapping these women and he's been at it since at least 1930, even though he looks about 25 years old right now in 2012? If I tell them he's a vampire? Do you think they're just going to say 'sounds great,

Danny, go get him,'?"

"I think I know a bit about how people will react if you tell them your suspicions."

"I'll end up in the god-damn psych ward. Especially with my reputation."

"What reputation is that?"

"A booze hound who's very tight-lipped about why he left Chicago homicide. A loner and a screw-up. A physical and emotional wreck whose life is in shambles. Do I need to go on?"

Amanda smiled. "That's okay. I think I get it."

Danny sat up and stared across the table at her. "I had an old friend at the FBI run through old missing person cases. There are cases that match this same criteria going all the way back to 1930. Young blond women or girls, going missing in December around the winter solstice, body never found and cases never solved…"

He watched as the color drained from Amanda's face.

"Oh, Christ, I'm sorry," he said. "I shouldn't be going on about all this with you."

Amanda rubbed the cross between her fingers. "No, it's okay. I was just thinking though how close I came to being on your friend's list of cases."

"I know. I'm sorry."

Amanda cleared her throat. "It's okay. Really. She sat up and folded her hands in front of her on the table. "What do you want though? What do you think I can do?"

"You can identify him. Even if you wouldn't be considered a reliable witness, I'd believe you. I'd know I'm right about him. I don't know how we'd get back up to Coldfoot right now in this weather, though. And there's no record on him. I don't have any pictures…"

"If he's a vampire, I don't think he would show up in photographs. Or at least not in mirrors. That's the legend, anyway."

Danny closed his eyes. "I still can't believe I'm talking about this." He shook his head and looked back at Amanda. "You think all that crap is true? Coffins and wooden stakes and all that?"

"I know the so-called crap about silver crosses is true. Maybe the rest is too."

Danny shook his head. "Jesus. I can hear my mother now, telling me I should have listened to her about alcohol. It's killed my brain."

Amanda laughed and glanced up at the clock. "You know, I'm actually off work right now. I was supposed to be off 15 minutes ago."

Danny looked around for another librarian and saw no one. "I'm sorry. I just assumed you were the only one here."

"My boss is in the back. She'll come out when I leave."

"So are you saying you want to get out of here?"

"Yeah, I am. I want to go home and have dinner." She paused. "You're welcome to come with me."

"You're inviting me to dinner?"

"Yeah. I'm a good cook, I promise."

Danny laughed. "You could be the worst cook in the world and you'd still top me. When I'm at home, I usually just eat Pop-Tarts."

"Then it sounds like you could use a decent meal."

"I could, I admit it."

Amanda got up from her chair. "Alright then. I'll just go tell my boss I'm leaving, and you can follow me back to my place. We can talk more about our vampire problem over dinner."

Danny watched her back as she retreated into the back room of the library. He stood up and grabbed his hat and gloves from the reference desk and marveled at his own behavior as he prepared to go back out into the cold. He couldn't believe he was going to the home of a potential witness, and telling her details of his case that he hadn't bothered to tell his captain, or even his fellow detective. Not to mention the fact that those details could easily land him in a psychiatrist's office, stripped of his badge and his job.

Never mind all that. If he lost his job and what little standing he had in Fairbanks, so be it. He'd lost more in one Chicago second than he'd ever had in Fairbanks anyway. There was nothing left for him to lose.

CHAPTER 29

Aleksei sat upright in his leather chair and listened to the sound of water running as Maria took her shower. She certainly was taking her sweet time about it. But at least she ought to be clean when she finally knocked on the door and indicated she was ready for him to let her out of the bathroom.

At long last, he heard the sound of the shower being shut off. It shouldn't take her too long now to towel off and dry her hair. He rubbed his hands along the arm of his chair and tried to calm his nerves. His irritability annoyed him. No, more than annoyed. It pissed him off.

He knew it was that damn cop who had ruffled his normally calm demeanor. He should just find the man, get rid of him, and forget he had ever darkened his doorstep. But he didn't want to risk sending other cops in his direction.

And, if he was being honest, he knew it wasn't just Danny Fitzpatrick who had set his nerves on edge. It was also his guest. He had to admit, he didn't think she was going to work out. He was starting to wonder why he had ever chosen her. She had the right look, but he hadn't paid enough attention when he had discovered her over the Thanksgiving holiday. He hadn't realized that she was too old for his Natasha. Too worn.

Or maybe he was just tiring of his ritual. So many years, and so many women, and he'd never found one who could really replace Natasha. Every year he was certain he had found the one. Every year he ended up disappointed.

Not for the first time, he considered making a permanent companion for himself. He hadn't wanted to deal with the baggage involved before, but maybe now was the time.

If he did go that route, he definitely needed to think younger. Maria Treibel was certainly too old and too sour. The woman's personality was severely lacking. He needed someone fresh and full of life. Someone like Natasha.

He listened to the sound of the hair dryer coming from the bathroom and knew Maria would be knocking for him soon. He'd give her a chance at least, and see how she managed his holiday plans.

But he was fairly sure he would be moving on to his backup plan. His mind drifted to Katie Bailey, the teenager who had visited Snow Creek with her family a few days earlier. She may just be the perfect choice. Young and beautiful, she was much more like Natasha than Maria would ever be.

He tried imagining how it would feel to turn her and make her his permanent companion. He felt exhilarated at the thought, and excited about the prospect of teaching Katie how to act like an adult. He would start by discarding her juvenile name and calling her Katerina.

Lost in thought, he jumped when he heard Maria knocking on the bathroom door. He stood up and ran his hand through his blond hair to smooth it, then headed down the hallway. He forced himself to put Katie out of his mind and focus on the guest at hand.

Aleksei opened the bathroom door and found it much easier to forget about Katie than he expected. He looked Maria up and down, taking in her long, thin frame under the thick white robe he had given her. Her hair was thick and shiny, and fell past her shoulders. With her face scrubbed and clean, she was indeed beautiful. In spite of the bruises and the split lip his manners lessons had given her.

He reached out to touch Maria's cheek, and she instantly flinched away from him. He frowned and grabbed her arm.

"I take it your shower met your needs?" he asked.

"It did, yes."

"Then I would expect some courtesy from you."

He pulled Maria down the hall before she could respond, and pushed her into a large windowless bedroom. In the center of the room was a large mahogany sleigh bed, covered with a plush lavender comforter, ivory sheets, and an assortment of ivory and lavender pillows. A matching mahogany nightstand and dresser, both adorned with old fashioned gaslights, completed the room. Maria's slippered feet sunk into the soft ivory carpet.

"This is your room," Aleksei said.

"It's nice," Maria said.

Aleksei opened a walk-in closet and pulled out a long grey flannel skirt and a matching tailored jacket. He tossed both on the bed, and reached into the closet again to bring out a long-sleeved white blouse. He walked to the dresser and pulled out a pair of grey tights, putting both the tights and the blouse on the bed next to the skirt and jacket. Finally, he returned to the closet and reached down to pick up a pair of black kitten heel shoes with a t-strap and buckle. He set the shoes on the floor next to the bed and returned to stand beside Maria.

"There you go," he said. "Get dressed."

Maria clutched onto her robe and made no move towards the bed.

Aleksei ignored her and walked towards the bedroom door. "I'll give you your privacy while you change. But I expect you to be quick about it. I want you presentable for dinner."

Maria walked to the bed and ran her fingers over the clothing. The clothes were beautiful, but looked straight out of the early 1900s.

"Where did you get these clothes?" she asked.

"Why do you want to know?"

"They look so old-fashioned. Like something you'd see on tv."

142

"Maybe they are. You've heard of costume shops?"

Maria turned back towards Aleksei. "But why?"

"Because they're what I want. I can't stomach the way women dress today. So classless and revealing. And I've never seen a worse trend than women wearing trousers."

"How old are you?"

"Your rudeness never ceases to astound me."

Maria's face turned white. "I'm sorry, I just…"

"Never mind. Let's just say I'm older than I look. Now hurry up and get dressed."

Aleksei walked to the bedroom door and stopped as he put his hand on the knob. He turned back towards Maria.

"What's your name again?"

Maria's face registered surprise. He didn't remember? "My name's Maria."

Aleksei gripped the door handle and tried to stifle his rage. "I'll ask you again. What is your name? And I warn you, you don't want to make me ask a third time."

Maria stared at him as her hands started to tremble. She tried to think of what he wanted, but she found herself completely unable to think. Her name??

"Natasha," she blurted out, suddenly remembering Aleksei's previous instructions. "My name is Natasha."

"Natasha what?"

Maria shook her head. "I don't know. I'm sorry, I don't remember."

Aleksei scowled. "Koslova. Natasha Koslova. You got it now?"

Maria nodded.

"I know I haven't discussed this with you yet, but you're a nurse. You help wounded soldiers. Like me."

"Like you? I don't understand.."

"Get dressed," Aleksei said. "I'll be back soon to get you."

He walked out of the room and slammed the door behind him. Maria looked at the door, already knowing what she would see. Or more accurately, what she wouldn't see. There was no knob on her side of the door.

CHAPTER 30

"You are a good cook," Danny said. He took another forkful of lasagna and smiled across the table at Amanda.

"Thanks. But lasagna really isn't hard to make."

"It is for me. Frankly, this salad would be a bit much for me to handle."

Amanda laughed and took a sip of red wine. "My grandmother taught me how to cook when I was a young girl. But, she only taught me Norwegian recipes. It pains her now that my favorite cooking is Italian."

"That's your background? Norwegian?"

"Yeah. On my Dad's side, anyway. My mother's family came to Alaska from Russia."

"Interesting. I don't think I've ever had Norwegian cooking."

"Well, if you like salmon or herring, you'd probably like it. The problem for me was that I hated fish. I still hate fish."

Danny laughed. "I like everything, really. I don't care what it is. I'll eat anything."

"I kind of figured that when you said your main diet consists of Pop-Tarts."

"What's wrong with Pop-Tarts? The blueberry pastries are especially excellent."

"I like Pop-Tarts. I just wouldn't want to live on them."

Danny took a drink of wine. "Well, I add beer, too."

"Oh, well, no problem then."

"Right, I've got it covered."

Amanda finished her glass of wine and debated whether to pour another. The debate didn't last long, as she grabbed the bottle and poured another glass. She leaned back in her chair and stared at Danny as he finished the last of his salad.

"So now that we've had a chance to eat, tell me about what happened when you met my would-be kidnapper."

Danny gulped the last of his wine and, following Amanda's lead, quickly re-filled his glass. "What do you want to know?"

"I guess a good start would be telling me his name. You didn't mention that. Who is he?"

"I know I didn't mention that. And there's a good reason for that. I shouldn't be talking about suspects with you."

"Oh, give me a break, would you? You've already broken your so-called rules. You said yourself, you don't care what this does to your career."

"Maybe I'm having second thoughts now."

"Bullshit."

"Alright, fine. But before I tell you anything more, I need you to make me a promise."

"What?"

"That you won't run up to the Arctic half-cocked, gunning for this guy. You won't go anywhere near him. And you won't talk to anyone but me about this case."

"That's more than one promise."

"Do you agree, or not?"

"What do you think? Of course I do. How crazy would I have to be to run after him? He almost got me once, that was more than enough for me. And I've

146

been having nightmares about him every night for a decade. You think I want to see him? All I want is for someone to stop him."

"And you'll keep quiet about all this?"

"Who would I tell? You already know how it's turned out every time I've tried."

"Will you keep quiet? Yes or no."

"Yes. Obviously."

"Alright then, his name is Aleksei Nechayev. He lives north of here, in Coldfoot."

Amanda felt the hair on the back of her neck stand up at the sound of Aleksei's name. Her mouth was suddenly bone dry. After all these years, the monster finally had a name.

Danny noticed the color draining from her face. "You okay?"

Amanda reached for her wine and gulped down what remained in her glass. She forced her hand to remain steady as she set the glass back on the table. "I'm fine. I've heard of Coldfoot. It's on the Dalton Highway, right?"

"Right. He runs a weird tourist attraction up there. It's an old asylum that people say is haunted. And after visiting there, I think they're right. Creepiest fucking place I've ever set foot in. Nechayev gives tours, and people stay overnight at his hotel on their way to the Arctic."

"I want to see him."

"You just swore you didn't!"

"That was before you told me this. He still didn't seem real then. Now, I need to see him."

Danny finished his wine and slammed the glass on the table. "God-dammit, no. I told you flat out, in no uncertain terms, no. You're not going anywhere near this psychopath."

"I just want to identify him, that's all."

"I'm going to try to find a picture of him for you to do that."

"He's a vampire. You're not going to find pictures of him."

Danny got up from the table, nearly knocking over his chair as he stood up. He paced back and forth through Amanda's dining room and adjoining kitchen.

"Listen," he said. "I told you I believe you. I don't think this guy is human. But I really can't handle this vampire shit."

"Well I think you need to learn to handle it, because that's what he is," Amanda said, her voice sharp.

"How can you be so sure? Just because of your cross? What if that was just a coincidence?"

Amanda rolled her eyes. "I've done research ever since I got attacked. There are actually a lot of vampire stories out there if you pay attention. I'm not the only person who's encountered one of them. And when you read the stories, it all adds up. He's a vampire, there's no doubt in my mind about that."

Danny continued to pace.

"I'll be honest," Amanda said. "I don't want to keep having this same argument. You just need to accept the truth, so we can move forward. Otherwise, it's a waste of my time. I'm not interested in helping you disprove what I know is true. And frankly, you're wasting the latest victim's time, too. If she still has time left, that is."

Danny dropped back down into his chair and ran his hand through his hair. "You're right, I admit it. I actually did some research myself and read quite a few stories about possible vampire sightings. I'm sorry."

"You don't have to apologize. I know it's still all very hard to digest. And I've had ten years to do it."

"It's more than hard. It's fucking impossible. But if there's a chance of Maria being found alive, I need to get over it."

Amanda got up from the table and headed for her kitchen, where she removed a second bottle of wine from the rack above her stove. She grabbed her glass as well as Danny's and walked into her living room, beckoning for Danny to join her.

She sat down on her cream colored sofa and put the wine and glasses on the coffee table in front of her. Danny joined her on the couch as she opened the new bottle and filled both of their glasses with wine.

"What are we having now?" Danny asked.

"Bordeaux. It's what I like when I need to relax."

Danny took his glass of wine and leaned back, making himself comfortable on the plush couch cushions.

"You can put your feet up on the coffee table if you want," Amanda said.

"I can?"

Amanda nodded and kicked off her own black heels. "I am," she said, doing just that.

Danny smiled and removed his loafers. He stretched out his legs on the coffee table and took a sip of wine. "This is the life."

"Can we get back to Aleksei now?"

"Yeah, I guess we better."

"Why can't you take me up to his hotel?"

Danny stared out the window at the snow, which was now even with Amanda's window, and still falling. "How do you expect to get there? You think we can just hop in the car and drive up the Dalton Highway in a blizzard?"

"First off, this isn't a blizzard. Second, no, I don't think we can just hop in the car. But obviously you got up there last night, so however you went, that's what I want to do, too."

"I chartered a plane through the police department."

"So we'll do that again."

"I can't go back up there without any evidence. I don't have anything on this guy, I told you. We searched the whole damn place and couldn't find anything."

"Maybe I'll just charter a plane myself."

"You promised me you wouldn't go there, remember? Do we need to get into another shouting match?"

Amanda stared into her wine, shifting her hand so that the liquid rolled in its glass.

"Listen," Danny said. "I was so far out of line when I got you involved in this, I would be fired tomorrow if it got out. But that's not even the issue. If you go up there and confront this asshole and get yourself hurt or killed, I don't think I could live with myself. In fact, I know I couldn't."

Amanda pursed her lips and remained silent.

"Please don't do it," Danny said.

Amanda sighed and let out a deep breath. "Alright, I won't. For now, at least."

Danny shook his head. "Okay, for now. I'm not sure how long now will last, so I'm going to have to nail this bastard before we get to that."

"Fair enough. How are you planning on nailing him?"

"That's the problem. I don't know." Danny downed his wine and put the glass on a coaster on the table. "I need to find something that connects him to these girls. I just need to find out more about him. Not so much what he is, but who he is. What's his background? How did he get here? And how long as he been at this game of his?"

Amanda polished off her glass of wine and refilled both her glass and Danny's. "You said his last name is Nechayev, right?"

"Yeah."

"So he's Russian." Amanda mulled an idea over as she drank more wine. "Like I told you before, he attacked me in Sitka, that's where I'm from originally. Sitka has a strong Russian heritage. It actually used to be ruled by the

Russians before the United States bought Alaska, it was the capital of Russian America. It still has heavy Russian influences."

Danny reached out and picked up his newly-filled glass of wine. "I know that," he said, thinking of his conversation with Rex the bartender. "You think he's from there?"

"I don't know. But I know the library there has the best Russian collection you're going to find outside of Russia. Primary sources, history, memoirs…"

"So you're hoping you can find something about Aleksei in there?"

"It's worth a shot. I can't really speak Russian, but I can read it. I studied the language in school. I have some time off now until after New Year's. I'm planning on leaving for Sitka tomorrow anyway to visit my parents. I'll go to the library and the historical society and see if I can find anything."

"That sounds like a plan. Maybe I'll go with you."

"You think I can't do research on my own? I'm a librarian, remember?"

"I'm not saying you can't do it, but maybe I could find something there." Danny took another gulp of wine. "God knows I'm at loose ends here."

"I think I'd be better off going on my own. You should stick with your files here. Maybe there's something you've missed."

"I wish I had more connections here. I knew everyone who was anyone in Chicago and I could find dirt on anyone, no matter how much they had it hidden. Here, I'm flying blind." He shrugged and put his glass of wine on the table in front of him. "But, I do need to follow up on those old cases I got. See if I can connect them to Nechayev somehow. Plus, I need to figure out what to do with him when I do nail him."

"What do you mean?"

"How the hell do I get rid of him? If he is a vampire, just arresting him isn't going to work too well, is it? So what the fuck am I supposed to do with him?"

"Kill him."

"Sure. Just call me Dirty Harry."

"I'd kill him in a heartbeat."

"Okay. I'll call you Annie Oakley, then. Although I guess she wasn't a killer was she, just a sharp shooter."

Amanda ignored Danny's rambling. "Do you know how to kill him? A gun isn't going to do it, you know."

"Yeah, yeah, I know all the bullshit about staking him through the heart. I did some research and watched Buffy the Vampire Slayer. That girl could kick some serious vampire ass."

Amanda couldn't help but laugh. "This isn't funny."

"You're laughing."

"I know, but this isn't a joke. You can't treat it that way. It's not going to be easy to get rid of him."

Danny let out a deep breath. "I know that. But all I can do is the only thing I've ever done. I'm a cop going after a killer, that's what I know how to do. The rest, I'll have to figure out as I go along."

Amanda stared at the blank screen of the television across from her couch. "You mentioned Chicago before," she said, wanting to talk about something besides the vampire who haunted her dreams. "That's where you're from?"

"Yeah."

"How'd you end up here?"

"I wanted to get out of there."

"Okay. So where else to go but Fairbanks, right?"

"Something like that. I wanted to get as far away as I could. This seemed as good a place as any."

"Why did you want to get so far away? Was there a reason?"

Danny bit his lip. "There was. But I'd rather not talk about it."

Amanda nodded. "Okay. I didn't mean to pry." She finished her wine and put the empty glass back on the coffee table. "I think I've had more than enough wine now."

"Really? I'm just getting started."

Amanda rested her head on the back of the couch, and turned her face towards Danny. "You know something I just realized? This is the first time since I got attacked that I've ever been able to talk about it without people calling me insane."

"What about your family?"

"They didn't want to talk about it. They thought I was nuts too." Amanda paused. "Ever since, we don't really talk about much of anything."

"There's something to be said for that. I'm not a big talker."

"Seems odd for a cop."

"Why? I get other people to talk about themselves. I never have to talk about me."

Amanda let out a deep breath and closed her eyes. "The wine is making me sleepy."

Danny poured himself another glass, finishing the bottle. He wasn't even feeling buzzed. Is this what people meant about getting to the point where you need alcohol just to feel normal? Maybe so.

Amanda opened her eyes and watched him as he sipped the wine. "Thanks for believing me," she said.

"You don't have to thank me. I wouldn't have believed you if I hadn't seen this asshole with my own eyes."

"It still means a lot to me though. After all this time...You just have no idea. So thank you."

Danny turned his face towards hers. "You're welcome. I'm sorry about what happened to you."

Amanda closed her eyes again. Within seconds, she was fast asleep.

Danny grabbed a throw from the back of the couch and covered her with it before getting up and heading for the window. He looked outside at the snow, and could barely make out his car on the sidewalk in front of Amanda's house. He really didn't want to drive home in this.

He finished his wine and picked up the empty bottle from Amanda's coffee table. He walked to the kitchen, and thought about cleaning up the dinner dishes. But he really didn't have the energy. He looked at Amanda's wine rack and debated whether he should open another bottle. Why not? He'd pay her back.

He decided to switch to white, and grabbed a bottle of Chardonnay. He walked back into the living room, where Amanda was now snoring softly.

Danny sat down in the chair next to the couch, and put his feet up on a matching ottoman. He opened the bottle of wine and filled his glass, lifting it in a toast to the sleeping Amanda.

"Cheers, sweetheart," he said.

Holding the wine bottle in one hand and the glass in the other, he rested his head on the hard back of the chair and closed his eyes.

CHAPTER 31

Maria's hand shook as she brought the spoon filled with chicken soup to her lips. She clasped hold of her wrist with her free hand to steady herself, frightened of the consequences if she ended up spilling the soup.

Aleksei watched her from across the table. "How's the soup?"

"It's good. Thank you."

"I thought you would want something hot since you were so cold earlier."

"It is nice."

"I'm normally not the cook here, I admit. But the cook is gone for the season so I manage."

Maria nodded and forced herself to smile before taking another spoon full of soup. She grabbed a roll from the basket in front of her and dipped it into the steaming broth before eating it. In spite of her terror, it felt good to eat a hot meal. She hoped she could get some of her strength and energy back.

She glanced at Aleksei, who had no soup of his own, and instead merely sipped a glass of vodka. "You're not hungry?" she asked.

Aleksei shook his head. "I am, but I'll eat later. I don't eat what you do."

"You mean you don't like soup?"

"Is it necessary for you to talk constantly?"

"I'm sorry. I just didn't understand what you meant."

"I meant exactly what I said. I don't eat what you do."

His sharp tone told Maria all she needed to know about continuing the conversation. She looked down at her bowl and focused on eating the rest of the soup.

The dining room was large and ornate, with a rectangular mahogany table in the center of the room. Four matching chairs with red pillows surrounded the table, and it was covered with a pristine white linen cloth. Aleksei had lit two tall red candles in the center of the table. The dishes looked like antique china and the napkins were starched and folded. A crystal chandelier hung from the ceiling and gave the room its light.

Maria felt as if she had traveled back in time when they had entered the room. Not only because of the furniture, but also because of her clothes. Due to her height, the skirt and jacket didn't fit her well, and were too short on both her arms and her legs. She felt restrained by the suffocating tights underneath the long tailored skirt. The shoes were also too small and her feet were pinched and cramped. Maria knew Aleksei had not been pleased with how she looked in the outfit he had chosen for her.

Maria stared out the arch windows that were spread along the wall, watched the falling snow, and realized it felt good to be able to see the outdoors, even if she couldn't see anything but a blanket of thick white flakes against the dark sky. She was also glad to see that at least one of the rooms in this house of horrors had windows. She may be able to use them to escape.

She took another roll and picked up her knife to spread butter on it. She glanced at Aleksei, momentarily thrilled to see that he was now watching the snow too instead of watching her. This could be her chance to slide the knife under her sleeve and bring it back with her to her room. It wasn't sharp, but it was better than nothing. At least it was a tool.

She barely moved her fingers to push the knife and immediately froze at the sound of Aleksei's voice.

"I really wouldn't do that if I were you."

"Do what?"

"Don't insult me by playing games. You were trying to hide the knife under your sleeve. Do you think I'm an idiot?"

"I wasn't…"

"Stop lying!"

"Okay, okay. I'm sorry. Please don't be angry. I'm sorry."

Aleksei rolled his eyes. "What did you expect to do with that anyway? Cut me? With a butter knife?"

"I don't know what I thought I could do with it."

Aleksei finished his vodka and placed his glass on the table in front of him.

"I thought I made it clear to you down in the root cellar the other day, but apparently you're quite dense. So let me say it again, and for your own sake, I hope you get it this time."

He leaned forward against the table, and stared directly at Maria, his blue eyes ice cold.

"If you try to take me on physically, you'll lose. Every time. There is absolutely no doubt about that." He sat back in his chair and folded his arms. His voice dripped with disdain. "If I were you, I'd get that through my thick head sooner rather than later."

Maria put down her roll and stared back at him. "I thought I was just disoriented when we were down in the cellar. But now I remember the way you moved. You were so fast, I couldn't even see you. How is that possible?"

"Because of what I am."

"What are you?"

"That's not something you need to worry about. Honestly, it's not worth my time to explain it to you."

"Who was Natasha?" Maria asked.

Aleksei stared at her, his disdain turning to barely masked hatred. "You were supposed to be her. I don't think that's working out too well though."

"You loved her, obviously."

"Yes, I loved her. I still love her. But no matter how many times I try, I can't find her again."

"How many times? So you've done this before?"

"More times than you can count, I'm sure."

Maria stared at him, chilled by his words. So there had been others in her shoes. Her terror increased exponentially with the realization that he was even more of a monster than she had already thought.

Aleksei grabbed the napkin in front of him and dabbed at his mouth. "Are you done with your soup?" he asked.

Maria had lost whatever appetite she had. "Yes," she said.

"Good. I'm bored with this conversation. It's time for you to retire for the night."

Before Maria could respond, he was out of his chair and next to her own. He grabbed her arm and pulled her up. "Let's go," he said.

He walked her down the hall to her room, never once loosening the painful grip he had on her arm. He nearly knocked her to the ground as he pushed her into the room. "You'll find a nightgown on the bed," he said.

He shut the door behind him without another word.

Maria shivered and walked to the bed, where she saw a heavy blue flannel nightgown. She looked at the dresser across from the bed, wondering if there was anything to be found in the drawers. She opened one, and was grateful to find a few pairs of thick socks. The room was very cold, and she couldn't seem to stop shivering. She opened the rest of the drawers and found old-fashioned corsets and lingerie, more flannel sheets, and a blanket. She took the blanket and a top sheet and carried them to the bed with her.

She pulled back the lavender comforter and started to remove her clothes, anxious to get out of the ill-fitting ensemble, when she remembered the walk-in closet Aleksei had gone in earlier to get the outfit. She crossed the room again, and opened the closet. It was a long shot, but it was worth a try.

Maria walked into the closet and pushed aside the dresses, jackets, and skirts hanging in organized rows. She ran her hands along the walls of the closet, hoping for the impossible. A hole maybe, or if she was really dreaming, another door. As she expected, she found nothing. There was no way out of this room.

Maria returned to the bed and finished getting undressed. Trembling from the cold, she quickly pulled on the gown and socks and slid under the sheets, putting the extra blanket and sheet she had taken from the drawer on top of her and pulling the comforter around her neck. In spite of her fear, she was relieved to be in a bed instead of on the floor of the root cellar.

She wondered how many women had been in this very bed, under these same circumstances. Aleksei's cold voice echoed in her head. "More times than you can count…"

Shivering, she forced herself to block Aleksei from her mind. Focusing on her fear accomplished nothing. She had to think about how to get away from him.

She wished she had some clue where she was. Was she still in Fairbanks? She didn't think so, but she couldn't be sure. And why had Aleksei seemed so familiar to her?

Her eyes opened wide and she sat straight up in the bed. She knew why he looked familiar and where she had seen him. She could see herself in the lobby of the Snow Creek Inn with Nate back at Thanksgiving. Hear Aleksei's voice as he gave them the tour of the haunted asylum.

Aleksei, the Russian owner of the Snow Creek. He had been so cordial and charming to her when she and Nate had stayed at the hotel. She had even joked with Nate about how hot she thought Aleksei was. She shuddered now as she realized he must have been stalking her since that trip. Aleksei must have chosen her then.

Maria lay back down in the bed and pulled the covers up around her again. The room was too cold to be without them. Her mind raced as she rested her head on the downy pillow, and she felt her heart pounding in her chest. Was she back at the Snow Creek? She must be.

For the first time since she had woken up in the root cellar, she felt a sense of hope. Would Nate be able to point the police in the direction of Coldfoot? Would he tell them about the Thanksgiving trip? In the back of her mind, she knew it wasn't likely that the trip would even come up, as Nate would have no way of knowing that it was significant. But she forced that from her thoughts. It would come up. It had to.

Maria closed her eyes and imagined the police showing up at Snow Creek and arresting Aleksei. Someone was going to find her, she was sure of it. She didn't allow herself to think that she might be dead before they did.

CHAPTER 32

Aleksei headed for the Snow Creek kitchen and opened his private refrigerator. He took out a bag of blood, and poured it into a crystal glass. He was so grateful for Alaskan blood banks. He could always make sure he was well stocked on food for the winter.

He felt himself relax as he sipped the blood and fed his hunger. He could have gone out to hunt, as there was an Inupiat tribe not far away, but he didn't feel like working tonight. He had neither the energy nor the ambition.

He returned to his study and to the comfort of his leather armchair. Staring at the wall, he went over the evening in his mind.

There was no longer any doubt that Maria was not making the grade. Not only was she too talkative, and too damn nosy, but she couldn't even wear the clothes he had given her with any sense of elegance. She was simply not suitable.

Besides that, he couldn't stop thinking of the Irish detective and his rude invasion of Aleksei's home. In the back of his mind, he knew the detective was on to him, and he'd figure out a reason to come back to Snow Creek eventually. He was thankful that at least all of this had come about early on in his cherished winter season. He would have to abandon his New Year's plans, but he had plenty of time to put his new plan in motion and enjoy the rest of the winter.

He would have no trouble finding Maria's replacement, since he had all of her family's contact information in his cherished guest book. It would be a piece of cake. And this time, he was going to make her his permanent companion. He knew it was time.

He finished his dinner of blood and put the glass on the table next to him. His groin tingled with anticipation.

He would bring Katie here, and she would be his. He shook his head, almost imperceptibly. No, it wouldn't be Katie at all.

It would be Katerina.

CHAPTER 33

Danny walked into his Chicago apartment and was immediately hit with the smell of something delicious. That was the norm for dinner time at his home. He didn't know how he had gotten lucky enough to find a French chef who wanted to marry him. For that matter, he didn't know how he'd managed to find anyone who wanted to marry him.

For most of his life, marriage had been the last thing on Danny's mind. Years of growing up in the middle of his parents' bitter and angry marriage, and even angrier divorce, had left him immune to the allure of the institution. He was happy with his job and, except for various girlfriends, his job was his life. But that had all changed when he had met Caroline Baudin during an investigation of a murder that had occurred in the neighborhood of her French restaurant.

After five years of wedded bliss, Danny now loved marriage as much as he loved his wife. He couldn't imagine how he had ever managed without her and wondered what he had eaten before falling victim to her addictive cooking.

He headed for the kitchen and the source of the yummy smell and found Caroline at the stove, her back to him as she stirred whatever was making Danny salivate. She was dressed in her favorite attire, blue jeans and a long-sleeved t-shirt and her brown hair fell in waves past her shoulders.

"Hi, Danny," she said, without turning to look at him. She lifted a spoon full

of broth from the pot and sipped at her creation, testing to make sure she had the taste she wanted.

Danny walked to the stove and slid his arms around her waist, kissing the back of her head. "What smells so good?"

"Coq au vin."

Danny stared into the pot. "I'm guessing the vin is wine."

Caroline nodded. "Burgundy, to be exact. And coq is chicken. Or actually rooster if you want to be precise. It was my grandmother's recipe and I'm testing it for the restaurant."

Danny's stomach growled. "How long until I get to eat it?"

Caroline smiled and put down her spoon. She turned away from the stove and faced Danny, her arms around his neck. "Are you hungry?"

"Starving." Danny leaned into her and kissed her lips. "I haven't eaten since breakfast."

"Why do you skip lunch so often? You're too skinny as it is."

"I can't help it. It was a busy day."

"Still the same case?"

Danny kissed her again and pulled away from her. He opened the refrigerator and grabbed a beer, twisting off the cap as he leaned against the sink.

"Yeah. It's driving me nuts, I admit it. Jackson and I aren't getting anywhere."

"What about the FBI? Are they any help?"

"Are you kidding? When are they ever any help?" Danny shook his head. "I did talk to John Fisher today. He's running the files I've got through some of their systems, but I don't expect him to find anything we don't already know."

"Which is?"

"That this creep's been raping and murdering women all over Chicago."

Danny took a swig of beer and placed the bottle on the counter. "I just can't figure out how he manages it without leaving a shred of evidence. It's like he knows everything we look for."

"Maybe he watches CSI."

Danny rolled his eyes. "God help us." He watched as Caroline opened the refrigerator and pulled out a puff pastry. "Ooh, desert?" he asked.

"Yeah. It's your favorite. St. Honore Cake."

"Let's skip the coq au vin and move right to that."

Caroline laughed and set the pastry on the counter. She opened the cabinet to take out her mixer, and turned to Danny, her face now pale and panic-stricken. Drips of blood began to drip from her neck.

"Caroline? What is it?"

The blood turned from a drip to a deluge, gushing out of her neck and turning her shirt bright red. It splattered all over Danny, instantly soaking his shirt and pants.

"Caroline!"

"Danny? Danny, wake up. Danny!"

Danny jumped in his chair, sending an empty bottle of wine across the room. Amanda was leaning over him with her hands on his shoulders. He shook his head, trying to wake up. Where the hell was he?"

"Are you okay?" Amanda asked. "You were dreaming. I heard you yell."

Danny sat up in the chair and rubbed his eyes. "I'm okay. I'm sorry." He looked around the living room. "I don't remember falling asleep here. I should have gone home."

"No, it's fine."

Danny glanced at the empty bottle he had thrown to the other side of the room. "I owe you a bottle of wine. I'm sorry."

Amanda smiled. "It's okay, really."

Danny looked down at his clothes. They were rumpled and he could only imagine what he looked like, but at least there was no blood.

Amanda moved back to the couch and sat down. "Who is Caroline?" she asked.

"What?"

"That's what you were yelling. Caroline."

"It doesn't matter. I'm sorry I woke you up."

"You sounded devastated."

Danny let out a deep sigh and rubbed his eyes. "Caroline was my wife."

"What happened to her?"

"She's dead. But I'd really rather not go into any more detail about it."

"Okay. I'm sorry."

Danny held up his hand. "You're not the one who needs to apologize. I'm the nut screaming like a lunatic in the middle of the night."

"Not to mention throwing bottles across my living room."

Danny smirked. "I didn't break anything, did I?"

Amanda shook her head. "No. No damage done."

"Except to my ego." Danny forced himself to get up from the chair and walked to the window, where he stared out into the night. The snow was still falling, now even faster than it had been earlier. "Jesus, is it ever going to quit?"

Amanda joined him at the window and peered over his shoulder. "It's a terrible night, no doubt."

Danny walked back to the couch and sat down with a thud. "If I haven't already imposed on you too much, can I sleep on your couch? I really don't want to drive in this."

Amanda sat down next to him. "Of course. I don't think you'd get very far if you tried to drive home anyway."

"Thanks. No more screaming, I promise."

"It's okay. I know all about nightmares."

Danny turned to face her and gently pushed a strand of blond hair out of her eyes. "I'm sure you do."

"I'm actually glad you're here. All this talk about Aleksei has my nerves so frazzled. I don't want to be alone."

Amanda stood up and extended her hand to Danny. "You don't have to sleep on the couch," she said.

Danny started to tell her he most certainly did, he had already broken enough rules and she was a victim and a witness for his case, but his mouth never formed the words. Instead, he took Amanda's hand and got up from the couch. He pulled her towards him and gently kissed her lips.

"I don't want to be alone either," he said.

Amanda took his hand and led him into her bedroom.

CHAPTER 34

Aleksei stood outside Maria's room, and listened. He heard nothing but the sound of her breathing, so he felt confident she had fallen asleep and wasn't attempting anything stupid. Not that she had any means of getting out of the room anyway.

He put his hand on the doorknob and considered going inside. His plans for Katie Bailey had excited him and he considered making use of Maria while she was here. His hand lingered on the doorknob, but he finally decided against going into the room. He felt nothing but disgust for Maria and he had no desire to ruin the good mood he had found himself in while developing his plans.

Making his way back to his study, he settled into his favorite chair once again. He leaned back and closed his eyes. He had gone way off track when choosing Maria. He needed to remember his Natasha if he was going to succeed in finally finding his new companion in Katie.

It was January and Aleksei couldn't believe he had survived to see 1916 end and 1917 arrive. His nurse couldn't believe it, either.

"I'm amazed at how well you're doing," Natasha said as she brought him a crust of bread and a cup of water, which had nearly frozen to ice.

"I'm starving," Aleksei said.

"I know. We all are."

"Any news from the front?"

"Just that everything is chaos. The troops are in disarray, there have been mutinies." Natasha paused. "It's like here in Petrograd. Everything is falling apart."

Aleksei shuddered. "I don't want to go back there."

Natasha put her hand on his arm. "I know. I hope you don't have to."

"I want to stay here with you."

"Well, you can for now. They can't send you back to the front when you can't even walk yet." Natasha patted his arm and stood up from the cot. "I'll be back to check on you later."

Aleksei watched as she walked to another soldier's cot and brought him his lunch, and frowned as she turned toward the entrance to the hospital tent and smiled. He felt his stomach tighten in knots that were beyond his hunger. He knew who that smile was for.

Natasha walked to her visitor and kissed him quickly on the lips. The two left the tent hand in hand.

Aleksei knew just who the interloper was. Maksim Bodrov, a soldier who had been assigned to guard the Petrograd barracks. A pathetically easy job while Aleksei and others served as cannon fodder at the front. He hated Bodrov, and hated that Natasha couldn't understand she deserved better than him. She deserved so much better than all of this.

He sighed and shifted on his cot, immediately feeling a burst of pain in his leg. He deserved better than this, too. Even if he didn't have to go back to the front, he knew he would eventually die here. They all would. They were starving, and freezing, and there was no food or warmth to be found.

Aleksei's mind drifted to his family and he wondered if any of them were still alive. His brothers had gone to the front at the same time he had, in different regiments, and he'd never heard a word about them since. His parents were most likely safe in their Petrograd home, not even particularly far from where he was now, but they might as well have been a million miles away. Aleksei felt no connection to them anymore. Although if he was being honest with himself, he knew he never really had. Once his grandmother had passed away, his interest in his family mirrored their interest in him, which meant that it was essentially non-existent. Now, his only interest was in Natasha and his plan to get out of this hellhole.

Aleksei already had the plan in place and he couldn't wait to share it with Natasha. He had seen the vampires haunting the hospital at night, looking for easy prey, just as he had seen them hunting along the front lines. He knew what they were as his grandmother had told him all about vampires when he was young. She had told him the tale of the man who encountered a vampire on the way back to his grave after the vampire had drained all of the blood from two young boys in the village, and how the vampire's burial shroud had brought the boys back to life. His grandmother had warned him to always be on the look-out for the creatures that belonged to the night, those who retained their human forms but were anything but human. They were the undead.

He had been afraid of them then, but now he welcomed them, and knew he would soon join them. He just needed his leg to heal and then he would offer himself to the vampires when he heard them rustling in the dark outside the tent. He would beg them to make him one of them and he'd never have to worry about being cold or hungry again.

The plan was the only thing that got him through the days of hunger and the nights of ice. He wished he could tell Natasha, but he knew she wouldn't understand yet. Eventually, she would, and she would be part of his new life.

He would bring her with him.

CHAPTER 35

Danny walked into the police station and stamped his boots on the carpet to shake off the snow. He had left Amanda's place a few hours earlier, thankful she was still asleep so he could slip out with nothing more than a note to let her know he would be in touch. He wasn't good at morning after conversations.

He was also thankful that the snow had finally stopped and the plow had come through during the night to do its job. That was one way Alaska reminded him of Chicago. In both places, snow rarely stopped people for long. Dealing with it was simply a way of life.

Danny hung up his coat and walked to his desk, unsurprised to see several more people in the office today than had been there the day before. The Christmas holiday was over.

He waved at Tessa, who was across the room talking to a fellow detective, and sat down at his desk. Before he had a chance to boot up his computer, Tessa was back at her own desk beside his.

"How are you doing, Danny?"

"I'm fine. Why?"

"You don't look fine."

Danny looked down at his clothes, surprised. He had gone home and taken a shower after leaving Amanda's, and had changed into clean clothes. He even considered them his best clothes, black pants and a grey crew neck sweater over a white oxford shirt. For him, he was dressed up. What was the problem?

"I don't?"

"No. Look at you. You've got circles the size of Texas under your eyes. And you look so drawn and pale. I don't think you're taking care of yourself." Tessa paused. "That two day old beard doesn't help."

"I'm sorry I don't meet your Tim Gunn standards."

"It's not that and you know it. I'm concerned about you. Ever since we started on this missing person's case, you haven't been yourself. You've been behaving strangely and you know it"

"Hate to break this to you, but you don't really know what strange is for me. You hardly know me."

Tessa folded her arms across her chest. "I know you well enough."

Danny sighed and pushed his chair back. "Maybe I just don't like the holidays, ever think of that?"

"That's still not a good reason to walk around looking like a combination of a corpse and a bum."

"Nice visual. Thanks. And here I thought I looked quite sharp today. This is my best outfit, and I was certain I'd earn your approval."

"This isn't a joke," Tessa snapped. "I'm just concerned, that's all."

Danny wheeled his chair back to his desk and logged in to his computer. "Don't be. We've got more important things to worry about than my appearance. Anything new on Maria?"

Tessa shook her head. "No. I went over the security camera footage from the lot where we found her car again, hoping I'd catch something new, but there was nothing."

"Still just see her walking towards her car?"

"Yeah. And the time lag is just so weird. It's like one second she's there and the next she's not. Like she saw someone and followed them maybe, got out of the range of the camera."

"Or someone followed her. Someone who wouldn't show up on the camera."

"What? Who wouldn't show up on a camera?"

Danny waved his hand as if dismissing the thought. "Oh, no one, I don't know. I was just thinking out loud I guess. Wondering if the camera could have just missed someone because of the time lag."

Tessa stared at him, obviously unconvinced.

"It's weird though, isn't it? The time lag, I mean. Normally those cameras are running constantly."

"Right, but the tech explained that. There was some kind of glitch."

"Of course there was."

"What are you getting at?"

"Nothing, I told you."

Tessa continued to stare at him.

"What?" Danny said. "I was just thinking out loud like I said. You got anything else?"

"Not really. I went through a bunch of those old cases your friend sent you. I can't see anything to link the girls."

"Except the way they look and the time they went missing."

"You know we need more to go on. We don't have anything to pin this on your Arctic guy."

"I'm gonna talk to the family members from some of those cases. See if those women ever went to Nechayev's house of horrors."

"I think that's smart, but I don't think I'll be able to help you."

"Why?"

"They're taking me off the Treibel case. Moving me to a homicide that came in this morning."

Danny nodded. "The holiday's over and people hurry and get back to murder, right?"

"Yep."

"I'm not surprised. The Treibel case has gone cold, except for Nechayev."

"And as far as the Captain is concerned, that's gone cold, too."

"That's because he hasn't met Nechayev."

"Danny..."

"You don't need to give me another lecture. I know we don't have any evidence on him. Doesn't stop me from also knowing that he's guilty. And, no one is gonna convince me a woman walks to her car on her way to a job she was excited about, and then just out of nowhere decides to abandon the car and run off instead. She didn't go missing by choice."

"You know I agree with you. I just don't know how to prove it." Tessa got up from her desk. "And with that I should probably get started on the new homicide and see if I can do a better job on this case than I did on Maria's."

Danny watched her, remaining silent as she put on her coat and walked out of the station. He knew she was right and he had absolutely nothing to go on, but that wasn't going to stop him from finding Maria Treibel and any other victims of Aleksei who might still be alive. He thought back to the barren landscape of Coldfoot, and shuddered at how easy it would be for Aleksei to hide his victims there. For all Danny knew, he somehow kept them in storage.

He heard a noise behind him, and turned to find his boss standing at his desk. Captain Jack Meyer was a man who was hard to miss, as everything about him was large. He was tall and beefy, with a big head and a round face that was a permanent shade of red. When he spoke, he always spoke loudly. In spite of this, Danny had liked him since his first day in the Fairbanks office.

"What can I do for you, sir?" Danny asked.

"I need to talk to you, Fitzpatrick. What have you been up to on the missing women?"

174

Danny considered how to answer and imagined himself telling the truth. *"Well, I had sex with our only witness last night and told her all the details of the case. Oh, and I know who the perp is, and he's a vampire."*

"Fitzpatrick?"

"Oh, sorry, just thinking for a minute." Danny imagined himself taking a one-way trip to the psych ward, and chose a different answer. "Well, you know the Treibel case has gone cold. But I'm still certain Nechayev up in Coldfoot is our guy."

"I thought you said you didn't find anything up there."

"I didn't. But I know in my gut he's the one. I just need another warrant and I'll go back up there."

Meyer sat down on the edge of Danny's desk, his burly leg taking up at least half of the desktop. "What judge do you think is gonna give you another warrant based on your gut?"

Danny sighed. "None. I know that. I'm trying to go through some of these old missing persons' cases and see if I can find a link. Something concrete to support another warrant."

"It sounds to me like you're spinning your wheels."

"I don't see it that way."

Meyer looked around the room before continuing, wanting to make sure the other detectives had all left. "Listen, I think you should step back from this. Take a few days off."

"What? That's the last thing I need to do. I don't have time for that."

"These cases are cold, Fitzpatrick. Time isn't of the essence here."

"I think it is for Maria Treibel."

"And yet you have absolutely no idea where she is. Are you thinking you'll just sit here at your desk and pull her whereabouts out of your ass?"

"I know exactly where she is."

"Here we go again."

"Is it wrong to want to find the woman?"

"No, obviously it's not wrong." Meyer sighed and rubbed his eyes. "Listen, there's no gentle way to put this and I've never been too good at all that anyway. But I'm not asking you about taking time off. I'm telling you that's what you're going to do."

Danny stared at him, unable to hide his surprise. "What? Why on earth?"

"Take a look in the god-damn mirror and that should answer your question! You look like you haven't slept in a month. Everyone can smell the alcohol on you. You've got circles under your eyes the size.."

"The size of Texas, I know." Danny shook his head. "I'm fine, sir. Really."

"I know about Chicago, Danny."

Danny sighed. "I know you do." It had been a condition of the job. Meyer was the only one who knew any details of Danny's departure from Chicago homicide. "Can I ask how that's relevant here?"

"I think the time of year is getting to you. The holidays and all that. The anniversary of your wife's murder coming up…"

Danny flinched. He had been doing all he could to not think of that upcoming anniversary.

"Or else this Treibel case is getting to you," Meyer continued. "I don't know which it is; maybe it's a combination of both. But I do know that you look like shit and I can't have you going out on cases looking like this. You need a break."

"Even if I don't want a break?"

"Right. Like I said, I'm not asking."

"So how long is this break supposed to be?"

"You covered over Christmas, so I thought you could take the New Year's holiday for yourself. Maybe a week off is just what you need to come back here

176

with a clear head."

"And by the end of that week Maria Treibel will probably be dead."

"We both know there's about a 1% chance that Maria Treibel isn't already dead. We'll find her body soon enough and this will be a homicide."

"They never found a body in any of the other cases."

"And if they don't find one here, odds are more than good that she left of her own accord. People walk away from their lives all the time, Danny. You ought to know that better than anyone."

"I do know that. And I also know that's not what Maria Treibel did. And Anna Alexander didn't either."

"Right. And we're back to square one again. You know that, but you don't have a shred of evidence to prove it."

Danny stared at the wall in front of his desk. "So when does this break start?"

"I think it would be a good idea to start now."

Danny nodded and turned off his computer. "I'll see you after the New Year, boss."

He stood up from his desk without saying another word, and headed to the doorway. He grabbed his coat, making sure to bundle up before he headed out into the cold. Meyer watched as Danny walked outside towards his car, got inside, and started the engine. There was no doubt in his mind where Danny was headed as he turned out of the police station parking lot. Meyer knew he was headed for a bar.

CHAPTER 36

Aleksei paced the length of his study, waiting for the sun to set for the day. It was typical of his luck that the snow had stopped and the sun had made a brief appearance on the one day he planned to travel. Luckily for him, he didn't have the same travel restrictions humans had, so he would still be able to get to his destination in spite of the delay. He just needed the sun to go away.

While he waited, he turned the problem of Maria over in his mind. He was going to just kill her when he roused her from her sleep that morning, but instead he had decided to give her a reprieve. He had given her breakfast and allowed her to get cleaned up, then locked her back in her room. While he didn't want to think about it, he knew there was a chance his plan for the rest of the winter could go awry. He decided to keep Maria around while he made sure all of his ducks were in a row. She was his backup plan now. It wouldn't be an enjoyable winter with her, but at least he wouldn't be alone.

He glanced at the clock on his wall, noticing the time was nearly 3:00. The sun should be gone now. He walked to his window and pushed the heavy shade slightly aside so he could peer out, happy to see the sun had indeed set, and the twilight now cast a purple glow across the snow surrounding his home. It was time to go.

Aleksei had already prepared several meals for Maria and left them in the root cellar, along with enough water to tide her over, a lantern, and a clean chamber pot. He had also tossed several blankets and a pillow down the stairs into the cellar. Now, he would toss Maria there as well, and be on his way.

He walked quickly to Maria's door and swung it open. She was sitting up in the bed, and jumped when he entered the room.

"Get up," he said.

Maria quickly rose from the bed. "What's going on?"

"No time for talking."

Aleksei opened the bottom drawer of the dresser and pulled out a pair of thick fleece pants and a heavy wool sweater. He threw them onto the bed.

"Put these on, it's going to be cold where you're going." He turned his back and faced the door. "I'll give you privacy."

"What do you mean, where I'm going? Where are you taking me?"

Aleksei bit his lip and swallowed his temper. "Did I not just say we don't have time for talking? Shut up and put the warm clothes on. I'm giving you one minute. If you're not dressed, you'll be left with nothing on but that nightgown. Believe me when I say you won't like that."

Maria suppressed her rising terror and quickly put on the pants and the shirt. She kept the heavy socks she had found the night before on her feet.

"Don't I need shoes to go somewhere? Where are my shoes? What did you do with my own clothes?"

Aleksei whipped around to face her, his face filled with rage. His mouth was open and two fangs protruded from his gums. Maria screamed and stumbled back onto the bed.

"I told you to shut up!" Aleksei yelled. He stood over Maria's shaking figure and purposely bared his fangs as he grabbed her arm. "Do you see what I am now?" he whispered. "Do you know how easy it would be for me to kill you right this second? To sink my teeth into your neck and drain every last drop of your blood?"

"Oh my God," Maria said. "Oh my God, please."

"Please what? Are you asking some god of yours to save you?" Aleksei drew in his fangs and stared down at Maria. "This may surprise you, but I can actually understand that. I've been there. And you know what? It doesn't do a damn bit of good."

He tightened his grip on Maria's arm and pulled her from the bed. "You're in luck today though. I'm not going to kill you. Mind you, I was. But I realized that I need you as my backup now."

Aleksei continued to talk as he dragged Maria out of the bedroom and down the hallway towards the kitchen. He knew his grip on her arm was the only reason she hadn't fainted dead away. As it was, she was too frozen with fear to resist him.

"I'm not sure how long I'll be gone," he said. "But don't worry, I've left supplies for you. If you learned anything from the start of your stay here with me, you'll be smart enough to conserve the lantern this time."

Maria's lack of resistance ended as she heard the word lantern. She stopped in her tracks, catching Aleksei off guard.

"No," she said, her voice cracking with panic. "No, please, not back there. Please!"

Aleksei recovered from his momentary lack of attention and continued pulling her into the kitchen. "You're wasting your breath," he said.

He opened the kitchen door and dragged a now kicking and screaming Maria outside. She immediately gasped at the burst of frigid air.

"Good thing you kept those socks on," Aleksei said.

He pulled Maria through the snow and opened the door of the root cellar. "I'll see you when I get back," he said, before throwing her down the stairs of the cellar as carelessly as he had previously thrown the blankets and pillow. At least she had those to break her fall, he thought. Not that he cared if she got hurt.

He slammed the door on her screams, and slid the lock in place. He smiled, unable to contain the thrill he got from knowing Maria was down in the cellar, fumbling in the pitch dark, and wasting her breath on screams no one but him would ever hear. Regardless of his disdain for her, he absolutely loved the power he had over her. He was glad he had decided to keep her in reserve. Killing her wouldn't have been nearly as fun.

He allowed himself time to savor the moment. If he blocked out Maria's tinny screams, there was nothing but silence in the still darkness around him. He could barely contain his excitement at the journey that lay ahead of him.

It was time to get going now and to leave Maria behind. He was moving on to his new companion and he knew exactly where to find her. Guest books and credit card invoices were such wonderful things.

He went back inside and took one last look around his home before locking it up for his trip. He felt a rush of adrenalin as he locked the front door behind him. Before he knew it, he would be in Seattle and in front of the Bailey home.

Aleksei paused for a moment, wondering what Katie Bailey was doing now. No doubt school was closed for the holidays, so she was likely to be out with friends. Maybe shopping or going to the movies. Wasn't that what young girls did nowadays? He smiled as he imagined her laughing and smiling with her friends, with no awareness of the fact that her days as Katie Bailey were numbered.

Katie had been so sullen when visiting Snow Creek with her family, it was obvious the girl needed something more out of life than boring vacations with her parents and imbecilic little brother. Aleksei could tell she had longed for excitement and adventure. He would give that to her, in ways she could never imagine. She would thank him when it was all over, he was sure of that.

Polar Night

She would never look back at the life she was soon to be leaving behind. Katerina would never be Katie again.

CHAPTER 37

Katie Bailey typed out a text to her friend Jessica as she walked to her car after finishing her shift as a waitress at her grandfather's restaurant. Her feet ached and her shirt was stained with the coffee she had managed to pour down the front of her instead of into her customer's mug. She had been lucky she hadn't been burned, but she didn't feel particularly lucky. It had been a crappy day.

Katie resented the fact that she had to work, when so many of her friends were able to spend all of their time on school clubs and teams. Why did she have to get stuck with parents who believed work experience was important for every young person to have? She could hear her mother talk about the importance of learning responsibility in her head and she rolled her eyes. She used to love hanging around her grandfather's restaurant before she had been forced to work there. Her mother managed to ruin everything.

She got into her car and slumped into the driver's seat. She sent Jessica another text, letting her know she would be picking her up at 8:00 that night, and stuck her phone into her purse. The last thing she needed was to be stopped under Seattle's new bullshit "texting while driving" law. Her mother's lectures would never stop then.

Katie didn't notice the tall blond man who was watching her from the group of trees surrounding the restaurant. She didn't know he had followed her mother and brother from their house when they had come to the restaurant for an early dinner a few hours earlier. She didn't know he had watched her while she waited tables and chatted with her customers. That he had watched with joyful anticipation while she hung up her apron and clocked out for the evening, giving her grandfather a hug before she left the restaurant.

She didn't know.

Katie pulled out of the restaurant parking lot and headed for home, just as the rain started back up again and she had to quickly turn on her wipers. There was no getting away from the Seattle winter rain. She just hoped it might slow down for a bit when it was time to head out with her friends. Within minutes, she had arrived home and she ran through the rain onto her front porch and into her house.

An hour later, Katie ran back out, having showered and changed into her favorite outfit, a black tunic dress and red platform pumps. She played with her large hoop earrings as she got into the car and turned on the ignition. She and Jessica were meeting Tyler and Ryan tonight and Katie couldn't wait.

She was so excited about her upcoming date that she didn't notice the tall blond man across the street from her house as she pulled out of the driveway and sped off down the road. She didn't see him as he stood on the sidewalk and watched her drive away.

CHAPTER 38

Aleksei opened the door of his Seattle hotel room and immediately closed the heavy drapes that hung across the window. He lay down on his back on the hard double bed in the center of the room. The sun would be coming up soon enough, and he needed to rest for the day. He had a big night ahead.

As he glanced down at his chest, he noticed a spot of blood on his black coat. He frowned and brushed at it with his fingers. He had obviously been careless when he had made the homeless woman down near the shore of Puget Sound his dinner. At least her body shouldn't be turning up any time soon and would probably be in the middle of the Pacific Ocean by the time he got back to Alaska. Still, he would need to remember to clean up the coat before he left the hotel.

He felt confident that he had watched Katie long enough to know her routine and it was clear that the restaurant where she worked as a waitress would be the best place for him to make his move. The parking lot was small and poorly lit and was apparently used only by restaurant staff. The customers seemed to all park along the street in front of the building. Best of all, there was no security camera anywhere in sight. Aleksei was sure he could distract Katie as she walked to her car and take her with him without anyone being the wiser.

Aleksei stared at the dull white ceiling and visualized how the evening would go in his head. He could see himself grabbing Katie around the neck and

185

stifling her screams with his large hand placed over her mouth. He would pull her into the woods next to the restaurant and choke her windpipe with his forearm until she lost consciousness. From there, it would be smooth sailing until he got her back to Snow Creek.

He planned to keep her in his home right away and he would prepare the bedroom Maria had defiled for Katie. He wasn't sure exactly when he was going to turn her, but he knew he didn't want to waste much time. His anticipation was getting to be too much for him. And he had decided that Maria would be the first kill he and his companion made together. That alone made him nearly giddy. Or at least as giddy as a nearly 100 year old vampire could be.

There was only one thing holding him back. If this was all going to work as he planned, he had to do everything correctly when he turned Katie. Aleksei was ashamed to admit, even to himself, that in all these years he had never turned a vampire. He just hadn't wanted the aggravation. He had been all about killing, feeding and moving on.

But there shouldn't be any problem turning Katie. Obviously he knew how it was done, because it had been done to him. All he had to do was remember.

Aleksei heard the rustle outside the torn walls of the medical tent and knew the vampires were back. He sat up in his cot and clenched his threadbare blanket in his hands, trying to calm his nerves. Tonight had to be the night.

It was February now, and his leg had completely healed. The only reason he had been able to remain in the relative safety of the field hospital was because the Russian troops had devolved into such chaos both at the front and in Petrograd, no one paid any attention to which soldier was where. No one had any idea anymore where anyone belonged. As long as Aleksei kept to himself and remained in the confines of the hospital, no one noticed him.

No one except his Natasha, that is. She continued to watch out for him, and seeing her smile was always guaranteed to be the highlight of his day. She regularly brought him the latest news about the city. Petrograd was in chaos, as workers organized industrial strikes and starving citizen staged marches in the streets that quickly turned into riots. Soldiers were deserting and joining in with the strikes and the city was rapidly turning into anarchy.

Natasha had been excited when she visited him earlier that day. Tomorrow was International Women's Day, and she was planning to join a march in honor of the occasion with her fellow nurses. Aleksei had no use for her enthusiasm, as he felt such activity was far beneath her. Who knew what kind of street trash she would encounter? Not to mention, he could barely hide his disgust when she shared that Max planned to desert his post and join in the march with her.

He tried to convince her that this march was no way for a lady of her caliber to behave, but Natasha merely shushed him and continued to chatter about Max and their plans. Aleksei could barely contain his rage. One more mention of that charlatan Max and he wouldn't be responsible for his actions.

Natasha didn't even notice his anger and left him with a smile as she always did. Aleksei watched her leave the tent and seethed as he imagined her meeting her precious Max. That was when he knew he couldn't wait any longer for the vampires.

Now that they were right outside the tent, he felt a pang of fear. He had seen what they had done to the soldiers on the battlefield, their fangs sinking deep into their necks. Did he really want that done to him? He looked around the tent of dying men and got his answer. Of course he did. What was the alternative?

Aleksei got up from the cot and folded his blanket into a neat square. He didn't look back at any of his fellow patients as he lifted up the door of the tent and walked outside. The cold air hit him in a rush. He had been so cold for so long he had been sure he was immune to the temperature, but leaving even the minimal shelter of the hospital tent proved how wrong he was. He shuddered,

187

wishing he had brought the blanket with him. But as he turned towards the sound of the vampires, he knew he wouldn't need it for long anyway.

There were three of them, two men and a woman. Aleksei could tell that one man was the leader just by his posture and body language. He was a stocky man, with dark hair and sallow skin, and the Asian-like features of the Russian Far East. The other man was tall and slender, with hair as blond as Aleksei's and skin so pale it was nearly translucent. The woman was nearly as tall as the blond man and her face was surrounded by an unruly mane of bright red hair. She was standing with her arm draped over the blond man's shoulder, as if she was marking her territory. The three turned and looked at Aleksei in unison and immediately bared their fangs.

Aleksei swallowed his fear, and continued to move towards the trio of vampires.

"Why are you disturbing us, soldier?" the stocky man asked.

"I want you to feed on me."

The vampires laughed, again in unison. The woman dropped her arm from the blond man's shoulder and walked seductively towards Aleksei.

"You're offering yourself as food, handsome?"

"I am. But not just that. I want you to turn me." Aleksei paused, remembering his manners. "Please."

The woman stared into Aleksei's eyes and ran an ice cold hand down his cheek. "You certainly are a gorgeous one." She turned back towards the leader. "What do you think? Should we do what he wants? I'd like a new toy."

Aleksei winced. "No, I don't want that. Please. I don't want to be part of your group. I just want you to turn me."

The leader approached Aleksei now, his power evident in every step. Aleksei forced himself not to back away.

"You think you can just strut out here and make demands on us? What's

stopping me from feeding on you right now, and letting you rot here with the rest of your kind?"

"Nothing. I know nothing's stopping you. I know you're going to feed on me. All I want is for you to turn me as well."

"Why?"

"Because it's the only chance I have at life."

"You think you're going to die?"

"I know I am. I'm starving. And the cold…"

The man nodded. "You're right of course. You'll all die here. But why is that our problem?"

"It's not. But I know you need to feed. So I'm offering you myself. You won't have to hunt or do any work."

"You think I'd have to hunt if I walked in that tent right now? I've got a buffet in there, lined up and ready for me."

"They'll scream and fight you. I won't."

The blond man spoke for the first time. It was clear from his voice that he was not Russian. Scandinavian, perhaps? "You really think you won't scream or fight? When the fangs sink in and your blood starts gushing out of you?"

"I know I won't."

The man chuckled. "You have no idea what you're in for, soldier." He turned back to the leader. "I'm inclined to give him what he wants. Just so I can hear him scream."

The dark-haired man shrugged. "Do whatever you want, Greger. I'm going inside to eat." He gestured towards the woman. "Come, Yelena."

The two disappeared into the tent, leaving Aleksei alone with the vampire he prayed would soon become his sire.

"What's your name, soldier?"

"Aleksei Nechayev."

"Do you know how this works? Obviously you knew what we were. Have you watched us feed?"

"I have, sir. On the battlefield. And some nights in the tent."

Aleksei now heard faint moans coming from inside the tent, and knew the vampires had begun to feed.

"So you've been watching us. Why are you offering yourself now?"

"Because I know I don't have much time. And I need to be able to turn someone myself. Before it's too late for her."

"Her?" Greger burst into laughter. "This is about a woman? You want me to turn you into a vampire so you can make yourself a girlfriend?"

"I need to save her."

"Is she dying too?"

"No. But she's getting herself into trouble with a fool. She belongs with me."

Greger continued to chuckle. "So you love her so much you want to kill her? How very romantic of you. And so Russian. All of you are mad."

"You're not Russian, sir?"

"I'm not. I'm Swedish. And don't ask me how I ended up in this god-forsaken place, I'd rather not discuss it."

Aleksei nodded and remained silent.

"So, I guess we might as well get on with it, shouldn't we?" Greger said. "No time to waste. Although frankly, you don't look like you're ready to die any time soon."

"It's time, sir. Please."

"Oh don't go back to your begging. I already told you I'd do it." Greger took a bite out of his own wrist and watched as red blood began to flow down his arm. "Do you know why I did that?"

"No."

"Because that's how it works. Once I bite you, I'll drain you to an inch of

your life. But right before you die, I'll give you my wrist. You drink my blood, and you'll turn."

"Right away?"

"No. You'll die first. But you'll wake up tomorrow a vampire."

Aleksei shuddered with a mix of fear and anticipation. "Will you be here?"

"I thought you said you didn't want to join our group?"

"I don't, but..."

"We'll be around. I'm not the type to desert my descendents." Greger grabbed Aleksei's arm and pulled him close, his fangs grazing his neck. "Ready then?"

Aleksei nodded as he felt the teeth sink into his skin. He jerked at the intense pain, and fought the urge to scream as his feet collapsed under him, and the world around him faded to black.

CHAPTER 39

The phone rang and buzzed at the same time, vibrating across Danny's nightstand. Desperate for the noise to stop, he reached out and grabbed the phone without raising his head from his crumpled pillow.

"Hello?"

"Danny?"

Danny didn't recognize the female voice on the other end of the line. "Yeah. Who is this?"

"It's Amanda."

"Oh, Amanda. I'm sorry. I'm a little out of it."

"Are you drunk?"

Danny glanced at his clock. "At noon? Are you kidding?"

"Hungover, then."

"Well, yeah. Guilty as charged there." Danny propped himself up on his elbow and winced at the pounding in his head. He needed coffee, as usual. "What's up?"

"Nothing in particular. I just wanted to check in with you. See if you found out anything more about Aleksei."

Danny sighed. "No, I haven't. I'm kind of on an unexpected vacation."

"What? Oh my God, you didn't get fired because of me, did you?"

"No, no. I'm not fired. And they don't know anything about you. My boss just wanted me to take some time off because he thinks I'm a wreck."

Amanda bit her lip and remained silent.

"What?" Danny asked.

"I didn't say anything."

"Yeah, but I know you wanted to."

"I was just thinking your boss might be on to something."

"Thanks a hell of a lot."

"Well it's true, Danny. Look at right now, for God's sake. It's 12:00 in the afternoon and the only reason you're up is because I called you. You were passed out drunk before I called, I know it."

"So?"

Amanda noticed the chuckle in his voice, and laughed herself. "You're right, never mind. There's nothing strange about that at all."

Danny swung his legs over the side of the bed and forced himself to sit up. "So what can I do for you, Miss Fiske? I know you weren't just calling to check in with me. Have you found anything useful there in Sitka?"

"Not really. Or at least nothing that could help us now."

"But you did find something?"

"Nothing concrete, just speculation on my part."

"Well spit it out, would you?"

"I did some research on the town where you said Aleksei is now, Coldfoot. It used to be a busy mining camp, but the place died out and the camp moved to a nearby town called Wiseman in the early 1900s. I looked into the history of the Wiseman area and starting around 1920, there were an unusually high number of murders and disappearances reported. And, the tribes in the region told stories about a white-haired monster that haunted the night."

"So you're thinking this white-haired monster is our Russian friend?"

"I'd say it's possible. There was a significant Russian migration to the US and to Alaska in the late 1800s and early 1900s, especially after World War I and the Russian Revolution. It's possible Aleksei came to Alaska then and never left."

"Possible. But it doesn't prove anything."

"I know it doesn't. I told you, it was just speculation on my part. I've still got a lot of material to research to see if I can track him."

Danny took a deep breath and rubbed his hand through his thick mop of hair. He couldn't believe the words that were about to come out of his mouth, but, what the hell. It wasn't like he had anything he could do here.

"I think I'll come there to Sitka too and help you search."

"What? You don't have to do that."

"I know I don't. But I want to. It will give me something to do. And since I've fully committed to chasing a creature instead of being a cop, I might as well go all out."

Amanda chuckled. "Well, okay. Since you put it that way."

"How long does it take to drive to Sitka from here?"

"You don't know Alaskan geography at all, do you?"

"No. But what kind of an answer is that? You care to enlighten me?"

"Sitka's on Baranof Island, so you can't drive here. Most of Southeastern Alaska is only accessible by plane or by boat."

"Yet one more reason to hate this god-forsaken state."

"Oh come on. It may be a tiny bit inconvenient to get here, but it's a gorgeous place."

"Well I guess I better see if I can get a flight down there. Is it a long flight?"

"No. My trip was about 5 hours, it's not bad. You'll have to switch planes in Anchorage though."

Danny got up from his bed. "Alright, listen. I'm going to see if I can book a flight for today. If I can, I'll send you a text and let you know I'm on my way."

"Okay. I can pick you up at the airport tonight. And I'll book a hotel for you too so you don't have to mess with that."

"Thanks. I'll get back to you in a bit."

Danny walked to his kitchen and made his customary pot of coffee. While he waited for the coffee to brew, he sat down at the table and booted up his Macbook. He brought up the travel ap, where he typed in his flight criteria. To his amazement, there was a flight leaving Fairbanks for Sitka in 3 hours. If he hurried, he could easily make it.

He quickly booked a seat, trying not to flinch at the exorbitant cost, and printed out his boarding pass. Still waiting on the coffee, he sent a quick message to Amanda, letting her know when he would arrive at the Sitka airport. It was an odd feeling, and not one he actually wanted to admit to himself, but he couldn't deny he was looking forward to seeing Amanda again.

He brushed the thought from his mind, rolling his eyes at his own silliness, and poured himself a cup of coffee. He gulped it down without bothering to add any creamer and quickly re-filled the mug. He took another sip and headed back to the bedroom to pack his suitcase.

CHAPTER 40

Amanda rapped her knuckles on the hotel room door and called out for Danny.

"Danny, are you up? It's me. Amanda."

She didn't have to wait long for an answer, as the door opened and Danny greeted her with a scowl.

"I knew who it was. Who the hell else could it be, anyway? You're the only person who even knows I'm here."

"Wow. Good morning to you, too. Are you always so charming in the morning?"

"Yeah, I am."

Amanda stepped around him and walked into the room. "Then I guess I can consider myself fortunate that you left my place before I woke up."

"I'm not a morning person, I admit it. But I'm up, even though I'm suffering from jet lag. What the hell else do you want from me?"

"Nothing. Silly me for expecting you to act like a mature adult and exchange the customary morning greetings."

"Fine. How are you, Amanda? Did you sleep well? How's the weather out there? I hope this morning finds you well."

Amanda chuckled. "Give it a rest, smartass. And give me a break on the jet lag. You're in the same time zone you were in yesterday."

Danny walked to the end table next to his king-sized bed, and picked up his mug of coffee. He took a drink, and plopped down onto the rumpled, unmade bed. "Well I don't know what it is then, but I'm suffering from something."

"I would guess it's a lack of alcohol."

"Good guess." Danny finished his coffee and set the mug back on the table. "So what's on our agenda today?"

"I thought you'd probably want breakfast first. Is that another good guess? Or did you bring your own box of Pop Tarts?"

"I wanted to, but they wouldn't let me carry them on the plane."

"Well you're in luck then. I know a great diner right down the street. You can eat a real breakfast for a change. Put some meat on those bones of yours."

"Who are you, my mother? I eat fine. And you're not the first one to tell me I'm too skinny. I can't help it that I'm naturally slim."

Amanda chuckled. "You're like a supermodel."

"Is there a point to this banter? Or should we think about discussing the reason I'm here?"

Amanda plopped onto the bed next to Danny. "I was thinking we should go to the Russian Heritage Center today. They have an extensive archives collection there on Russian immigrants to Alaska."

"You know, that's one thing I was thinking about on the plane. If our friend really is a vampire, would he register himself through whatever process immigrants used? It seems to me he'd just come and go as he pleased."

"Yeah, I know. But we don't know for sure that he was already a vampire when he came here."

"Good point."

"Plus, they have a collection of materials from early 20th century Russia there as well. Photos, diaries, news accounts. We might find something useful. Based on the fact that you found related disappearances as far back as the 30s, and I learned about the mysterious deaths in the mining camp, I think it's a good guess that Aleksei was around in the early 1900s."

"Yeah, I agree. Good a place to start as any, at least."

"We might actually get lucky. That time period was so tumultuous for Russia. World War I, the downfall of the Tsar, the Revolution…I would imagine we'll be able to find a lot of material."

Danny shook his head. "This is so strange to me. Trying to solve a case by looking at incidents from 100 years ago. It seems completely impossible."

Amanda patted his knee with her hand. "You know what I think since I got attacked? Nothing's impossible. The fact that Aleksei exists at all proves that to me."

Danny stood up from the bed. "Well that's the spirit. Let's give it the old scout try or something like that."

"I think it's the old college try."

"Whatever. I could swear there's some kind of saying about scouts."

"I don't think so."

Danny walked towards the door of his room and waved his hand dismissively, as if to surrender the point.

"Maybe you're thinking of live by the Girl Scout way," Amanda said.

"Yes, yes, that's exactly what I meant. Always been my mantra."

Amanda laughed and followed him out of the room towards the parking lot and her car.

CHAPTER 41

After a breakfast of eggs, bacon, hash browns, biscuits, and several cups of coffee, Danny and Amanda left the Early Bird Diner and got back into her rented Toyota Corolla.

"Off to the Archives now?" Danny asked, rubbing his full belly as he fastened his seat belt.

"I was thinking maybe we could make another stop first. I want to take you to the regular public library."

"Why?"

"Remember I told you about the research I did about Coldfoot and Wiseman? I wanted to show you the materials I found there. I thought it couldn't hurt to have fresh eyes looking at what I found."

"Alright."

"They have a special exhibit there about early Alaskan history. That's where I found the primary sources about Wiseman."

"Primary sources?"

"You know, artifacts, original documents, first-hand accounts." She paused as Danny looked at her with a befuddled expression. "Sorry, librarian talk. There are primary sources and secondary sources."

Danny searched the recesses of his brain. "I'm sure I've heard of that. Sometime in college, no doubt."

"Probably. Anyway it doesn't make any difference. I just want to show you the materials."

They drove along Airport Road and turned onto Harbor Drive. As its name suggested, the road faced the Crescent Harbor, and it was immediately obvious why Sitka had a reputation as both a fishing village and a tourist destination. Danny couldn't help but be reminded of Lake Shore Drive as Amanda drove alongside the water and finally came to the Kettleson Memorial Library.

Amanda nodded a quick greeting at the librarian at the desk and led Danny back to the Historic Alaska display that filled the back quarter of the library. She pulled two chairs together and sat down to find the materials that had caught her interest.

Danny sat down next to her and sorted through a selection of old books that had been arranged on the table in front of him. A title caught his eye.

He picked up the book, called "*A Portrait of Wiseman, Alaska*," and held it up for Amanda to see. "Isn't Wiseman the town you mentioned? The one with the murders and disappearances?"

"Yeah."

Danny put the book down on the table and leaned forward to browse through it. "This was written by some guy who was there in the 1930s. I wonder if he wrote anything about our friend."

Skimming the book, Danny came upon a selection of black & white photographs. A photo of an old cemetery filled with tiny headstones sticking awkwardly out of the frozen ground caught his eye. He brought the photo closer to his eyes and squinted, trying to make out the blurry inscriptions.

"What do you see?" Amanda asked.

Danny shook his head without answering. He wasn't sure yet. He skimmed through more of the book, keeping his finger on the page with the photograph. Finding what he was looking for, he read quickly through a stilted account of the population of the tiny village.

"Look at this," he finally said. "According to the book, there were only about 120 people in Wiseman at the time this was written. Mostly white males, miners and trappers, and a handful of white women and children. The rest were native to the area, an Eskimo tribe I guess."

"So?"

"So look at all the headstones in this cemetery," Danny said, returning to the photograph. "There's a hell of a lot of them for that small of a population. And I could make out some of the dates. They're all from around the same time."

Amanda grabbed the diary she had found, written by a miner who was terrified of the creature the tribes called the "white-haired monster."

"This guy wrote about the so-called monster in 1928. He says he knew the monster was killing people in the village, but the rest of the villagers chalked the deaths up to bear attacks. They thought he was crazy."

"Almost all of these headstones are dated 1927-1929."

Amanda let out a deep breath. "I'm sure there could be another explanation. I doubt people lived very long in those conditions. The cold alone would do a lot of people in."

"True enough. But I know you're thinking the same thing I am. That diary writer wasn't crazy at all. The monster was Aleksei."

"I wonder if he's been in the area ever since."

Danny put the book back where he had found it. "I doubt it. He couldn't have opened Snow Creek until much later; the asylum itself wasn't even built at this time. But if he got a taste of the Arctic and enjoyed it, he could have easily returned."

Amanda glanced down at the diary in her hand. "This guy writes that most of Wiseman was abandoned by the time he finished this diary. He writes about planning to leave the Arctic and go back to Fairbanks, but that's where the diary ends."

"I wonder if the white-haired monster got him before he could carry out his plan to move to Fairbanks. Aleksei probably wiped them all out."

Amanda shuddered. "God, it's so awful to imagine."

"It is. But I think it fits. I think Aleksei came to Wiseman from who knows where and found he liked the Arctic quite a bit."

Amanda put the diary back in its place in the display rack and glanced up at the clock on the wall in front of her. "We've probably been here long enough. We should get over to the Archives so we have enough time to look for Aleksei."

Danny nodded and stood up from his chair. "Maybe we can find out what he was up to before he became the white-haired monster."

CHAPTER 42

Aleksei paced through the trees outside the restaurant, grateful for the infamous Seattle rain. While he knew all about Seattle's reputation for rain, he still couldn't believe his good luck. He had been concerned he'd have to alter his plans and wait until evening to capture Katie and bring her home to Alaska with him. But thanks to the rain, he would now be able to snatch her up as soon as she finished her shift and returned to the car he had watched her park a few hours earlier. He was certain this unexpected dose of good fortune was a sign that he was making the right move in abandoning his quest to replace Natasha. It was fate, and he knew without a doubt that it was finally time to say goodbye to his beloved Natasha and start a new life. Katie was meant to be his Katerina.

Aleksei's body tingled as he watched the back door of the restaurant open, and Katie step outside. She was wearing her work uniform of khakis and a navy t-shirt and she smiled at the older man at her side carrying two bags of garbage. Aleksei knew the man was the owner of the restaurant, Katie's grandfather. He also knew this was the last time the man would ever see his granddaughter.

He heard Katie laugh at something her grandfather said and watched her hug him before he disappeared back into the restaurant. Aleksei and Katie were alone in the nearly empty parking lot. If his heart was still beating, he knew he would have felt it beating right out of his chest. He licked his lips and approached Katie's car. He made no sound as he came up to Katie from behind.

"Excuse me," he said.

Obviously startled, Katie whirled around to face him. He thought he saw a glimmer of recognition on her face. "Yes," she said, her hand on the open door of her car.

"Do you remember me?" Aleksei asked. He pushed the car door closed, and leaned in towards Katie, his body towering over her 5"4' frame.

Katie tried to swallow her rising fear. She glanced towards the restaurant, willing her grandfather or one of the other employees to come out the back door. "Do you need something?" she asked.

"Just you."

Katie's eyes widened and she moved away from the car. She turned to run to the restaurant, dropping her purse and phone on the ground next to her car.

Aleksei grabbed her and pulled her back towards him, immediately covering her mouth to silence the scream he knew would be coming next. He pulled Katie into the trees and out of sight of anyone in the restaurant, and turned her face towards his. He couldn't deny, he relished the terror in her eyes and the tears that had now mixed with the raindrops spattering her face.

"You're coming with me," he whispered.

Katie tried to shake her head, but Aleksei held her still. He wrapped his arms around her neck, being careful not to break it. Sometimes even now, he forgot his own strength. It was a delicate balance, applying enough pressure to bring on unconsciousness but not enough to bring on suffocation. But he was used to the process by now. And Katie was putty in his hands.

Within seconds, she was unconscious in his arms. Aleksei smiled and lifted her off the ground, tossing her limp body over his shoulder. He had Katie out of Seattle and on the way back to Alaska long before anyone noticed the purse and phone left on the wet concrete of the restaurant parking lot.

CHAPTER 43

Danny rubbed his eyes and stared at the piles of papers and photos in front of him. The sheer amount of materials in the Russian archives was overwhelming and trying to find something about Aleksei Nechayev was worse than searching for the proverbial needle in a haystack. He was frustrated, irritated, and wishing he had a drink.

He glanced over at Amanda, who was poring over a diary written by a WWI Russian soldier and wincing as she tried to make out the Russian scribbles.

"Have you found anything useful at all?" he asked.

"Don't you think I would have told you if I had?"

Danny shook his head. "This is a waste of time."

"I don't think so."

"I thought crap like this was supposed to be cataloged? Shouldn't we be able to just search for Nechayev?"

"We should, but the Archives doesn't have enough personnel to catalog and index everything. They try, but they're always behind." She set the diary aside and picked up a folder stuffed with photographs from the Russian Revolution of 1917. "We're on our own."

Danny sighed and rolled his chair across the room until he was next to Amanda. He grabbed an envelope containing photographs of WWI soldiers. "I guess I'll browse through these," he said.

Amanda ignored him and continued to sift through her own stack of photos. Danny opened his envelope, and poured the contents on to the table in front of him. Faded black and white and sepia toned photos scattered, with a few dropping to the floor around his chair.

Looking up from her own work, Amanda frowned at him. "Be careful. These photos are valuable."

"Spoken like a true librarian."

"I'd say I'm speaking as a courteous person. The archivists are giving us free rein here. The least we can do is make sure we don't damage their materials."

"You're right. I'll be more careful."

Amanda nodded and returned to her photos, as Danny reached down to pick up the pictures he had dropped. He leafed through them, wandering about the serious young men he saw staring back at him. All were wearing the uniform of the Russian Imperial Troops, cloth caps tilted on their heads, loose-fitting tunics, and trousers tucked in boots. In addition, all of them looked much too young to be heading to war. He supposed that was one thing that never changed.

Danny flipped through more photos, and stopped on a shot of the Ninth Army Unit, dated November, 1916. Unlike the photos from the start of the War, these soldiers stared at the camera with eyes haunted by fatigue and hunger. The men were gaunt, and their uniforms hung loosely on their nearly emaciated bodies. Their cloth caps had been replaced by tattered fur hats, and their tunics were now covered with threadbare overcoats. He shook his head, wondering if any of these long-ago soldiers had survived the war.

He was about to place the photo back in the envelope when a soldier standing at the edge of the photo caught his eye. Unlike the majority of his comrades, his head was bare, leaving his obviously blond hair visible. While it was impossible to make out the color of his eyes in the black and white photo, they were clearly unusual, and their gaze pierced the camera lens. The man was significantly taller than any of the men around him, and his face was immediately recognizable to Danny. The man was Aleksei Nechayev.

"Amanda," Danny said. "Look at this."

Amanda lifted her eyes from her own work, and glanced at Danny. "Look at what?"

"This photo. Do you recognize this guy?" Danny pushed the photo towards her, and pointed to Aleksei.

Amanda picked up the photo and stared at it, her eyes instantly filling with tears. "That's him," she said. "I know it. It's him."

"I think so too."

"He looks the same."

"Exactly. This is the guy I saw in Coldfoot."

Amanda's hands started to shake, and she set the photo back on the table. "So he was a WWI soldier?"

Danny leaned back in his chair, causing the wheels to screech on the tile floor. "We probably shouldn't jump to conclusions. Maybe this is his grandfather or some other relative."

"Are you kidding me? Do we have to go over this again? Come on."

"Alright, alright. I admit it. I think it's him, too."

"So he is a vampire. I was right."

"He's something, that's for sure. He's more than 100 years old and he looks the same as he did in 1916."

"He's a vampire."

Danny held up his hands. "Okay."

The two stared at the photo in silence. Danny felt a return of the same chill he had felt in Coldfoot. If Amanda hadn't been seeing the same thing, he'd swear he was having some sort of hallucination. How could this be the same guy?

"So now what?" he said.

"Now we find out more about this unit. What happened to them in the War. If this was 1916, the start of the Revolution was right around the corner."

"This is interesting, I'm not gonna deny it. But what the hell does it mean for my case? So we know Aleksei was a Russian soldier. So what? That doesn't help me find Maria."

"But maybe it will if we can find out when he came here and where he started out. He must have another home here besides Coldfoot where he keeps his women..."

Danny rubbed his eyes again and shook his head. "Okay. It's not like I have anything else to go on. And I'm not wanted back at work anyway."

Amanda looked over his head at the clock behind him. "Damn," she said.

"What?"

"The archives is about to close. We need to clean all this up."

"What? I'm not stopping now, not when we finally got something. I'll flash my badge at them and demand to stay longer."

"That's not really fair to the employees. And you said yourself, it's not like we're going to find something you can use to nail Aleksei here. We can come back tomorrow bright and early."

"I guess. We can do some searching for this unit on the Internet. I've got my Macbook back at the hotel." Danny's face turned red as his stomach growled loudly. "And I guess I could use some dinner, too."

Amanda smiled. "So could I. I can't believe we've been here all day and I didn't even think about lunch. I know a great place we can go. You can even get some beer."

"That sounds a lot better than the food."

The two stood up and hastily arranged the archival materials back into tidy piles, leaving their photo of Aleksei out so they could continue their research in the morning. Amanda grabbed Danny's hand and smiled at him.

"It's amazing to find him, isn't it? After all this time, I know he really is what I said he was."

Danny tried his best to smile in return. "I'm glad for you. I know it must be satisfying."

He watched as Amanda nearly skipped out the door ahead of him. He could understand her excitement, but he couldn't share it. He had already known Aleksei was a monster, but he had still hoped for some rational explanation, something that would prove Amanda had been wrong. He knew how to stop a human monster. But a real monster was something all together different. Whatever Aleksei was, Danny had no idea how to stop him.

CHAPTER 44

Danny bunched up his flat pillows against the headboard of his hotel room bed and sat half up in bed, his back resting against the pillows. He reached his hand out to brush a lock of Amanda's hair out of her eyes, and tucked it behind her ear with his fingers. Her eyes were closed, but he knew she wasn't sleeping. Her mouth curved into a smile as he caressed her cheek.

Danny hadn't planned to bring Amanda back to his hotel room, as he had sworn he would never sleep with a potential witness again, but after the two had finished their dinner at the restaurant Amanda had chosen, it seemed like the logical step. After all, what difference did it make if he slept with a witness again? He'd already crossed that line, so why worry about ethics now? And, what the hell else was there to do in Sitka, Alaska in the dark?

It dawned on him that Amanda was the first woman he'd slept with more than once since Caroline had died. He glanced down at her, and said as much.

"You know something? You're the first woman I've slept with twice since my wife died."

Amanda opened her eyes and looked up at him. "Really?"

"Yeah. I've stuck to drunken one-night stands." And not to many of those either, if he was being honest.

"I guess I should take this as a compliment, then."

"I guess so. Especially since I'm not even drunk."

Amanda chuckled and rolled over onto her back. "I'm honored." She exhaled deeply, and stared at the ceiling fan above the bed.

"What are you thinking about?" Danny asked.

"Aleksei."

"Go figure."

"Seeing him there in that photo, it's just so bizarre. He looks exactly the same..."

"You're the one who said he was a vampire. I would think you'd be happy it looks like you're right."

"I guess thinking he's a vampire, and seeing it with my own eyes are two different things. It just gave me the creeps."

"I can understand that. Everything about him gives me the creeps. And I wasn't even attacked by him."

Amanda moved onto her side and bent her elbow, propping her head up on her open palm. "Why don't we talk about something else?"

"Sounds good to me."

"Tell me about your wife."

"I'd like to talk more about Aleksei."

"I'm serious."

"So am I."

"I know her name was Caroline. You told me she died..."

"Right on both counts."

"So what happened to her? It's obviously had a huge impact on you. Anyone can see you're not over her."

"Why do you say that?"

"You really have to ask? You're a complete wreck."

Danny laughed drily. "Thanks."

"What happened to her?" Amanda asked again.

"She was murdered."

Danny felt his throat close up as the words left his mouth. He bit his lip, and eyed the hotel mini-bar.

"Right in front of me," he said.

"Oh my God. I'm sorry."

Danny rolled his eyes and got up from the bed. He grabbed the pants he had tossed on the floor earlier, and pulled them on as he walked across the room to the mini-bar. He chose a bottle of scotch and tossed it back.

"And that's exactly why I didn't want to talk about what happened," he said. "You'd be amazed how unbearable it can be to hear people telling you how sorry they are."

"I don't know what else to say."

"I know you don't. And it's not your fault. I just can't stand hearing it."

"Who killed her? Why?"

Danny's eyes welled with tears. He reached for another bottle of Scotch and plopped onto the chair next to the mini-bar, stretching his legs out in front of him.

"A guy I knew at work. A cop. Actually, he was my partner."

"Oh my God," Amanda repeated. She stopped herself before adding her sympathy. "Why?" she asked.

Danny shook his head and took a drink. "It's a long story. Are you sure you want to hear this? Don't you have something better to do than listen to 'This is Your Life, Danny Fitzpatrick?'"

"No, I don't. What happened?"

"His name was Stephen Jackson. I was only partnered with him for a few years, before that I'd been with the same guy since I first became a cop. He retired, and I got put with Jackson, who had just moved to Chicago."

"So you didn't know him that well?"

"Well enough. I thought I did anyway. He and I started working on a string of murders in the area. Women who'd been raped before they were murdered. We already knew about a serial rapist who'd been busy in Chicago, and Jackson and I got put on the case when it was clear the rapist had escalated and added murder to his game."

Danny paused and took another drink. Amanda stared at him, wondering if he was still aware she was in the room. He looked as if he were miles away.

"I told you this was a long story so I'll make it short," Danny said. "I had no idea Jackson was playing me for a fool, working this case with me while he was the god-damn perp. I kept talking about how it seemed like the asshole was so careful, he seemed to know just what cops would look for, but it never dawned on me that there was a good reason for that. Then one day he slipped, made a comment about how one of the women looked when she took her last breath. I guess he was getting so fucking cocky he didn't even think about what he was saying, he just wanted to brag about it. He tried to play it off as soon as he realized what he'd said, but I knew then. I knew what an idiot I'd been."

"I started looking at the rape cases and realized they'd started right around the time Jackson moved to Chicago. I looked up unsolved cases in Des Moines, where he'd come from, and sure enough, there was a serial rapist who miraculously stopped right after Jackson moved out of the city. He knew I was after him, but I didn't have any evidence. He threatened, told me if I knew what was good for me, I'd stop. I told him to fuck off and I was going to keep going until I could nail his ass to the wall."

"So he went after Caroline?"

Danny nodded. "That night I walked into my apartment and found him in the bedroom with Caroline. He told me she was going to be his next victim, and I was welcome to watch. He had a knife to her throat.." Danny's voice cracked and he quickly downed the rest of the Scotch.

"You don't have to keep talking about it," Amanda said. "I'm sorry I brought these memories up for you."

"Don't worry about it. These memories aren't ever gone, believe me."

Danny tossed the empty bottle into the wastebasket, and stared at the painting of a beach scene on the wall. Why advertise the beach in an Alaskan hotel? He supposed the proprietors were just trying to help guests forget they were in this god-forsaken Arctic wasteland.

He turned towards Amanda, who was now sitting up straight in the bed, hugging her knees to her chest.

"He sliced her throat right in front of me," he said bluntly. "I had a gun on him and I was about to fire, I knew I could blow his head off, but I waited too long. I was trying to make sure I had a perfect shot, but my fucking hands were shaking so god-damn much..."

Danny let out a deep breath. "Her blood splattered all over me at the same time I pulled the trigger and blew his brains out. Have you ever seen how much blood comes out of jugular veins?"

Amanda shook her head.

"A hell of a lot. Pumping everywhere, all over me. All out of Caroline. I still see that blood everywhere I fucking look."

Danny got up from his chair and grabbed a bottle of vodka out of the minibar. He held it up to Amanda. "Time to move on to the alcoholic's choice."

"So that's when you moved to Fairbanks? After Caroline was murdered?"

"You got it. I quit homicide, and left Chicago right after her funeral. I didn't care where I went. I just knew I couldn't stay there." He sat back down and stared at Amanda. "So now you know all about Caroline. Satisfied?"

"I really am sorry. I shouldn't have pried."

Danny waved his hand, dismissing her. "You didn't. I'm the one who screamed her name in your apartment and threw bottles across your living room. I can't blame you for being curious."

"Still..."

"And I don't want you feeling sorry for me, okay? I can't take that shit."

"Okay."

"You don't feel sorry for me?"

"I don't, no."

Danny chuckled. "Good. Because no matter what happened, I'm still a total fuck-up. I haven't done a single useful thing since I came to Alaska."

"I don't agree with that."

"No?"

"No. You listened to me. You're the only person that ever believed me about Aleksei. I think that was very useful."

"Did it ever dawn on you that the only reason I believed you is because we're both fucking nuts?"

"Oh, sure. I definitely think that." Amanda couldn't keep the smile out of her voice.

Danny smiled in return. "As long we're on the same page then."

He walked back to the bed and lay down next to Amanda, drawing her mouth to his. He closed his eyes, forcing himself to ignore the line of red drops he had seen along her neck and the blood he was sure was splattered all over the hotel room wall behind her.

CHAPTER 45

Aleksei opened to door to his guest room, and saw Katie still unconscious on the bed where he had left her. He had foolishly hoped that sedating her wouldn't be necessary, but her high-pitched, piercing screams when she had first regained consciousness and saw him standing in front of her had quickly dispelled him of that notion. Not that he was worried about anyone hearing her. He knew that wasn't an issue here in Coldfoot. But he could only take so much of the screaming himself. Katie had a lot to learn before she became his permanent companion.

He had gagged her now and left her on the bed to sleep off the sedative. When she woke up, he'd start teaching her about good manners and ladylike behavior, neither of which included screaming loud enough to wake the dead. He left the room and closed the door behind him before heading to the kitchen. There was something he couldn't put off any longer.

Not bothering to put on a coat, as he knew no one would see him here and there was no need to blend in, Aleksei opened the kitchen door and walked outside towards the root cellar. He hoped Maria was still alive, as he wanted her to be Katie's first kill, but he couldn't deny that it wouldn't bother him if she wasn't. He almost wished he hadn't left her the food and water he had before he went to Seattle. He had moved on, and his mind was too occupied with Katie to deal with her. Plus, Maria had disappointed him, and he'd never had any tolerance for those who didn't live up to his expectations.

Aleksei brushed the snow from the root cellar door, and opened it. He walked down the stairs into the cellar, holding a lantern in front of him, and found Maria curled up in a ball in the corner of the dirt floor, her fingers clutching her blanket around her face. He could tell instantly that she was still alive, but he knew she was pretending to be sleeping, regardless of the fact that she'd tried this trick with him before. He was amazed at how truly tedious she had turned out to be.

"Time to wake up, Sunshine," he said. "I'm home. Did you miss me?"

Maria opened her eyes and remained silent, staring at him with a vacant expression.

"I see you still have some food left," Aleksei said, glancing at the plates he had left on the cellar floor. "So you took my advice about conserving your resources."

"Don't you even want to know where I was?" he asked. "What I was doing?"

"I don't care," Maria whispered.

Aleksei grinned. "You'll care soon enough."

He walked over to Maria and squatted on his haunches in front of her, bobbing up and down on the balls of his feet. It was all he could do not to tear her neck open right now, but at the same time, she looked so gaunt and frail that it hardly seemed worth the effort. She wasn't going to be any challenge for Katie at all.

"Sit up," he said. "Now."

"Why?"

"Because I said so."

Maria pushed herself up with arms that were starting to become bony and leaned against the wall. "Satisfied?" she said.

Unable to control himself, Aleksei bared his fangs. He couldn't conceal his delight at the fear that invaded Maria's face, and the whimper that escaped from her mouth. So much for the vacant expression.

"I am now," he said.

He stood back up and paced around the cellar. "I see you still have food so I won't bother to bring you more just yet. Nice job of conserving your water, too."

"So you're leaving me down here now?"

"Yeah, the house is off-limits now, sorry. I have a new guest."

"What are you?" Maria asked.

"I'm a man with very sharp teeth," Aleksei said. "I don't have time to tell you anything more, and maybe if you hadn't asked so damn many questions you wouldn't have found yourself back down here in the first place."

Before Maria could respond, Aleksei headed up the stairs. "By the way," he said, turning back around. "You don't have to worry about being Natasha anymore. That was a hopeless cause. I know that now. And you won't have to be down here too much longer anyway."

He turned away and walked up the steps, stopping again when he got to the door. Unable to resist, he yelled back to Maria before pushing the door off its hinges.

"You'll be dead soon enough," he said. "My new guest and I will see to that."

Ignoring her cries, he let the heavy door slam shut behind him.

CHAPTER 46

Aleksei prowled into his study and poured himself a tall glass of vodka before taking a seat in his favorite chair. Maria had riled him up and he found himself regretting the strong sedative he had given Katie to knock her out. He should have gone a bit lighter. He wanted her to wake up now.

But for now he'd have to be content with planning the life he would give her and imagining all they would do together. It wouldn't go wrong now. He wouldn't be too late this time.

Aleksei was starving. He needed to feed, and he needed to do it soon, but he had to find Natasha first. He didn't have time to hunt.

He felt so confused, more powerful than he ever could have imagined, but also more lost. He should have joined Greger and his group of vampires. He needed to be among his own kind and learn how to manage his new life. He'd find the group again once he had Natasha. They'd learn from Greger together.

He raced through the streets of St. Petersburg, moving so quickly he was a blur to the hundreds of injured protestors and beggars who shuffled through the streets like zombies. He occasionally grabbed blond women he thought could be Natasha and tossed them into the gutters when they disappointed him.

Desperate, he knew the only way he could find Natasha was to turn to the one person he loathed above all others. Maksim Bodrov. Aleksei hated to admit it, but he knew Bodrov was the person most likely to know where Natasha was. Once he got the information he needed, he'd kill Bodrov and feed on him to ease his hunger.

Finally, he came upon the St. Petersburg barracks.

"Bodrov!" he yelled. "Maksim Bodrov! Where are you?"

He knew it was possible Bodrov would not be at his post, as most of the St. Petersburg guard had deserted amid the chaos of the protests. He nearly shook with relief when he heard Bodrov answering his calls.

"Who wants to know?" Bodrov yelled, walking towards the sound of Aleksei's voice.

"It's Aleksei Nechayev. I want to speak with you about Natasha."

Aleksei heard footsteps behind him and turned to see Bodrov entering the room. He dragged his right foot behind him and moved with a stilted gait, his face wincing in pain with every step. Aleksei didn't bother to ask Bodrov what had happened to him. It was of no interest.

"What about Natasha?"

"I need to know where she is. She hasn't shown up at the hospital. It's urgent that I find her!"

Aleksei felt himself losing control as he talked. It was all he could do to keep from jumping on Bodrov and finishing him off.

"You're a little late."

"What do you mean?"

Bodrov stared at Aleksei, feeling a sense of unease. He had never liked Nechayev and had tried to convince Natasha that he was a nutcase, but he seemed ever stranger now. What was wrong with him?

"I asked you what you mean!" Aleksei yelled.

"I mean you're not going to find her. Natasha's dead. She was killed yesterday in the protests. Knocked over and trampled by a god-damn herd of

idiots."

Aleksei stumbled backwards as if reeling from a physical blow. He stared at the floor and tried to maintain his composure. Surely this couldn't be true? Why had he bothered to find this piece of trash Bodrov?

"Sorry, man," Bodrov said.

Aleksei saw movement out of the corner of his eye, and looked up to see Bodrov shuffling, pulling his dead leg behind him. He leaped forward and grabbed Bodrov's collar, pulling him half off the ground.

"What the fuck?" Bodrov said. "Get the hell off of me."

"Where is she?"

"I told you, she's dead."

"Tell me where she is."

"I can't..."

"Tell me!" Aleksei screamed.

Bodrov stared into Aleksei's eyes and felt a rush of terror. "They moved the bodies to the Summer Garden, by the Field of Mars. You can probably find her there."

Aleksei loosened his grip on Bodrov's shirt. "Right. Of course. She's taking care of them. That's what she does." He stared outside the barracks, imagining Natasha in her nurse's uniform, tending to the wounded, just as she had done to him.

He felt Bodrov shift, obviously trying to pull away from him. He pulled Bodrov's shirt tighter, bringing him closer.

"You didn't take care of her," he said. "What good are you? What kind of a soldier are you?"

"There was nothing I could do..."

"Shut up!" Aleksei said. He stared at Bodrov's neck, watching his vein throb with fear. He looked back at Bodrov's face, and bared his newly-made fangs.

Bodrov shook with terror, and futilely tried to pull away from Aleksei's grip. "What the hell? Help! Someone, help me, please!"

Aleksei chuckled at his cries and moved within an inch of his face. "There's no one here to help you. And now that I know where Natasha is, I don't need you anymore. I'm done with you," he said, and sunk his teeth into Bodrov's quivering neck.

The screams intensified before Bodrov slumped in Aleksei's arms. Aleksei drained the last drops of blood from the body, and let it drop.

He was gone before anyone responded to Bodrov's screams, or found his dead body crumpled on the floor of the barracks.

CHAPTER 47

Danny tossed aside a folder of documents pertaining to Russia's role in WWI, wondering what on earth he was doing back in the archives for a second day. He couldn't read Russian, and the odds of finding another picture of Aleksei were clearly slim to none. And he couldn't get behind Amanda's idea that all this could somehow lead to finding Maria. He'd never been a history buff and that's all these materials were as far as he was concerned. History. And ancient history, at that.

He rocked back and forth in his swivel chair and let out an exasperated sigh.

"This is a waste of time," he said. "We're not going to find anything else."

"Do you always give up so quickly on your cases?" Amanda asked.

"None of my cases involved sifting through 100 year old documents."

"Well there's a first time for everything."

"Maybe I'll just leave this to you and go do some exploring around Sitka. It's a lot warmer here than it is in Fairbanks."

"It's balmy here compared to Fairbanks. Sitka is totally different."

"I think I will go look around then. I can't stand being cooped up in here anymore."

"Suit yourself. If I find anything, I'll call you."

Danny was about to get up from the chair when his phone rang. He took it from his pocket and glanced at the incoming number, noticing a Chicago area code. He considered not answering, but realized that would be childish to say the least.

"Hello?" he said.

"Danny? This is John Fisher."

"Fisher? What do you want? How'd you get my number?"

"You called me to ask for help, remember? What the hell?"

"Right, right. Sorry."

"Besides, I'm an FBI agent. You think I'd have trouble getting your number if I wanted it?"

"Alright, fine. We've cleared up the phone number mystery. How about telling me what you want."

"I don't want anything. I just came across a case that I thought might interest you, so I decided to call."

"What is it?"

"We're investigating a sex trafficking ring in Seattle, so I've been monitoring their police reports. I noticed a call about a missing girl, and when I looked at the report and saw her photo, I thought she looked a lot like the women you asked me to run a report on for you. Same physical characteristics you told me to look for anyway. Tall, slim girl, long blond hair."

"That's hardly an unusual physical description."

"I know, but something about this girl just hit me. And apparently her parents mentioned visiting Alaska recently. I thought you might want to take a look at the report."

Danny rubbed a hand through his hair and nodded. "Alright," he said into the phone. "I don't think it has any connection to be honest, but it can't hurt. Send it through to me."

"You'll get it in a minute."

"Thanks, John."

"You had any luck with your case?"

"No. It's basically dead in the water."

"Well that sucks, sorry to hear it." He paused for a moment. "Did you get the file?"

Danny clicked on his messages. "Yeah, it's here. I'll let you know if it leads to anything."

"Okay, buddy," John said.

Danny ended the call without further comment. He wasn't interested in any of his old "buddies."

"What was that about?" Amanda asked.

"My old friend from the FBI ran across a case he thinks might be connected to mine. He's the one I asked to run the report on the old missing women cases."

"Do you think it's connected?"

Danny shook his head while he waited for John's attachment to download onto his phone. "It doesn't sound like it. Apparently it's a missing girl case in Seattle."

"Why does he think it's connected?"

"Apparently the girl looks like our cases." He glanced over at Amanda, who was pushing her long blond hair behind her ears with slim and elegant fingers. "And you."

Danny turned back to his phone and opened the report from Seattle. Katie Bailey, 17 years old, disappeared from her grandfather's restaurant the day before. Purse and phone found next to her parked car. He looked at the photo of a smiling Katie, and looked back at Amanda, who was watching him with questioning eyes. No doubt about it, Katie had the right look for Aleksei.

"She does look like you," he said. "And like Maria and Anna."

"Let me see."

Danny pulled his phone away. "I know we're kind of working as partners here but there are limits. I can't show you a police report that technically I'm not even supposed to have."

"Well then keep reading it and see if you find anything interesting."

"Okay, Chief."

Danny returned to the report. He felt a twitch of adrenalin as he read through the detective's report of her interview with Katie's parents. She had asked if Katie had any travel plans, and the parents had mentioned that the family just returned from a trip to Alaska. To the Arctic. And Katie had hated it as Katie was at the age where she hated traveling with her parents and brother.

It was clear the parents were desperate and babbling, but Danny was quickly convinced that their off-handed remark about the Arctic might just be the most important information they had shared.

"What is it?" Amanda asked. "You look like you've found something."

"I might have. The missing girl recently went on a trip to the Arctic."

"To Coldfoot?"

"I don't know. I need to find out though."

Danny continued paging through the report files. "But this doesn't fit his pattern. He just got Maria. Why would he be going after another victim so soon?"

"Maybe he doesn't stick to a pattern. Maybe he kidnaps women whenever he feels like it, and the Solstice was just a coincidence."

"Maybe," Danny said, unconvinced. "But I still think the Solstice is significant. Too many went missing on that day for it to be a coincidence."

Danny sat up straight in his chair. "I need to contact this detective." He skimmed back through the report for a name. "Lauren Cooper. She needs to ask the parents if their trip included Coldfoot."

Amanda felt her heart beating in her chest. "I can't believe he got someone else. And a young girl? My God."

"Yeah. Looks like Aleksei's branching out and going younger." Danny remembered the list John Fisher had given him, and the girls he believed were among Aleksei's earliest victims. "Actually, I think he started out with young girls. Maybe he's decided to go back to his roots."

Danny stared at the photo of the pretty teenage girl smiling back at him from the pages of the police report, and was overcome with nausea. He stood up and paced the room as he called Seattle PD, and Detective Lauren Cooper.

CHAPTER 48

Lauren Cooper chewed her lip as she sorted through her notes on the missing Katie Bailey. She didn't even want to look at the girl's photo, but couldn't shake the feeling that the smiling blond teenager was staring at her and willing her to find her before it was too late. Lauren tasted blood and realized she had chewed a bit too much. Better switch to a stick of gum.

She reached down into her purse and pulled out a pack of peppermint gum. She shoved two sticks into her mouth for good measure and returned to her notes. Twirling a strand of her short brown hair around her index finger, Lauren racked her brain for anything she could have missed on Katie Bailey. She was certain the girl had not run away of her own accord. Teenage girls don't leave their phones behind when they take off on some planned adventure.

Lauren had talked to every family member and friend Katie had and all she had was one dead end after another. By all accounts, the girl had left her job at her grandfather's restaurant and simply disappeared into the Seattle night. Her frustration mounting, Lauren sighed when her phone rang. Now what?

"Lauren Cooper," she said, struggling to talk over the mouth full of gum she had forgotten she had.

"Detective Cooper, my name is Danny Fitzpatrick. I'm a detective in Chi… in Fairbanks, Alaska, and I need to talk to you about your case."

Lauren spit her gum out in a tissue and leaned back in her chair. "What case?"

"Katie Bailey. The missing teenager."

"How do you know about my case? Who are you, again?"

"Danny Fitzpatrick. Fairbanks PD. I think your case is connected to some missing women here in Alaska."

Lauren's ears perked up. "How so? And how did you even know about Katie?"

"I have a colleague in the FBI who forwarded the information to me. He came across your case while working on one of his own, and thought there might be a connection."

"Why?"

"I'll explain that soon enough, but right now I need you to do something for me. You have to find out if Katie and her family have ever been to a resort called Snow Creek in Coldfoot, Alaska."

"What??"

"You heard me. And trust me, you don't have any time to waste. I know they mentioned a trip to the Arctic they went on last week. If they stayed in Snow Creek, I know where Katie is."

"What the hell are you talking about? How do you know what the Baileys told me?"

Danny felt himself losing his patience. "Did I not just tell you I have a contact in the FBI who forwarded your case to me? What the hell is wrong with you? You've got a kid missing there and I'm telling you I think I know where she is!"

Lauren matched his scowl on her end of the call. Just who the hell did this guy think he was talking to? For all she knew, he was some quack playing games. But, it wasn't as if she had any other leads to go on. She'd talk to the Baileys and then find out what this pushy pain in the ass from Fairbanks was on about.

"Alright," she said. "Let me talk to the Baileys. I'll call you back." She glanced at the caller ID on her cell. "Will you be at this number?"

"Yeah, I'm on my cell. If you can't get through for some reason, call me at the Bay Inn in Sitka, Alaska. I'm in room 115."

"Okay. I'll get back to you as soon as I can."

"Hurry up. You don't have time to waste, trust me."

Lauren ended the call and scrolled through her notes for the Bailey's phone number. Danny Fitzpatrick was pushy and rude, but Lauren felt a tingle of adrenalin just the same. She might just be dealing with a quack, but it would be easy enough to determine that soon enough. For now, all she wanted to do was follow-up on what looked like her first solid lead.

CHAPTER 49

Christine Bailey paced back and forth in her kitchen, ignoring the untouched sandwich and now cold cup of coffee on the counter. While her friends no doubt meant well when urging her to eat, she knew she'd vomit if she put the sandwich anywhere close to her mouth. She couldn't do anything right now but wait to hear from Katie. There had to be an explanation for her disappearance and she knew her daughter would be calling any minute with a bizarre story of what had happened, something they would laugh about in the years to come.

Christine jumped at the sound of the phone in her pocket ringing.

"Katie?" she answered.

"Mrs. Bailey?"

Christine's heart sank. It wasn't Katie.

"Who is this? Do you have news on Katie?"

"This is Detective Lauren Cooper. I'm sorry, Mrs. Bailey, I don't have any news. But I did want to ask you a question."

"What is it?"

"You mentioned Katie accompanying you on a trip to the Arctic, correct?"

"Yes. We went last week. Why? What does this have to do with anything?"

"Did you stay at a place called Cold Foot?"

"Yes. At the Snow Creek. That's where we stayed overnight before we went to Prudhoe Bay. Why are you asking?"

"I'm sorry, I can't tell you that. But.."

Christine interrupted Lauren before she could complete her sentence. "What do you mean you can't tell me? My daughter's the one who is missing! You certainly can tell me. Do you think she's there? Katie wouldn't go there. She hated it there!"

"Mrs. Bailey, I will let you know as soon as I know anything about your daughter, you have my word on that. Thank you and I truly am sorry."

Lauren ended the call before Christine could yell at her again. She heard Christine's anguished voice as she hung up and felt guilty for causing the poor woman even more grief, but there was nothing she could do about it.

The important thing now was to call this Alaskan detective back and find out what the hell he knew about Katie Bailey and the Snow Creek resort. She wasn't getting anywhere here in Seattle. She'd need to talk with her captain, but she was starting to think her next move should be to head to Alaska herself.

CHAPTER 50

"Thanks for the ride to the airport," Danny said as he tossed what little he had packed back into his overnight bag. He took a quick look around his hotel room to make sure he hadn't left anything, and headed outside.

"You're welcome," Amanda said. "It's not like it's any trouble anyway."

"I'm just glad I could get a flight today. I need to get back to the office."

"You really think Aleksei has the Seattle girl?"

"Lauren Cooper said the parents told her they stayed at Snow Creek. Do you think that's a coincidence?"

Amanda shook her head as she unlocked her car. "I hope it is. I hate to think of a young girl with that monster."

"I agree, but it can't be a coincidence. And if it is, it should be in some kind of record book. Snow Creek is a hell of a dangerous place for blond women. And now, blond teenage girls, too."

Danny stared out the window at the huge flakes of snow that were just beginning to fall. "Great," he said. "I hope the weather doesn't delay my flight."

"Can't you just call your Chief and let him know what's going on?"

"I tried. He was supposedly in a meeting."

"What do you mean, supposedly?"

"I was told he was in a meeting, but I think it's more likely he just didn't want to take my call. He thinks I've gone off the rails and he told me to stay away so he didn't have to deal with me. And, I tried calling Tessa but she's swamped with a new homicide case, somebody ran over a drunk who had passed out outside Anthony's Bar and apparently it wasn't an accident."

"I'll keep going through the archives," Amanda said. "See if I can find anything about Aleksei's history here in Alaska."

"More power to you. But you know I don't think there's any point to it."

"Maybe not. But it can't hurt anything. And I'm interested in it anyway."

Danny shrugged. "Suit yourself."

"Let me know what happens when you get back. I want to know if Aleksei really does have Katie."

"Sorry, but that's not gonna happen."

"What? Why not?"

"Because I've already involved you in this too much as it is. I never should have told you a damn thing about what's going on. We're not partners and I'm not going to keep you up to date on my case."

"You're a real jackass."

"Fair enough. I've fucked up from start with you. It has to stop now."

"Great time for you to decide to be ethical. Can I help it if I'm curious to know how this all turns out?"

"Watch the news and maybe you'll find out."

"Asshole."

"Like I said, fair enough."

Amanda turned into the airport parking lot a little too quickly, causing her rear tires to fishtail in the street.

"Watch out," Danny said. "Don't run your car off the road just because you're pissed at me."

Amanda ignored him and drove to the departure terminal for Alaska airlines. She pulled to the curb and put her car in park.

She turned away from the road and towards Danny. "Good luck," she said. "Thanks. Do I get a kiss?"

Amanda rolled her eyes. "Get the hell out of the car. You're going to miss your flight."

Danny grinned and pulled his overnight bag from the back seat. "Thanks again for the ride," he said as he stepped out of the car and shut the door behind him.

Amanda turned back towards the road and drove away without another look in Danny's direction.

CHAPTER 51

"You don't have to be afraid of me," Aleksei said to a terrified Katie, who was trembling and crying on the bed in his guest room.

"You'll actually come to love me, I'm sure of it," he said. "We're going to do so many things together. Travel the world. See things you never even imagined existed. You'll thank me for rescuing you from a mundane life with nothing to look forward to but getting married and having babies. You'll wonder how you ever tolerated working at that common restaurant for even a minute. You're not a commoner. You're so much more than that."

Aleksei stood up from his chair and crossed the room to the bed. He moved towards Katie, his face less than an inch from hers. He heard her whimper through the gag.

"It's a rush you won't believe, becoming like me," he whispered. "Just wait and see."

Katie shifted backwards and tried to kick Aleksei with her legs. He had a tight grip on her ankles before her feet ever made contact.

"Bad girl," he said. "Didn't your parents teach you any manners? Ladies don't kick and fight like dogs."

Aleksei sat down on the bed, still holding Katie's ankles with a grip like a steel trap.

"Does that hurt?" he asked.

236

Katie nodded, and increased her whimpering.

"Good. Think of this before you try anything else stupid." He squeezed the ankles harder, prompting a yelp from Katie, before letting her legs drop back onto the bed.

"Do you remember me?" he asked, changing the subject. "Do you know where you are?"

Katie nodded yes.

"The trip to Coldfoot with your family, right?"

Katie nodded again.

"I watched you all the while we toured the asylum and heard the ghosts. I knew you would be mine at some point. Granted, at that time I didn't think it would be this soon. But, sometimes you have to go with spontaneity, right?"

Aleksei watched impassively as the girl's eyes darted around the room. "If you're looking for an escape, you're wasting your time," he said. "There's no way for you to get out of this room until I let you out. So tell me, how was your trip to Prudhoe Bay? Did you enjoy it?"

Katie stared at him without responding.

"A simple nod for yes or shake for no will do just fine," Akeksei said.

Katie shook her head no.

"I'm not surprised. What's in Prudhoe Bay for a beautiful young woman like you? That proves my point. You're going to be grateful I took you away from that life. Your parents were obviously nice people, but so very boring. And your little brother didn't have any of your spunk."

Large teardrops fell down Katie's cheeks at the mention of her family.

"You might miss them at first," Aleksei said. "But trust me, soon enough you'll barely be able to remember their faces. You're better than they are."

Aleksei moved closer to Katie again. "If you promise not to scream anymore, I'll take the gag out," he said. "Do you promise?"

237

Katie shook her head yes.

"Alright. I'm warning you, though. One scream and it goes back in, but the next time it'll be tighter."

Aleksei moved his long fingers behind Katie's head, and untied the gag. He gently pulled it out of her mouth. Katie gasped at once, as if trying to breathe for the first time, and immediately began to sob. Aleksei put a finger on her chin and lifted her face to his.

"I told you, there's no reason to be afraid of me. You're going to be my partner. I'll love you."

Katie's sobbing turned into blubbering. Aleksei frowned and wiped the tears from her cheeks. It was obvious he needed to just get on with things. A crying kid was no fun at all.

"You can stop crying," he said. "This is all going to be over soon."

He bared his fangs, causing Katie to abandon her promise not to scream. Her terror filled the room with a piercing shriek that made Aleksei cringe. There were times he was sorry to have such exceptional hearing.

He clamped his hand over Katie's mouth, and let his mouth hover over her neck, taking in her living scent so that he would remember it once she was dead. She smelled like citrus, a tangy mix of orange and grapefruit. No doubt the result of body lotion she had rubbed on the last time she had showered. Aleksei liked the scent, and knew he would remember it.

Aleksei pulled himself away from Katie's neck, and took a bite out of his own arm, just as he had watched Greger do so many years before. He never broke eye contact with the terrified teenager.

"It's all over now, Katerina," he whispered. "Next time you see me, things will be very different."

He sunk his fangs deep into her neck and felt a rush of arousal at the taste of her blood in his mouth. Forcing himself to stop drinking, he removed his hand from Katie's mouth and instantly pushed his bleeding arm in its place. He gripped the back of her head so she couldn't move away from him, and forced her to drink his blood before he returned to sucking her own blood out of her neck. Ignoring her futile thrashing and attempts to escape his clutch, he was overcome with a feeling of euphoria as he drained Katie's blood from her body.

Within seconds, Katie stopped struggling, and slumped against him. He removed his arm from her mouth, and used it to steady her drooping head. He felt the fight leave her body along with her blood as her body crumpled into his arms.

CHAPTER 52

"How can you just dismiss this?" Danny asked, trying unsuccessfully to keep his voice calm.

Captain Jack Meyer stared at him, trying to remain calm himself. He was no more successful than Danny.

"Danny, didn't I tell you to take a break?"

"I did!"

"By going to Seattle and sticking your nose in one of their cases?"

"No, god-dammit, I told you I didn't go to Seattle. I was in Sitka and got a phone call from an old FBI contact. He told me about the Seattle case. Have you been listening to me at all?"

Meyer waved his hand in a dismissive gesture. "I've been listening to as much as I can stand."

"What the hell is the problem?"

"The problem? I don't know; where do you want me to start? How about with the fact that I helped you get a warrant to search this Snow Creek place you're so obsessed with, and you couldn't find a damn thing. Or, how about that I've got enough cases of my own to deal with without worrying about a missing Seattle teenager. If that's not enough for you, you're really stretching to try and tie this Seattle kid to your missing women here. And while we're at it, it would have been nice of you to let me know you'd involved the FBI in our cases. Why the hell did you call the FBI anyway?"

Danny scowled. If he told Meyer he had been looking at cases from nearly 100 years ago, he'd surely lose his badge and be sent to the psych unit before the day was over. "I just asked him to run a check to see if he could find any cases that were similar to Maria and Anna." He decided to go on the offensive. "I'd call that good police work. Didn't think you'd have a problem with it."

Meyer refused to take the bait. "The problem I have is that you didn't tell me you'd involved the FBI. Makes me wonder what the hell else you've been up to that you haven't bothered to share. But really, that's the least of our issues. How can you possibly justify meddling in a Seattle case?"

"Because I know it's connected to ours."

"Right. Because a teenager in Seattle is obviously connected to two women in Alaska. Are you going to track down every case of missing blond women and girls in the whole country and try to pin them all on this guy in Coldfoot? Why stop there? Surely there must be some missing blonds in Europe you can search for too?"

"How can you ignore the fact that all three of them were at Snow Creek before they disappeared?"

"I'm not ignoring it. I supported you when you got the warrant to go up there. But you didn't find anything, Danny. How can YOU just keep ignoring that fact?"

"Because I know Nechayev is guilty."

Meyer shook his head. "Jesus Christ."

"He just got Katie Bailey. I need to go to Snow Creek again. Last time, he had plenty of time to hide Maria or do God knows what with her. Now, he'd be caught off guard."

"You know as well as I do that you can't harass this guy again. We've got nothing on him. And, by all accounts, he hasn't bothered a soul in Coldfoot or anywhere else up there, and has been nothing but a responsible business owner."

"He's a hell of a lot more than a business owner. He's a kidnapper and, most likely, a murderer too."

"Because you say so."

"Because I know so."

The Captain circled around his desk to his chair, where he sat down with a sigh. "Danny, I know your record back in Chicago. I know you were a good detective. One of the best. So how about your take yourself back there and think about this from the perspective of the cop you were then. What would that guy think about this situation?"

"I can't tell you that, Captain. That guy doesn't exist anymore."

"This is exactly why I told you I wanted you to take a break."

"And I told you, I did."

"I'd say you need to take another one. And this time, don't fuck it up by digging around trying to find something to pin on Aleksei Nechayev. Take a break and clear your head. I mean it."

"You're willing to just let this guy walk because you're pissed at me?"

"I'm not pissed at you, you jackass! I'm trying to help you. You're going off the rails and you need to get yourself under control. I told you before, I know all about your history. I think you're transferring too much personal baggage onto these missing women. The fact is, we don't even know if they were kidnapped."

"We don't? Are you kidding me?"

"You think teenage girls don't run away from home? You think people don't walk away from their lives? You did, for crap's sake!"

The Captain continued before Danny could respond. "How many times do you read about people presumed dead and turning up years later in some

California beach town or in Mexico or wherever? What about those guys in the news recently who were supposedly victims of John Wayne Gacy? Turns out, both of them were alive and well and living in other parts of the country. They just didn't want to be found. And in every case, family and friends say they never dreamed the missing person would choose to disappear. It happens all the time, and you know it."

On a roll, the Captain went on. "I wouldn't be surprised if 10 years from now someone finds Anna Alexander soaking up the sun in the fucking Florida Keys. Hell I'd be willing to bet on it."

"If I were you I wouldn't put too much money on that bet."

"When you never find a body, there's no way you can be sure. That's the simple truth, and you know it as well as I do."

"So your philosophy is that when someone goes missing, if they don't turn up dead, our best course of action is to assume they moved to Florida?"

"Don't try to make me sound like an idiot. You're on thin ice as it is."

"Alright. So what now, Captain?"

"What now? I already told you. Take a god-damn break. And get a handle on your drinking."

"My drinking has nothing to do with this situation."

"I'm not convinced of that."

"Oh for Christ's sake. I haven't even had much to drink lately. Don't try to use that as an excuse to fuck me over and ignore this case."

The Captain's already red cheeks turned scarlet. "I'm trying really hard to hold my temper, Fitzpatrick, but you don't make it easy. You're officially on leave, and I don't want to see your face in here for two weeks."

Danny stood up and gave a mocking salute. "Aye, aye, Captain."

He turned on his heel with military precision and left the office.

CHAPTER 53

Danny immediately regretted leaving the station without buttoning up his parka when he got outside. The temperature had fallen to a frigid -40, and he ran to his car to avoid turning to ice. Inside the car was not much of an improvement, but at least he could button up and get his thick driving mittens on. He needed insulated pants if he was going to stay in this hellhole though. This cold was more than even a born and bred Chicagoan could take.

He held his breath as he turned the key in the ignition, praying that the car would start. It was a crap-shoot in temperatures like this, even with the engine heaters, and Danny let out a sigh of relief when he heard the ignition turn over. He sat in the car and shivered as he waited for the heater to make the inside of the car bearable. If he was being honest, he had to admit he was also shaking from anger. He knew he was right about Aleksei Nechayev and he didn't appreciate being taken for a drunken, crazy fool. Even if he couldn't particularly blame anyone who came to that conclusion about him.

If there was a bright side to the cold, at least the snow was no longer falling. Of course, with snow packed on the ground since October, it hardly made much difference. Danny wondered if it was in fact now too cold to snow. He'd always wondered if that was possible. If it was, surely this temperature fit the bill.

Instead of the snow, the air was now filled with ice fog, a phenomenon Danny had never heard of until this morning. Apparently, when the temperatures were this cold, car exhaust, steam from buildings, and even the air people breathed turned to ice crystals that hung suspended in the air. The more cold days in a row, the thicker the ice fog would get.

According to a guy he was listening to on the radio when he was driving to the office, the native tribes had called the ice fog "white death," because they believed that the crystals would invade their lungs and kill them. As Danny looked around him, noticing the crystals blanketing everything in sight and making the buildings around him nearly invisible, he could understand their fear. The whole thing was just plain creepy.

Danny fumbled for his phone, and called Amanda. As was her way, she answered almost immediately.

"Danny?" she said.

"Hello to you, too."

"What's up? Did you talk to your Captain about Katie Bailey?"

"Yeah, I talked to him. Didn't do me much good though."

"Why? What happened?"

"He told me I needed to vacate the premises for two weeks and get myself under control."

"Oh."

"He also said he thought I was bringing my personal baggage into this case, and was on some sort of crazy crusade against Aleksei."

"He knows about Caroline?"

"He knows about why I left Chicago. I've never talked to him about Caroline, but he knows enough."

"I'm sorry."

"Don't be. I don't give a shit what he thinks. I know we're right about Nechayev."

"I did find another picture of him today."

"Really?"

"Yeah, from before the War this time. It looked like he was from one of the wealthier families in Russia at the time. I'm actually surprised he ended up in the army. The Nechayevs weren't peasants, that was clear."

"Well no wonder he acts like such a stuck-up asshole now then. How'd you find this, anyway?"

"I was just looking through a photo album of the Russian bourgeoisie in St. Petersburg around the time of the War. His face jumped out at me, just like with the military picture."

Danny stared out at the icicles hanging on the gutters of the police station. "That's interesting, but it still doesn't help me with this case."

"I know, I'm sorry…"

Danny cut her off. "Don't be, nothing to be sorry about. In fact, I don't think I'm going to just sit here and feel sorry for myself, either."

"What do you mean?"

"I was thinking about just going to Rex's Tavern and drinking myself into a stupor. But, that's exactly what Meyer would expect me to do. I'd basically just be proving him right."

"That's true."

"I don't need him, though. I'm spent most of my adult life as a homicide detective in one of the biggest cities in the world. What the fuck do I need from these yahoos in Fairbanks?"

"What are you talking about?"

"I'm talking about the fact that I can deal with this on my own. I know Aleksei has Katie and I know where he is. I can charter a plane myself and deal with him on my own."

"Oh my God, Danny, no you can't!"

"Why not?"

"Why not? Because he'll kill you, that's why. You know what he is. You can't handle him yourself."

"Bullshit. I've dealt with plenty of monsters in my time. He's no different just because he's 100 fucking years old."

"He is different and you know it. Please, think rationally."

"That's not really my strong suit anymore, sweetheart."

"Danny, please!"

"Listen, I need to go. There's nothing for you to worry about, though. I'm not going to do anything stupid; I just need to figure out my next move. I'll talk to you soon."

Danny ended the call, cutting off Amanda's pleas for him to go home and stay in Fairbanks. He shifted his car into gear and drove out of the police station lot. He called the airport and made arrangements for chartering a plane that would be waiting for him when he got there. He wasn't going to bother to go home first. He didn't have any time to waste.

CHAPTER 54

"I'm surprised to see you again, Detective," Doug Matheson said as Danny climbed into his 4X4. "I thought you were finished with your business with Aleksei."

"I just need to talk to him again."

"Strange that you'd come all the way up here instead of just calling him on the phone."

Danny nodded. "I've always been a little strange."

He hoped this ended Doug Matheson's chit-chat, but he wasn't optimistic. He couldn't blame the man for being curious. But Danny was much more interested in thinking about what he was going to do when he got to Snow Creek than he was in talking. And, he wondered how he was ever going to pay off the credit card he had used to charter a plane. It was a hell of a lot easier to fly places as a cop. Between his last minute trip to Sitka and his $400 per hour adventure now, he'd be filing for bankruptcy any day. Assuming he survived his meeting with Aleksei.

Fortunately, Doug Matheson was apparently tired of talking and it was clear he thought Danny was a basket case anyway. They spent the rest of the drive to Snow Creek in silence. Danny felt his heart leap in his chest when Matheson pulled onto the Snow Creek drive. He stopped a good 15 yards from the front of the building.

"I can't take you any farther," Matheson said. "Aleksei's the worst about keeping his drive plowed when Snow Creek is closed. Even my truck can't get through that."

Danny stared at the drive and knew the man was correct. He was going to have a long walk.

"Are you sure you want to do this?" Matheson asked. "That's a hell of a long walk in this kind of weather," he said, echoing Danny's thoughts.

"I can drive you back to the airport," he continued. "Hell, you can use my phone and call Aleksei from there if you want, I'm always able to get service there."

"Thank you, Mr. Matheson. I appreciate the offer. But I really need to talk to Mr. Nechayev in person. I stopped at the camping store on my way to the airport and got some brand new snow pants and boots for this trip, plus snow shoes, so I'll be fine. I'm finally learning to dress like a real Alaskan," he said, attempting to lighten the mood.

"I think most Alaskans stay indoors when it's this cold. It's gotta be 15 below out there."

"That's warmer than it is in Fairbanks right now."

"Still damn cold."

Danny nodded and pulled his ski mask over his face before zippering his parka up around his neck. He pulled the hood up, and clasped it around his chin. He turned towards Matheson with only his eyes visible under the layers of winter clothing, and gave him a thumbs-up with his mittened hand.

"I'm prepared," he said, his voice muffled. "Thank you for driving me."

"I'll wait out here for you."

Danny waved the idea away. "No, no, that's not necessary. I'll call for a ride as soon as I'm done with Mr. Nechayev. I wouldn't want you to freeze sitting out here."

"I think you're certifiable, Detective."

"You're not the first one to think so, believe me."

With that, Danny lumbered out of the car and waved goodbye to Doug Matheson. As he watched the tail lights of the 4X4 disappear and felt the frigid wind whipping around him, he decided Matheson was right. He was indeed certifiable. But, there was no turning back now.

CHAPTER 55

Aleksei paced the floor of his study, impatient for Katerina to wake up. He knew it would take some time yet, but he had never been good at waiting. He felt edgy and anxious to be on the move. The walls of the study seemed to close in around him and he felt suffocated by his own home. There was a whole world waiting for him and Katerina and he wanted to say goodbye to Alaska for good. He spent enough time here and he was ready for his new life. For starters, he wanted to take Katerina to Russia.

He wondered what his homeland would be like now. He had kept up with the goings-on in Saint Petersburg in recent years thanks to the Internet and he had regularly visited the Sitka Russian library to keep up with news from his homeland before the days of the World Wide Web. He'd come to Alaska specifically because of its Russian heritage and it had been a great fit for him. But all good things came to an end.

Aleksei had left Russia originally because he was repulsed by the Soviets and their rise to power not long after he had been turned and he blamed the Revolution for Natasha's death. He'd been completely disgusted when the name of his hometown had been changed to Leningrad in 1924. He'd thought the change to Petrograd in 1914 was ridiculous, and in his mind he always called his home St. Petersburg, but that had at least been tolerable. It made sense to give the city a more Russian sounding name when the country was at war with the Germans. But naming the city for the architect of the Revolution was more than Aleksei could stomach. He had nothing but contempt for Lenin and his Soviet gang of thugs.

But the Soviets were long gone now and Russia remained. And after nearly 100 years, it was high time Aleksei went home.

His ears picked up a sound coming through the howl of the wind outside his home and he immediately stopped in his tracks. He twitched his nose, picking up the distinctive smell of an animal. A human animal.

He walked to the window and looked out, scanning the Snow Creek grounds. He didn't see anyone, but he knew someone was there. He left his study and headed for the lobby and the front door of the hotel.

CHAPTER 56

Danny tried to pull the hood of his parka tighter around his face, desperate to keep out the frigid wind. Unfortunately, it was already as tight as it would get. And it didn't seem to be keeping the wind out at all. His ski mask was soaking wet from the blowing snow and was starting to turn to ice. As were his gloves. He was starting to realize that he had completely underestimated how cold 15 below could be. Or maybe he underestimated how long 15 yards could be. He felt like he'd never reach the Snow Creek front door. And at this point, he was so damn cold that death by vampire didn't seem like that bad of an option. It couldn't be worse than this cold.

He let out a breath that immediately turned to ice in the air around him. Stumbling in the deep snow, he lumbered on to the Snow Creek Asylum.

CHAPTER 57

Aleksei stared out into the frigid night and saw a tall figure trudging through the snow of his unplowed drive. He knew the figure was a man, but his huge parka and face mask made him completely unrecognizable. Aleksei briefly wondered if the man was one of the townspeople in need of assistance, but instinct told him this wasn't a friendly visitor. His nose twitched as he picked up the man's scent. A scent he immediately recognized.

Aleksei turned on the Snow Creek outer lights and started to head out the door, before he remembered he was wearing nothing but his customary t-shirt and pants. He stopped himself, and went to the closet to get his own coat and gloves. He had no idea why Danny Fitzpatrick was here on his property, but he knew it wasn't good news. And he didn't need to complicate things by letting Fitzpatrick see that temperature had no impact on him. He'd always made sure to blend in and this was no time to stop that pattern.

He bundled up, and walked outside to face the man who was stumbling towards him in the snow.

"Hello?" he called out. "Who's there?"

Danny heard Aleksei's voice over the wind and a chill beyond anything he was experiencing in the cold went up his spine. This was it. And he really didn't have a plan for what he was going to do.

He plowed forward until he was nearly face to face with Aleksei.

254

"Mr. Nechayev? It's Detective Danny Fitzpatrick, Fairbanks PD. I need to speak with you, please."

Aleksei stood stiffly under the light on Snow Creek's deck. He bit down on his lip to control his anger, drawing blood as he did so.

"This is quite a surprise, Detective."

By now, Danny had made it to the deck and stared up at Aleksei. He briefly thought about the man's towering height, and the fact that it made him hate Aleksei even more than he already did. Danny was over 6 feet himself, and wasn't used to staring up at anyone. But this jackass could have played for the NBA.

"I'm sure it is," Danny said, struggling for breath. "But here I am."

He glanced at Aleksei, who seemed completely unfazed by the cold wind whipping around them.

"This cold doesn't seem to be bothering you too much, but for a mere mortal like me it's a killer. How about we go inside?"

Aleksei stood rigid, momentarily stunned at Danny's mortal remark. No one had ever suspected the truth about Aleksei, at least not unless he wanted them to. Had this rude, low-class detective figured it out? Or was he just playing some sort of game?

Danny stomped his boots on the deck. "Can we go inside, Mr. Nechayev?"

"Of course," Aleksei said, regaining his composure. He held the door open against the wind. "After you."

The two walked inside, and Aleksei quickly turned on the light over the front desk. He pulled off his gloves and coat and set them gently over the back of the office chair, then watched as Danny removed his wet ski mask, and the face Aleksei already knew he hated came into view.

Danny smiled at Aleksei. "There, now you can see I'm really who I say I am. You remember me, right?"

"Of course I do. You were here about that missing woman."

"Maria Treibel. Right. You know she's still missing?"

"That's unfortunate. But as I told you then, I don't know how I can help you."

"Yeah, right. I remember." Danny pulled off his parka and revealed the gun attached to the holster around his waist. "The thing is, I'm not here to talk about Maria this time."

Aleksei glanced at the gun and fought the urge to smirk. He knew Fitzpatrick's gesture was intended to unnerve him, but he actually hoped the cop would try to use the gun on him. Try it and see what happens, Detective, he thought.

He stared at Danny, an accommodating smile on his face. "So what is it you came all this way to talk about? I do have to ask, have you ever heard of a phone?"

Danny chuckled. "What can I say? I prefer to talk in person."

"So are you going to share what it is you want to talk about, or do you plan on keeping me in suspense?"

"Not what I want to talk about. Who."

"Okay, who?"

"A teenage girl by the name of Katie Bailey. Disappeared a few days ago in Seattle. Her name ring any bells for you?"

"No. Why would it?"

"Because her family stayed here at your place a few days before Christmas."

Aleksei nodded. "Of course. I remember the Bailey family now, parents with two children with them. Lovely family. They were my last guests before I closed for the season, so I couldn't help but remember them."

"Katie made an impression on you, I imagine?"

"I can't say that she did, no. But what's that you said about her disappearing in Seattle?"

"Right, she's gone missing. Just like Maria Treibel."

"Have you started working Seattle cases now too, Detective? It's odd. I would think a big city like that would have enough of their own cops."

"I'm just doing a little freelancing."

"So what does your freelance work have to do with me? It must be quite important for you to come all this way and brave an Arctic winter. I wouldn't have expected a Chicagoan to be so keen on Alaskan winters. It's a whole new world up here, isn't it?"

"How do you know I'm from Chicago?"

"I looked you up after you came up here last time. Surely you know how easy it is to find information on the Internet nowadays."

Danny stared at Aleksei, recognizing a threat when he heard one. The Russian's calm smile never wavered.

"Don't you find it odd," Danny said, "that so many people go missing after they come here to your fine establishment? Actually, not just people. Blond women. Blond girls. You like blond girls, don't you?"

"I don't know what you're talking about, Detective. I will say it's a strange coincidence that two of my guests have gone missing in recent weeks, but I think you are taking quite a leap. Two people are hardly "many," are they?"

"There's been a hell of a lot more than two."

"Then you're going to have to enlighten me on who they are. All I know about are this Maria woman you're apparently obsessed with, and the unfortunate disappearance of the Seattle teenager."

"How about Anna Alexander? Kristen Barrowman? Samantha Sharapova? Any of those names sound familiar? How about Betty O'Neill? Anna Maria Thiessen? She was a military kid here in Alaska. Disappeared in 1950."

Aleksei stared at Danny, and gripped the edge of his desk to maintain his calm façade. He knew, then. This bastard detective really did know. He cleared his throat.

"Did you say the last girl, Anna Maria something, disappeared in 1950? Interesting. I've always been told I look good for my age. How old do you think I am?"

"How about you answer my question? What did you do with those women?"

"Have you gone mad, Detective? I can't imagine what you're talking about."

Danny took two steps forward, and kept his eyes on Aleksei's. "I know you've got Katie Bailey and I want her back, okay? I admit I'm probably too late for the rest, but give me Katie."

"As I said, I don't know what you're talking about."

"Listen, asshole. Let's cut the crap, okay? I know you killed all those women I just mentioned. I know you've been in Alaska a hell of a long time. I'm fairly sure you went on a killing spree in Wiseman way back when you first came here. Natives called you a "white haired monster." I don't care about all that right now. I just want Katie."

Aleksei moved closer to Danny, staring down at him. "You know I did all that, do you? What else do you think you know about me?"

Danny felt as if his blood had turned to ice. "I know you came from Russia. And I know you were a soldier. In World War I."

"I was in World War I, was I? That would make me a very old man, wouldn't it? How do you suppose I've managed to keep my youthful good looks all these years?"

"I don't understand it. But I know it's because of what you are. And it's not human."

"You do know quite a bit."

Before Danny could respond, Aleksei had passed him in a whoosh of sound and was suddenly behind him, his long fingers around Danny's neck.

"Yes, I have to hand it to you," he whispered into Danny's ear. "You know a great deal about me."

Danny struggled as the fingers tightened around his neck, blocking his windpipe. He gasped for air, and found nothing.

Aleksei didn't break a sweat as he strengthened his grip on Danny's neck. "That's a problem though, I'm sorry to say. You simply know too much."

He continued to squeeze until he felt Danny slump in his arms. "It's nothing personal, Detective. I do hope you know that, too."

He turned off the light and left the hotel lobby, dragging Danny's limp body behind him.

CHAPTER 58

Aleksei sat on the edge of the guest room bed and waited for Katerina to wake up. He ran his finger along the curve of her face, relishing the cold marble feel of her skin. Now that he had her, he couldn't imagine why he had waited so long to make a companion. He had been such a fool, pining for a love he would never have again. He had so much time to make up for now.

Fortunately, time was not an issue for him. And wouldn't be for Katerina now, either. They had thousands of years ahead of them.

Katie's eyelids fluttered, and Aleksei felt his dead heart leap in his chest. She was waking up, finally. He grabbed her small hand, and covered it within his own strong grip.

She opened her eyes, and immediately widened them in terror when she saw Aleksei's face. She struggled to sit up, and pull her hand out of Aleksei's grasp.

"Calm down, Katerina," Aleksei said. "There's nothing to be afraid of. Not anymore."

Katie blinked and glanced around the room, trying to orient herself to her surroundings. She felt herself waking up and feeling increasingly strange. She felt so cold and sluggish. What had happened to her?

"It feels very weird right now, I know," Aleksei said. "But just give yourself a minute. You'll be fine."

Remaining silent, Katie forced herself to sit up on the bed. Within minutes, she realized Aleksei was telling the truth. She no longer felt sluggish, and found herself struggling with almost overwhelming sensations.

"What did you do to me?" she finally asked, barely able to keep the fear out of her voice. "What's happening?"

"I saved you," Aleksei said. "I made you better. Can't you tell? It's extraordinary, isn't it?"

Katie had to admit that it was. She looked down at herself, still wearing her work clothes from her grandfather's restaurant, but they were now splattered with blood. Was it her blood? It must be. Except for the blood, she looked the same. But somehow, she was completely different.

"What did you do to me?" she asked again.

"I made you like me. We're the same now. We're one."

Aleksei reached out and ran his fingers down Katie's cheek and along the curve of her chin. "You're perfect now," he said.

He gently touched Katie's lips with the tips of his fingers. "You don't have to worry about anything anymore. No sickness, no death. You can move like lightning now, you'll see. And wait until you find out how strong you are."

"How?"

"Because you're like me. A vampire."

Surprisingly, Katie didn't even flinch at Aleksei's words. It was as if she already knew before he told her. Her curiosity and fear had already started to be replaced by acceptance.

"But..."

Aleksei interrupted her. "No buts," he said. "It's done now. I'll teach you everything you need to know, don't worry."

"What about my family?" Katie asked.

"What about them?"

"Did you hurt them? Do they know what's happened to me?"

"No and no. Why do you care?"

Katie stared at him, surprised to find that she really didn't. She should be missing her family and calling out for her mother. But she didn't. And she wasn't.

"No," she finally said. "I guess I don't."

"That's because you're not Katie anymore. Katie Bailey's gone. You're Yekaterina. That's Russian for Katherine. But I'm going to call you Katerina. Or maybe Katya, if the mood strikes."

"Why Russian?"

"Because that's my home. And that's where we're going."

"Really?"

Aleksei nodded. "Yes, and soon. We don't have a lot of time to waste. I wanted to spend the winter with you here in Alaska, one last winter for me, but my plans have changed. We need to leave very soon."

"What will we do there?"

"Whatever you want to do. I'll show you the country, it's beautiful. And we'll just start there."

Aleksei leaned in closer to Katerina. "I told you I saved you, right? I did. Saved you from a boring, trivial life in Seattle." He dropped his voice to a seductive whisper. "There's a whole big beautiful world out there, Katerina. And we're going to see it all."

She continued to stare at him, taking it in, and feeling stimulated in ways she couldn't begin to understand. In spite of her excitement, she felt overcome by waves of hunger. She was craving something and feeling as if she'd go mad if she didn't have it. But she couldn't put her finger on what it was.

"I'm starving," she finally said.

Aleksei smiled. "Of course you are. And I know what you need; I've got it ready for you. Just give me a minute."

He stood up from the bed and walked across the room to the closet, where he had stored a small red cooler. He opened it and carried it back to the bed, where he retrieved a plastic bag full of blood. He held it up to Katerina.

"Did you ever donate blood before, Katerina?"

"Yes."

"Then you know what these bags are. Courtesy of the Alaskan blood bank. Of course, we don't need any needles."

Aleksei opened the bag, and Katerina felt a rabid rush of hunger. She leaped up, and grabbed the bag from his hands. She brought the bag to her lips and clamped down on it, drinking its contents in gulps. Within seconds, the bag was empty and Katerina turned back to Aleksei, her mouth covered in blood. She smiled at him.

He felt a wave of love wash over him and handed her another bag of blood. She was the most beautiful creature he'd ever seen.

Katerina finished a third bag of blood and leaped off the bed with a speed that surprised her. She twirled around the room with the grace of a ballerina and stopped at the closet door.

"Do you have better clothes for me?" she asked, looking down at her restaurant uniform. "If we're going to travel the world, I need something better than this."

Aleksei smiled again. "I don't yet," he said. "But we'll get some, don't worry. We'll get whatever you want. I've got a few things you can change into before we leave though."

Katerina danced back over to Aleksei and stood on her tiptoes so she could slide her arms around his neck. "So are you hot for me?" she asked.

Aleksei fought his arousal. "That's not the type of question a polite young woman asks," he said.

"Who says I'm polite?" She ran a hand down his chest and moved towards his groin. "I think you are," she said.

Aleksei stared down at her minx-like expression, amazed that there was no longer any sign at all of the sweet teenage girl who had been so terrified of him. He shouldn't have been surprised, but he was. He forced himself to step away.

"We don't have time for that right now," he said. "And I still have so much to teach you first."

Katerina ran her tongue over her teeth. "I don't think you have to worry about teaching me too much."

"I don't mean about that. I mean about what you are."

Katerina laughed, and suddenly sprouted fangs from her gums. She gasped, covering her mouth with her hand. "What the hell?"

Aleksei walked to her and removed her hand from her face. "See, that's what I'm trying to tell you. You have a lot to learn." He let his own fangs out, and smiled. "But like I said, I can teach you."

Katie grinned back, displaying her fangs. "Can I bite you with these?"

"You can bite lots of things."

She grabbed Aleksei's arm and pulled it to her mouth, sinking her fangs in his skin before he had a chance to pull away. He again had to fight his arousal as he watched her sucking his blood.

Katerina lifted her head, letting Aleksei's blood drip from her teeth. "That's awesome," she said.

Aleksei didn't feel like fighting his arousal any more. "It is," he said, his voice husky. "But you haven't seen anything yet."

He pushed her down on the bed, knocking the cooler of blood onto the floor. He tore off the uniform she would never wear again, and quickly removed his shirt, tossing it onto the floor next to the fallen cooler.

Katerina arched her back to meet him as his lips crushed into hers, the taste of blood mingling in both of the mouths. He moved his lips down her neck, giving gentle bites as he did. Katerina moaned, and worked her hands towards his belt. For a short time, Aleksei was sure no one else in the world existed. He forgot all about the dying woman in his root cellar and the Alaskan police detective he had locked into a room in his asylum.

CHAPTER 59

Amanda paced back and forth in her living room, waiting for Danny's phone to go to his voice mail. She'd already called 15 times, so it was a fairly safe bet that he wasn't going to answer this time, either. She snapped the phone closed when she heard his recorded greeting. 14 messages begging him to call her were probably enough.

She took a deep breath and fiddled with the silver cross around her neck as she tried to figure out what to do. She knew exactly where Danny was, so it shouldn't be too hard to get somebody to help her get to Coldfoot and find him. Shouldn't be, anyway. But in reality, she remembered what Danny had told her about his police captain forcing him to take time off. She didn't know what kind of reception she'd get from Danny's colleagues if she went asking for help now.

Regardless, she had to give it a shot, as she knew without a doubt that Danny's life depended on it. She picked up her phone again, and dialed the number for the police station. Amanda knew Danny had been working with another detective on the Maria Treibel case. If she was lucky, she would be able to get through to that detective.

"Fairbanks Police," a man's voice said.

"Hello," Amanda said. "Could I please speak with the detective working on the missing woman case?"

"What case?"

266

"The woman who went missing around the Solstice party. I think I might have a lead on where she is."

Amanda could imagine the policeman rolling his eyes, sure she was some nutter trying to get involved in an investigation. She knew all about how cops treated people they thought were crazy.

"That would be Detective Washington," the policeman finally replied. "Let me check and see if she's available."

A few seconds later, the man came back on the line. "I'll transfer you," he said.

Amanda breathed a sigh of relief. One step closer.

"This is Detective Washington. How can I help you?"

"Hello, Detective. My name is Amanda Fiske. I'm a friend of Danny Fitzpatrick's."

Tessa leaned back in her chair. "Oh? Is this about the woman who went missing, Maria Treibel?"

"Sort of," Amanda paused. "But not really. It's about Danny. He's in trouble, and I need your help."

Tessa sat up straight. "What do you mean he's in trouble?"

"He went after the guy he thinks kidnapped Maria Treibel."

"What?? He's supposed to be taking a break."

"Yeah, I know. But he's not. He went up to Coldfoot by himself and he told me he was going to take him down."

"Oh my God. He went after Aleksei Nechayev? Up there? Alone???" Tessa's voice rose with each question.

"Yes to all three."

Momentarily speechless, Tessa stared out at the falling snow that had returned with a vengeance. "Oh, Danny," she finally said.

"We need to get up there and help him."

"What do you mean, we? How do you know about all this anyway?"

"I told you, Danny's my friend. And…"

"And what?"

"And I've been helping him research Nechayev."

"God in heaven. What the hell has he been doing?"

"He knows Nechayev's guilty and he's right. I know it too. Aleksei's very dangerous."

Tessa shook her head. "Listen, I don't even want to know what you two have been up to. If you're telling me Danny is up there in Coldfoot by himself I need to get him some back-up. What the hell was he thinking? He didn't say a word to me about this!"

"He couldn't after the Captain had ordered him to go on leave."

"He sure as hell could have. He just knew I would have talked some sense into his thick head."

"Listen, I know you think we're crazy and I don't blame you. But please believe me when I tell you Danny is in huge trouble. I've tried calling him so many times, and he's not answering his phone. I'm so scared we might already be too late."

"What do you mean, too late?"

"I mean I'm afraid Aleksei killed him." Amanda took a deep breath. "I met Danny because I was one of Aleksei's victims. One who got away. I know what a monster he is, and I know Danny is exactly right about him. Please, you have to believe me."

Tessa rubbed her eyes. "I need to help Danny. Whatever else is going on can wait. I'll get some reinforcements and charter a plane up there."

"I need to go with you."

"Like hell you do."

"Please, I have to. I'll stay out of your way, I promise. I just need to go."

Tessa sighed. "Listen Miss… what did you say your name was again?"

"Fiske. Amanda Fiske. I can help you with Aleksei. I know things about him you can't possibly know. Please."

"Alright, listen. I know you and Danny are friends and you want to help him. And I appreciate you calling in and letting us know what he's been up to. But this is where your involvement ends, Ms. Fiske. This is a police matter now and we'll take it from here."

"But, you don't understand, please…"

Tessa cut Amanda off. "I don't have time to talk any more. I don't know what the hell Danny's got himself into, but I know it can't be good. We can't have civilians involved in this. Now I need to get going. Goodbye, Ms. Fiske."

Tessa hung up her phone without listening to whatever Amanda said next. She blew out a breath and stared out her window again at the heavy snow. "Danny, you god-damn idiot," she muttered to herself. "What have you done?"

CHAPTER 60

Tessa knocked on Captain Jack Meyer's door, and entered his office as he motioned for her to come in. He finished whatever call he was on and hung up his phone just as Tessa closed the office door behind her.

"God-damn that Fitzpatrick," Meyer said.

"Danny? What about him? He's why I was coming to talk to you."

"I just got off the phone with the Seattle detective he was working with while he was supposed to be on break. Her name's Lauren Cooper and she's on her way here to get information on her missing kid. She's in a god-damn plane right now."

"She's not going to be able to land here. Not with this snow."

"She already knows that. Her plane is circling the city as we speak." Meyer ran a beefy hand through his nearly non-existent hair. "God-damn it all. We don't have enough to do here? Now we gotta deal with some Seattle cop on a wild goose chase?"

"I'm afraid there's more than that, Sir," Tessa said.

"What do you mean?"

"I just got off the phone with a friend of Danny's. I think he's in big trouble."

"Yeah well, I'm not so sure that bothers me."

270

"I'm serious. This friend of his said he's gone up to Cold Foot to confront Aleksei Nechayev himself."

"What?! Are you kidding me?"

"I wish I was. But his friend has been unable to reach him, and he hasn't answered my calls either. He told this woman he was heading up to Cold Foot so he could find Katie Bailey before it was too late."

"Oh my God. Is he fucking nuts?"

"He's obviously not thinking clearly. We need to get up there."

Meyer stared out the window. "You got any ideas how we can do that? No planes will take off in this weather."

"Maybe we can get the National Guard involved."

"Jesus Christ. You think the National Guard's gonna get involved because one lunatic cop went off the rails? This is our problem to solve. And frankly, I'm not sure I think we all need to risk our own necks because that idiot went off half-cocked and didn't think about the fact he could freeze to death up there."

"It's not just the weather. This friend of Danny's, Amanda, she insists that Danny is right about Aleksei Nechayev. She said he attacked her and she got away from him, that's how she met Danny in the first place. She swears Nechayev really is dangerous."

"And Fitzpatrick knew all this and still went up to the Arctic by himself to chase after him?"

"To be fair, he did try to get you involved."

"And I suppose you think I was wrong to not get wrapped up in his Seattle craziness?"

"I don't think that, no. Really all I'm thinking now is I want to find Danny. I think he's right about Nechayev too, I have all along. I think he's in big trouble, Sir."

Meyer let out a deep breath. "Let's see what we can do about finding him, Detective. But I can't promise I won't kick his ass all the way back to Chicago when we do."

Chapter 61

Danny struggled to open his eyes and orient himself to his surroundings as he slowly regained consciousness. His head pounded with a pain that was worse than any hangover he'd ever had, and his hands were stiff and cramped behind his back. Worse, his neck throbbed and his throat felt as if it had been slowly constricted by a snake. In fact, this wasn't far from the truth.

He shifted his head, and realized he was sitting up against the column of a four poster bed, and his hands were bound tightly to the bed's leg by a thick braided rope. To his surprise, his legs and feet were unbound. He had been left in a cross-legged position, with his feet under the weight of his legs. As a result, his feet and calves were now hopelessly numb.

Danny moved to unknot his legs and feet, and immediately winced as pain shot through them. He slowly stretched his legs out in front of him on the plush ivory carpet he was sitting on, and waited for the feeling to fully return and the numbness to subside.

He leaned his head back on the wooden column of the bed and forced himself to take stock of his situation. He was cold, and realized that Aleksei must have removed his parka before tying him to the bed. The parka was hung neatly on the doorknob of the closet across from him. Like his gun and phone, which were on top of the dresser next to the closet, the coat was tantalizingly out of reach. Aleksei apparently enjoyed taunting his prey.

It was clear to Danny that he was in one of Aleksei's guest rooms, where tourists stayed when they visited the asylum. He remembered touring this and similar rooms himself when he had first come to Snow Creek with a search warrant and Terry Yazzie to accompany him. It was his own fool fault he didn't have that accompaniment now, he thought bitterly. He could imagine Tessa shaking her head at him and giving him one of her patented looks of disapproval.

He deserved it, and now that he was in this predicament, he realized he wasn't as keen on dying as he had previously thought. A suicide mission to save a damsel in distress had seemed quite gallant when he had ridden through the snow and cold with Doug Matheson but, at this moment; it merely seemed like the height of stupidity.

While he couldn't deny this fact, he also couldn't deny that self-pity wasn't going to get him anywhere now. He struggled to loosen the ropes that held his hands, realizing quickly that it was a futile gesture. Aleksei wasn't stupid and he was also stronger than any person or thing that Danny had ever encountered. The knots he had made would only be broken by a knife and, even then, Danny wasn't sure how easy it would be to undo them.

If he was going to survive, he would have to use his wits and somehow convince Aleksei to untie him. But, he wasn't arrogant enough to think he had such superior wit or intelligence. His current situation would suggest that he wasn't likely to outwit anyone at this point. Perhaps his mother really had been right about alcohol and his brain.

His only consolation was that Aleksei had kept him alive and had merely rendered him unconscious instead of killing him immediately. Danny knew this could simply be because Aleksei enjoyed teasing his prey, or perhaps he had grander plans for Danny before he killed him but for now, it was all Danny had to work with.

Before he could ponder the issue further, the door of the room opened and Aleksei walked inside. He had changed clothes since the last time Danny had seen him, and now wore a gray suit with a white dress shirt, but his face held the same arrogant smirk. Aleksei knew he had won and he had every intention of reveling in that fact.

"Glad to see you're awake, Detective," he said. "I trust your accommodations are satisfactory?"

"They're great," Danny said.

"I'm so glad. I was hoping you'd be awake by now, as I have a friend I want to introduce to you."

"I'm not sure that I'm up to having company. I'm not really at my best."

Aleksei chuckled. "It's not really up to you, I'm afraid. And, I'm only giving you what you said you wanted, anyway."

"What was that? My memory's a little fuzzy."

"You came trudging through the snowy night to storm into my office and demand to see Katie Bailey. Does that ring a bell?"

Danny felt a pang of alarm. "It does, yeah," he said.

"Great." Aleksei held the guest room door open and stuck his head into the hallway. "Come in, darling," he said.

Danny watched as Katie Bailey walked into the room. She wore a black velvet dress that barely covered her hips and looked as if the fabric had been torn away to expose her legs. On her feet, she wore black buckled heels that looked straight out of the Edwardian era. In spite of her strange clothing, Danny knew from the picture he had seen in the police report that it was Katie. But at the same time, it wasn't.

"Katerina, allow me to introduce you to Detective Danny Fitzpatrick. He's been so concerned for your safety he came all the way here from Fairbanks.

Isn't that something? Quite noble, don't you think?"

Katerina didn't answer, but looked at Danny with a mixture of amusement and contempt. Danny looked into her eyes and felt his heart sink.

"As you can see, Detective, Katerina is fine. More than fine, actually. Show him, Katya."

Katerina opened her mouth in a wicked smile, and displayed the fangs protruding from her gums. "So nice to meet you, Detective," she said.

Danny looked away, unable to stand the sight of the new monster in front of him. "Oh my God," he said. "What did you do to this kid?"

"I should think it would be obvious. You know so much about me, I assumed you'd figure this out, too." Aleksei showed his fangs in a smile that matched Katerina's. "She and I are one now. And Katerina is anything but a kid."

"So is this why you kept me alive?" Danny asked, his throat as dry as the Sahara. "Are the two of you going to kill me now?"

"No, no, don't be silly," Aleksei said.

He turned to Katerina. "Can you leave us alone now, darling? I need to talk to the Detective for a moment before we go."

Katerina nodded and left the room without giving Danny so much as a glance.

CHAPTER 62

Aleksei shut the door behind his offspring, and pulled in his fangs. He walked to the bed and crouched down in front of Danny, bouncing on the balls of his feet.

"She's quite something isn't she?" he asked.

"That she is," Danny said, forcing himself to look Aleksei straight in the eyes.

Aleksei smiled. "I know you think I'm going to kill you and, the truth is, I was, initially. I thought you could be Katerina's first kill. But then I thought more about it and I realized how much I owe you. Truly, you've done me a great service."

Danny fought to contain his surprise. "How do you figure that?" he asked.

Aleksei stood up and walked towards the window, where he gazed out at the falling snow. "Have you ever been in a rut, Detective?"

Before Danny could answer, Aleksei continued.

"I think you have. I know all about your past in Chicago. That messy business of your wife's murder."

"How do you know about that?"

"I told you before, I looked you up after you so rudely visited me and searched my home. I was curious about you. And, it wasn't very hard to find all I needed to know about you."

"Alright, so you know about my wife. What does that have to do with any of

277

this?"

"I couldn't help but relate to you." Aleksei turned away from the window and stared back at Danny. "I think you and I are a great deal alike."

Danny scoffed. "You think wrong, asshole. I have absolutely nothing in common with you."

Aleksei seemed unfazed by the insult. "I think you're the one who's wrong. But regardless, I was going to kill you anyway. Until I realized that without your visit and your search, I never would have gotten out of the rut I had found myself in."

He walked back to Danny and towered over him, his height seemingly doubled by Danny's position on the floor.

"Since you know all about me, you know I've been around for quite a long time. And let me tell you, I've been in this rut for what feels like forever. Vainly trying to replace my Natasha, going from one pathetic woman to another..."

Danny interrupted Aleksei's musing. "So is that why you killed all those women? You were trying to replace some vampire bitch?"

Aleksei's face darkened as he crouched down to glare at Danny. "She wasn't a bitch. And she wasn't a vampire. I'll warn you not to defile her memory again."

Danny swallowed hard. "Fair enough. But you didn't answer my question. This Natasha. She's why you killed all those women?"

"I was trying to find a replacement for her, yes."

"Let me guess. Natasha was tall and slender, long blond hair..."

Aleksei nodded. "The women had the right physical requirements. But that was where the resemblance ended. None of them were worth a damn."

"So where do I come into all this?"

"You forced me to re-evaluate what I'd been doing here in Alaska. You caught me off guard. No one had ever violated my home here in such a manner.

I knew it was only a matter of time before my cover here at Snow Creek was blown. And, I already knew my current replacement was a failure..."

"Maria Treibel?" Danny asked.

Aleksei waved his hand dismissively. "Yes, yes, her. She was a dismal failure and I finally realized that they would always be failures. I didn't need a replacement for Natasha. I needed to let go of her and move on."

"So you kidnapped a teenager and killed her?"

"I prefer to look at it as saving her. She can live forever now. Just like me."

Aleksei stood back up and walked back to the window. "Katerina is more than I ever could have dreamed. So like I said, I owe you. If you hadn't figured out the connection between Maria Treibel and Anna Alexander and shook me out of my comfort zone here, I might never have realized that what I needed was a partner, not a replacement."

"What did you do with the bodies? Where did you bury Maria?"

Aleksei grinned. "Can you imagine a more perfect place to bury bodies than the Arctic? Where else is so remote? So completely free of human interference? You and your colleagues could search until the end of time, and you'd never find those bodies. But, Maria, she's a different story."

"How so?"

"It's funny, actually. When you came here the first time, Maria was very much alive. You just didn't know where to look for her."

Danny could hear his heart beating in his chest. He tried to respond, but found he had no voice.

"Have you ever heard of root cellars?" Aleksei asked. "I doubt there's much use for them in Chicago, but here in Alaska they're quite common. We can't have basements here, you see. The permafrost makes it impossible. But root cellars are perfect. People used to use them for food storage. But there are all kinds of things you can store in them."

"You son of a bitch," Danny said, his voice thick with rage.

"You could have found her if you'd only looked hard enough." Aleksei looked at Danny with mock concern. "It's a shame, really. Your personal failures keep mounting up, don't they? Too careless to save Maria. Too late to save Katie."

Danny felt his throat closing up.

Aleksei returned to Danny and crouched down again. "I am curious. How did you figure out what I am? You people aren't supposed to know creatures like me exist."

"I got lucky," Danny said, reminding himself to keep Amanda's involvement to himself. "I guess I don't have any trouble believing in evil."

Aleksei smiled. "Well, like I said, I'm indebted to you. So you have my eternal gratitude. And when I say eternal, I actually mean it."

"Are you saying you really aren't going to kill me?"

"No, I'm not. Katerina and I are leaving Alaska and I'll leave you here. If you manage to escape your predicament, more power to you."

"What's to stop me from coming after you?"

"Nothing. But you'll never find me. My travel abilities are quite superior to yours. And, think about it. Who's going to believe you about me? How will your colleagues react when you tell them about your very own interview with a vampire?"

"I don't care what they think. I'll find you."

"But you have to find your way out of this room first, don't you?" Aleksei smirked. "Give it your best shot."

He stood up and walked towards the doorway before turning back to Danny.

"Did you ever see The Silence of the Lambs?"

"Yes," Danny said, thrown by the change of subject.

"One of my favorite movies. Do you remember the ending?"

"You mean when Lector goes after the psychiatrist?"

"No, no, before that."

Danny shook his head. "I don't know. Why the hell are you asking?"

"Never mind. Katerina and I need to get going. We've got a whole world waiting for us. Goodbye, Detective."

Aleksei closed the door behind him, leaving Danny alone.

CHAPTER 63

Aleksei raced through the streets of Petrograd, certain Maksim was wrong about Natasha. Wrong, or purposely lying just to piss Aleksei off. See where that had gotten him.

He came to the Summer Garden, and held onto the pillar of stone outside the gates before he went inside. Just as Maksim had said, dead bodies were everywhere. Crows and vultures picked their way through the corpses and rats braved the frigid air to nibble on fingers and toes. This was no place for the living. And no nurses were anywhere to be seen.

Aleksei knew he could find Natasha now, as he knew her scent and he could sniff it out. Even here where the stench of death permeated every molecule of air. He walked through the bodies, refusing to admit that death was all he could smell.

He saw a dark blue nurse's cape out of the corner of his eye and froze in his tracks. He hardly dared to turn his head and see what he knew to be true. The cape was Natasha's and her body lay crumpled beneath it.

Aleksei collapsed beside Natasha and took her stiff, lifeless body into his arms. Her head still bore the imprint of a boot that had thoughtlessly stomped on it and her chest was caved in where the stampeding herd had crushed the breath out of her.

"Natasha?" Aleksei grabbed her shoulders and shook as if willing the body

back to life. "Natasha!"

"I can save you," he said. "You can come with me."

He opened his mouth and bared his fangs as he gently cradled Natasha's head against his chest. He sank his fangs into her neck and quickly pulled back, spitting out the taste of death and decay.

Aleksei leaned back on his heels and stared out at the sea of corpses rotting around him. He couldn't save Natasha now; it was much too late for that. He was too late.

He set her body gently back on the ground and kissed her cheek. He could feel the skin already beginning to decay and it repulsed him. This whole country repulsed him. He couldn't tolerate a place that would kill something as beautiful and good as Natasha.

He left the Summer Garden, straightening his shoulders and regaining his composure as he walked back to the street. Natasha was gone, but he could find her again. He just needed to leave Petrograd.

He briefly wondered if he could find Greger and the others, but he knew he had no interest in traveling with anyone else. He'd always been better off on his own. He didn't know where he was going but he knew he wasn't coming back here. It was time to leave his homeland behind.

CHAPTER 64

Aleksei double-checked the guest room door, making sure the lock held tightly. Not that he thought Danny would manage to get out of his ropes any time soon, but it never hurt to be safe.

He smiled at the thought of Danny struggling against the knots he had made and couldn't help but wish he could stick around to watch. But there wasn't time for that. He and Katerina needed to go.

As if on cue, Katerina walked up behind him.

"Are you ready, darling?" he asked.

"I'm ready to get out of this dump if that's what you mean."

Aleksei smiled. In the past, he would have been offended by the insult to his home, but now he felt the same way about the place. He couldn't wait to leave it behind.

"You know, I've always loved the New Year. It's a huge holiday in Russia. We should go there and celebrate it properly."

"That's where you're from, right? Russia?"

"Right, that's where I'm from. St. Petersburg, to be exact."

Aleksei looked down at Katerina and playfully kissed her nose. "Let's get going. It's time for me to go home."

CHAPTER 65

Lauren Cooper hurried into the Fairbanks police station and stomped the snow from her boots onto the carpet before she headed for the front desk.

"I'm here to see Captain Jack Meyer," she said. "Lauren Cooper, Seattle PD."

The receptionist nodded cordially and picked up the phone on her desk. Lauren shivered involuntarily as she removed her hat and shook the snow from her long brown hair. To think she had complained about Seattle rain. She'd never been as cold as she was now and couldn't imagine how anyone lived in this climate.

She turned at the sound of footsteps approaching and saw a large, beefy man with a red face heading towards her.

"Detective Cooper," he said, his hand extended. "I'm Jack Meyer."

Lauren shook the man's huge hand. "Nice to meet you."

"You just made it in time. We've finally got the all clear to get out of here and head up north."

Lauren shivered again at the mere thought of heading north and what she presumed would be worse snow and cold, but she forced herself to keep her game face intact.

"Great," she said. "Thanks for letting me come along."

"Not a problem. We all want the same thing here. I'm hoping we can get up there and return with your teenager."

Jack led Lauren into the office and towards a petite woman who was hurriedly getting into her parka and snow boots.

"Tessa, this is Lauren Cooper. Detective, this is Detective Washington."

The two women shook hands and nodded a greeting.

"Is everyone ready to go, Captain?" Tessa asked. "I can't stand any more waiting."

Terry Yazzie walked in the office before Meyer had a chance to answer. "I've got the 4X4 warmed up and ready," he said. "Michaels and Franklin are meeting us at the airport."

"Let's go then," Meyer said. "Detective Cooper, you're going to want to put that hat and those gloves right back on."

Tessa grabbed her gun from her desk and checked her supply of bullets before holstering it to her waist. She knew perfectly well the gun was fully loaded, but she needed some kind of reassurance before heading up to what she knew in her gut was going to be a nightmare situation.

Watching her, Lauren met the other woman's eyes as she gripped her own gun. She suddenly felt chilled in a way that had nothing to do with the cold and snow, and was briefly frozen, not from the cold but from a fear she couldn't explain. She wanted to run out of the office and fly back to Seattle as quickly as she could. As she followed the three police officers back out into the cold parking lot, she couldn't shake the sensation that heading up into this dark and frozen Arctic wasteland was a terrible mistake.

CHAPTER 66

Danny's head drooped onto his chest and he struggled to keep his eyes open. He had given up trying to wiggle out of the tight knots that held his hands behind his back, and his arms and hands were now completely numb anyway. It was almost as if they were disconnected from the rest of his body. He found he didn't have the energy to care much anymore.

The room had become steadily colder since Aleksei had left and closed the door behind him and Danny felt sure that Aleksei had turned off the heat when he and the monster that used to be Katie Bailey had departed for wherever the hell they were going. It was a safe bet that Aleksei no longer cared about burst pipes. Danny could hear the wind howling outside and remembered the frozen night he had stumbled through to get to Aleksei's front door. It felt nearly as cold inside now. The extreme cold was taking a toll on whatever energy Danny had left.

Danny heard a voice howling along with the wind, and immediately snapped his head up. Was someone else here? Maybe Aleksei hadn't left after all.

"Hello?" Danny said, his voice a frog's croak. "Is someone there?"

The howling continued, and sounded like a man in agony. Danny felt every hair on his body standing on edge.

"Who's there?" he croaked. "Hello? Can anyone hear me?"

The howling abruptly stopped, and was followed by the sound of a slamming door.

Danny jumped as much as the ropes that bound him to the bed leg would allow. Another howl, and he heard his own heart pounding out a beat to accompany the ferocious wind.

He glanced at the doorway to the guest room, and saw the doorknob slowly creaking in a clockwise turn. He pushed himself back against the bed, wanting to disappear before whoever was on the other side of the door joined him in the room.

But the door never opened, and the knob stopped moving.

Danny stared at the door, his breath coming so fast and shallow he was close to hyperventilating.

"Hello?" he said, his voice barely above a whisper. "Is someone out there?"

There was no answer, and the howls that had filled the room were now gone. Danny heard nothing but the wind, and his heart pounding in his chest.

He leaned his head back against the bed and willed himself to relax. Had he simply hallucinated the whole thing? Or, was Aleksei still here and playing games with him?

He suddenly remembered the visit he and Terry had made to Snow Creek, and the screaming voices and slamming doors they had heard.

"Fucking haunted house," he said, rolling his eyes.

He closed his eyes and tried to stop the shivering that was now overtaking his body. He nearly jumped out of his skin when he heard another voice. Her voice.

"What were you thinking of coming up here alone, Danny?"

Danny didn't want to open his eyes as he wasn't sure if he could bear seeing her in the room with him. He finally did, and felt a tear run down his cheek when he saw her across the room, looking alive and beautiful and exactly as he remembered.

"Caroline," he said.

"Will you answer my question?"

"I don't have an answer. Except that I think it's fairly obvious I wasn't thinking. I've got myself in one hell of a mess, haven't I?"

"Espèce d'andouille"

Danny chuckled. "Yes, thanks for the reminder. I'm an idiot, I know. But please, lay off the French. I'm having enough trouble remembering English right now."

"It's freezing in here."

"I've noticed."

"I'm worried about you. You're shivering terribly."

"I think that's probably a good thing, isn't it? I think you're really in trouble once you stop shivering."

Caroline pushed her dark hair behind her ear in a gesture that Danny knew was as normal to her as breathing. Except she wasn't exactly breathing anymore, was she? Did ghosts breathe?

"So why are you here, Caroline? To keep me company while I die?"

"I don't want you to die."

"Yeah, well, I didn't want you to die, either. We don't always get what we want."

"Do you want to die?"

"Why do you ask that?"

"I can't think of any other reason you would go after a monster in the Arctic alone. Why not just put a gun to your head if you're so intent on suicide?"

"It would have been a hell of a lot easier, wouldn't it? But so messy..."

"I'm not joking, Danny."

Danny's shivering increased in intensity, and he found it difficult for his mouth to form words.

"Why not? This whole situation is a fucking joke. And you're not even here anyway. You're a god-damn ghost. Which, honestly, makes you fit right in up here in this psycho place. Have you met the other ghosts in residence?"

"Why do you want to die?"

"You're not letting it go, are you? I don't want to die. I just don't think I have any say in the matter at this point."

"I don't blame you for what happened to me, you know."

Danny felt his throat closing up. "You don't? That's good I guess. I sure as hell do."

"It wasn't your fault. Nobody knew about Jackson."

"Nobody else was his partner."

"Danny..."

"And besides, that's really not the point. The issue is I didn't just shoot him in time. I could have stopped him from cutting you..." Danny's voice trailed off as he blinked back tears.

"If you would have shot him he would have jerked and cut me anyway. You know that."

"Maybe so. But he might have missed."

"I don't blame you," Caroline repeated. *"And I'm tired of watching you live like some kind of zombie."*

"Well then go ahead and leave. I don't ask you to hang around, do I? Get the fuck out of my life already. It was till death do us part, remember? So go ahead, you're clear. Shit it's so god-damn cold!"

Danny cursed as his shivering became more violent. He swallowed hard as Caroline stood up and moved closer to him before kneeling down on the floor in front of him. For a brief second, he stared into her green eyes and felt sure she was the flesh and blood Caroline. Not a ghost, but really there with him.

"Caroline," he sputtered.

Julie A. Flanders

Caroline stroked his cheek with her hand, and made a shushing sound as she put her finger to his lips. Before he could kiss it, she was gone.

Danny blinked furiously, hoping each time he opened his eyes that she would be there in front of him again. But the room was empty.

"Caroline?" he called out. "Caroline!"

Danny's anguished cries mixed with the howls of the wind, and echoed down the deserted Snow Creek hallway.

CHAPTER 67

Danny heard voices yelling and feet stomping in the corridor, and was certain the ghosts had returned to keep him company. He wasn't going to be frightened of hallucinations this time.

"Danny? Are you here? Danny!"

Danny jerked his head up. That was Tessa's voice. He wasn't hallucinating at all.

"Tessa," he whispered.

He stomped his feet on the ground to make more noise, but any sound he could make was muffled by the thick carpet. He tried to swallow, but found no moisture in his mouth. "Tessa!" he croaked.

Within seconds, the door of the guest room opened and Tessa burst inside.

"Danny!" she yelled. "Oh my God, you're okay!"

Danny tried to speak, but couldn't form any words. Instead, he let out a deep sigh of relief as tears stung the corner of his eyes.

Tessa fell to her knees at his side and began working on the ropes that bound his hands. Terry Yazzie and Jack Meyer filed into the room behind her, followed by Doug Matheson and a woman Danny had never seen before.

"What the hell were you thinking coming up here?" Tessa said as she struggled with the ropes. "You damn fool."

Danny couldn't help but chuckle. "Never mind that," he said. "Just get these fucking ropes off me. And give me a coat. I'm freezing to death."

Tessa leaned back on her heels and grabbed Danny's arms, trying to calm his violent shivering. "Can one of you get us a blanket?"

Terry walked quickly to the bed and pulled off the down comforter. The blanket was cold to the touch.

Tessa grabbed the blanket and wrapped it around Danny. "It's alright, it's alright," she murmured, frowning as she noticed Danny's pale and bluish skin.

"He's got hypothermia," she said. "That son of a bitch must have turned the heat off completely in here."

Terry knelt down next to her and began to work on the ropes. "We need a knife," he said.

"I'll get one from the kitchen," Doug Matheson said, sounding happy to have a task. "I saw it when we were looking for the Detective here."

Danny's teeth chattered as he glanced around the room. Jack Meyer grabbed Danny's parka from the closet door and tossed it to Tessa, before opening the closet to find Danny's hat, gloves, and scarf. Danny ached to get into his warm clothes, and felt sure he'd never take them off again. His eyes returned to the brunette woman standing near the doorway.

"Who are you?" he asked.

The woman appeared startled. "I'm Lauren Cooper," she said. "From Seattle."

Danny nodded and glanced back at Tessa. "Nechayev?"

Tessa shook her head. "There's no sign of anyone here but you. Looks like Mr. Nechayev packed up and left."

"He took her with him," Danny said.

"Who? Katie Bailey?"

Lauren perked up. "Was Katie here? Did you see her?"

Danny thought back to the sultry vampire who had bared her fangs at him with such wicked delight. "I saw her, yes. But she's gone now."

"What do you mean, gone? Did Nechayev take her with him?"

How could Danny ever explain this? He stared at Lauren Cooper and forced his muddled brain to think. No one in this room would believe him if he told the truth about Katie Bailey. It was much better to tell a lie. A lie that had some truth to it.

"No," Danny finally said. "He killed her. I saw her."

"Oh no," Tessa said. "That poor kid."

"What do you mean, you saw her?" Jack asked. "You saw him kill her?"

"No. I saw her dead body."

Danny saw the hope drain from all of their faces just as Doug Matheson returned with a thin utility knife.

"This ought to do it," Matheson said. "I think we can cut the ropes without cutting your hands at the same time."

Danny cringed. "God, I hope so." He watched as Tessa grabbed the knife and set to work behind his back. "Be careful with that, would you?"

"I should give you a little slice just to teach you a lesson. I've seen some stupid stunts but damned if this doesn't beat all."

"I think I already learned my lesson without you adding to it. Just cut the god-damn ropes."

Danny nearly cried as he felt the ropes fall from his wrists. He brought his arms to his front and laid his limp hands in his lap. He tried to move his fingers and was immediately met with stabs of sharp pain.

"Give it a minute," Tessa said, wrapping the blanket tighter around Danny's body. "You'll be alright."

Lauren cleared her throat. "I'm going to try to find some bandages," she said. "His wrists are a bloody mess."

"I'll go with you," Doug said.

As the two left the room, Danny stared at his wrists. The ropes had cut deep gashes into each one, and his attempts to loosen the knots had only added to the rope burn around each gash. It struck him how odd it was to be staring at his cuts and yet not be able to feel them, but he knew that wouldn't last for long.

He suddenly had a flash of memory. "Oh my God," he said. "Maria!"

"What?" Tessa said. "Maria Treibel?"

Danny nodded. "A root cellar. You need to find a root cellar. Hurry!"

"What are you talking about?"

Danny stumbled to his feet, leaning on Tessa as his numb legs gave out under him. "Aleksei told me she was alive when I was here last. He had her in a root cellar. I didn't see it, but we need to find it. She might still be alive."

Jack and Terry both headed for the doorway.

"We'll see what we can find," Jack said.

Danny heard their heavy footsteps running down the hallway.

"I need to find her, Tessa. We could have saved her if I hadn't been so damn stupid last time. Why didn't I look outside?"

"Don't beat yourself up now," Tessa said, gasping as she tried to support Danny's weight. "You need to rest here, Danny."

"I'm fine," he said. "I just need to walk this off."

He pulled away from Tessa and stumbled to the door of the room, holding onto the frame as he caught his breath and steadied himself. The feeling was returning to his hands and legs, and it wasn't pleasant. Still, at least he could walk. He barreled past Lauren and Doug into the hallway, brushing off her bandages.

"I need to get outside," he said.

"What??"

Tessa followed Danny, shrugging her shoulders at Lauren as the two passed. Lauren set the bandages down on the bed, and followed behind.

"Danny, you can't go outside without your coat," Tessa said. "You're already hypothermic as it is!"

Ignoring her, Danny continued to follow the voices of the Jack and Terry to Aleksei's bungalow and the kitchen, where they had discovered what looked to be a root cellar outside the door. It was half covered with snow, but a strong wind had blown enough snow to the side that they could see a wooden door in the ground.

Danny opened the kitchen door and ran outside, ignoring both the yells of his colleagues and the bitter cold that bit into his skin. He fumbled with the door of the root cellar and reluctantly moved away for Jack and Terry to pry it open.

"Maria?" he yelled as soon as the door was open. "Maria Treibel!"

Danny pushed past Jack and Terry and made his way down the stairs of the root cellar, calling Maria's name with every step.

"It's the police, Maria," Tessa said as she descended the stairs behind Danny. "We're here to help you."

Tessa felt an increased sense of dread with each step, as the rotten stench of filth, urine, and feces was impossible to ignore. She knew the smell of death, and she feared what she and Danny were going to encounter at the bottom of the staircase.

It wasn't long before she saw what she feared, as they found Maria crumpled on the floor in the corner of the root cellar. She was covered by a tattered blanket and her hands were crusted in blood. Bloody fingerprints lined the walls, remnants of her futile attempts to claw her way out of her dungeon.

Danny kneeled down beside Maria and gently shook her shoulder. "Maria?"

"Check for a pulse," Tessa said, before kneeling down and grabbing Maria's frail and tiny wrist herself. She almost didn't believe it when she felt a pulse.

"I think she's alive," Tessa said.

Danny pulled Maria into a sitting position, and clutched her neck. The pulse was undeniable. "She is!" he yelled.

Tessa blinked back tears. "Thank God," she said.

Jack stood in the center of the root cellar, stunned at the scene in front of him. He turned to Terry. "Get an ambulance here, a helicopter or something. We need to fly her to a hospital."

Tessa turned towards Jack and Doug Matheson, who had now entered the cellar and was standing behind the Captain. "Can you two carry her out of here?" she asked. "We need to get her inside where it's warm."

Jack and Doug gingerly picked Maria up and carried her towards the stairs.

"She's so frail I could carry her myself," Jack said. "God help us."

Danny collapsed onto the floor of the cellar as he watched Jack and Doug carry Maria's limp body up the stairs. He put his head in his hands, and burst into tears.

Tessa wrapped her arm around his convulsing shoulders. "Danny, we need to get you inside too. And to a hospital."

"I'm fine."

"You're anything but."

Danny laughed and took in a deep breath. "No point in arguing with you, I know that."

"None at all." Tessa hugged him, and stood up. "I need to put an APB out on Nechayev. How long ago did he leave here?"

"I have no idea. I don't know how long I was out before you found me."

"We had a terrible time getting here because of a storm in Fairbanks. Airport was closed. It was 24 hours after Amanda told me about your foolhardy stunt before I could even get a plane."

"Amanda. So that's how you knew I was here."

"Lucky for you she called me."

Danny nodded. "About Nechayev, you're wasting your time with the APB.

He's long gone."

"Well he couldn't have gotten that far. This weather grounded everyone."

"Not him. He's different. He's a monster."

"I know that. But that doesn't mean…"

Danny interrupted her. "I'm not speaking metaphorically, Tessa. I mean it. He's not human. He's some kind of creature. I know it's crazy but I swear it's the truth."

Tessa held out her hand to him. "Danny, you're in shock. And confusion is common with hypothermia, I know. God knows you must be dehydrated too after being stuck in that room for so long. I don't even know how you're talking."

Danny started to protest again, but thought better of it. It was clear no one was going to believe him about what Aleksei really was, and he couldn't blame them. A month ago, he wouldn't have believed it either.

"We need to get you to a hospital," Tessa said. "Let Captain Meyer and me worry about Nechayev now."

Danny took hold of Tessa's outstretched hand, and slowly got to his feet. Feeling dizzy, he clutched onto her arm for support as the two made their way up the stairs of the root cellar and back to the kitchen of the Snow Creek Asylum.

CHAPTER 68

Lauren walked slowly through Aleksei's living quarters, buttoning her coat against the burst of cold that had engulfed the bungalow as soon as the other officers had opened the kitchen door to the outside. She ignored the chaos of the root cellar and the kitchen, as she knew the others had that situation well in hand. She wanted to get back to the reason she was here in this Arctic nightmare in the first place. Katie Bailey.

She searched the master bedroom and found nothing out of the ordinary, except for the fact that Aleksei had covered the king-sized bed with black. Black comforter, black pillows, and a black blanket. Very cheery place, Lauren thought. The closet looked as if it had been recently emptied, which fit with Danny's insistence that Nechayev had left the premises for good.

Lauren walked down the corridor, passing a bathroom with no knob on the inside of the door, and wondered if Katie and the rest of the women had been locked into that bathroom with no way to even try to open the door from their end. As she had always struggled with claustrophobia, Lauren shuddered at the prospect.

She shuddered more when she came to what had to be a guest bedroom, and immediately realized that this bedroom door was also missing an inside knob. Lauren had no doubt that this room was where Aleksei had kept his prisoners. Unlike Aleksei's own bed, this one was unmade, and the sheets and blankets were bunched haphazardly across the bed. Lauren winced as she noticed drops of blood staining the sheets and pillow cases. Was that Katie's blood?

Looking down at the floor next to the bed, Lauren came to a dead stop. A pile of clothing lay on the floor, khaki pants, brown socks, and a blue polo shirt with an insignia on the chest. A lacy bra and a pair of panties had been tossed on top of a pair of taupe boat shoes. Lauren crouched down to get a closer look at the lettering on the shirt. "George's Place."

Lauren immediately recognized the name of Katie's grandfather's restaurant and she knew she was looking at Katie's work clothes. The clothes she had been wearing when she was abducted. Lauren noticed blood stains covering the collar of Katie's shirt. Had Aleksei sliced her throat? That would be Lauren's guess.

She stood back up and pulled an evidence bag out of the bag she had been carrying over her shoulder since she had landed in Fairbanks. She snapped on a pair of gloves and picked up Katie's clothing and shoes, making a mental note to herself to make sure she got a team in place to analyze the bedclothes and the rest of the room.

Satisfied she had seen everything that could possibly be of interest in Aleksei's bungalow, Lauren carried the bag of Katie's clothing out of the room and returned to the kitchen.

CHAPTER 69

"There you are," *Jack Meyer* said as Lauren joined the rest of the officers. "I was about to send a search team out. We thought you were still back in the asylum."

Lauren shook her head. "No, I've been searching the bungalow."

"What do you have there?" Jack asked, gesturing towards the evidence bag in Lauren's hand.

"Katie Bailey's clothes. I'm sure it's the uniform she was wearing when she was abducted. The shirt has the name of her grandfather's restaurant on it."

Jack's heart sank. "Aww shit. What a god damn ugly business this is."

Danny thought back to the Katie he had seen with Aleksei. What was Aleksei calling her? Katerina?

"When I saw her body, Aleksei had dressed her in one of his costumes," he said.

"What do you mean, costumes?" Lauren asked.

Terry answered for Danny. "When we searched this place last week, we found a closet full of old-fashioned costumes for women. Long dresses, old shoes, that sort of thing."

"Right," Danny said. "And that's what he put her in. It was a long velvet dress."

Danny didn't mention that Katie had torn the dress to a much shorter length, and a much more revealing v-neck.

"So he dressed up her dead body in a costume?" Lauren said. "What the hell did he do with it then? There's not a body here. There's nothing."

"He took the body with him," Danny said.

Lauren shook her head, incredulous. "Holy shit, what kind of freak is this guy?"

"Well it doesn't matter," Jack said. "We'll find him soon enough. He couldn't have gotten far on his own, let alone carting around a corpse."

Lauren rubbed her eyes and forced herself to concentrate on her case. "We're going to need a forensics team up here. We need to go over this place with a fine-toothed comb."

"Already in the works," Jack said. "I'm hoping they'll get here soon with our transport." He stared at Maria, who was listless and non-responsive on the floor, bundled in as many blankets as the team could find. "We need to get Ms. Treibel to a hospital ASAP."

To everyone's relief, they heard footsteps marching towards the kitchen, and two National Guardsmen carrying blankets and a stretcher entered the room.

"We've got a jeep for two injured patients," one said. "There's a hospital plane waiting back at the air field.

Danny scowled. "I don't need special transport."

"Shut up and let us take care of you," Tessa said, silencing him with both her words and her expression.

Jack pointed to Maria. "Take this lady first, she's critical."

As the Guardsmen bundled Maria onto the stretcher, Lauren turned to Jack.

"I'm going to stay behind and wait for the team," she said.

"Figured you would. Keep me up to date, please."

"Of course."

The Guardsmen returned, and Tessa forced Danny onto the stretcher. They carried him out of the bungalow and back through the asylum, with Jack, Tessa, Terry, and Doug following behind.

CHAPTER 70

Danny swung his legs over the side of the Fairbanks hospital emergency room bed, and tapped his feet on the tile floor. For the hundredth time, he glanced at the clock across the room from his bed. He wondered if he'd ever get out of this hospital.

"Knock, knock," Amanda said as she entered the room.

"Well look who it is," Danny said. "I understand I have you to thank for saving my life."

"If you mean I let your co-workers know about your psychotic mission, yes."

"See, I wasn't totally nuts. I let you know what I was doing."

"You were still totally nuts. In fact I think that may be the understatement of the year."

Danny smiled. "The way Tessa's acting, I don't know if she'll ever let me out of her sight again."

"I don't know if I will either." Amanda shook her head. "I'm not even going to ask you what you were thinking."

"Good. Tessa's asked that enough for ten people."

Amanda chuckled. "I have a feeling she won't be the only one asking," she said. "Anyway, I'm your ride home."

"Thank God. It's about time."

"I don't think I've ever known anyone as impatient as you are."

"Impatient? I've been here for hours. And there's nothing wrong with me anyway."

"Oh, right. Nothing but mild hypothermia, dehydration, a bruised esophagus, shock…"

"I'm fine now," Danny said. He started to get up from his bed. "So let's get the hell out of here."

"Not so fast. The nurse is still processing your discharge."

Danny slumped back down onto the bed. "Oh, Christ."

"I talked to Tessa," Amanda said. "It sounds like Maria's going to be okay."

Danny breathed a sigh of relief. "Well thank God for that."

"She was totally dehydrated and had severe hypothermia so there was concern about organ damage, but the doctors said they got her in time. Or I should say you got her in time."

"We all did. No one would have known to come for either of us if it wasn't for you."

"What happened to that teenager from Seattle?"

"You don't want to know."

"I heard she was dead, but they haven't found her body."

"They won't. Aleksei took her with him."

"What?"

Danny stared straight at Amanda, imploring her to understand without making him say too much. "He made her like him. A vampire."

Amanda's face drained of all color. "Oh my God. How do you know?"

"Because he introduced me to her."

"Oh my God," Amanda repeated, clutching the cross around her neck. "That poor girl."

"Trust me. That poor girl is long gone."

"What about her family? What will you tell them?"

"What can I tell them? What can I tell anyone? All I can say is Aleksei told me he killed her and I saw her dead body. Honestly, that's not even a lie. And even if they're never going to find a body, I hope that will give the family some peace of mind eventually. I can't leave them to just wonder where she is or what happened to her for the rest of their lives."

Before Amanda could respond, Captain Jack Meyer entered the room behind her.

"Fitzpatrick," he said, "you're even crazier than I thought."

Danny couldn't help but chuckle. "Guilty as charged."

"I'd love to chew your ass out but how can I when you not only found Maria Treibel, you solved God knows how many cold cases as well? Maybe I'll force you to go on leave more often."

"Have the search teams found any bodies?"

Meyer shook his head. "Nah. There's not much point in even searching now, to be honest. Everything is too frozen. We'll have to wait until spring to really search in earnest. But, both you and Maria say Nechayev talked about killing a bunch of other women. Obviously you were right about Anna Alexander, too."

Danny nodded. "Aleksei admitted that one to me."

"Yeah. He is one crazy son of a bitch, that one. Tessa's got an APB out, but we haven't turned up a thing yet. It's like this bastard just disappeared into thin air. Or into the snow, at least. It doesn't make a damn bit of sense. Especially if he had that poor kid's body with him. There aren't any tire tracks leaving the house, his truck is still in the garage... If he left there on foot maybe we'll find him in the spring, too. Nobody could have gotten far in that weather on foot."

Danny and Amanda caught each other's gaze, but remained silent. Danny knew Aleksei was going to be an Alaskan mystery that would never be solved. Years from now, children would tell ghost stories around campfires about the murderer who disappeared into the Arctic snow.

"There's one thing I really don't get," Jack said.

"What's that?"

"Why the hell did he let you live? I get the feeling he assumed Maria was dead already anyway, or at least close enough to it that she wouldn't be found in time. But why take the chance with you?"

"I think in his own perverse way, he liked me," Danny said.

"Odd way of showing it."

"I said it was perverse. And honestly Captain, I think it was just arrogance on his part. The whole thing was a game to him, and he was toying with me. And he was so sure of his ability to escape our grasp that he didn't see it as a risk."

Jack shook his head. "Like I said, crazy son of a bitch."

"You mentioned Maria," Danny said. "She's well enough to talk?"

"Barely. She's weak as a kitten, but she could answer a few questions."

"I'd like to see her before I leave."

"I'm sure you can. She's up in the ICU but I've no doubt they'll let you in as soon as they know who you are."

The room suddenly became crowded, as a nurse entered carrying Danny's chart and a packet of papers. She set the packet on the bed beside Danny.

"You're clear to go, Detective," she said. "These are your discharge instructions. I just need to go over them with you and then you're all set."

Danny barely listened as the nurse read over the obligatory instructions and quickly leapt to his feet as soon as she finished.

"Do you mind waiting while I go see Maria?" he asked Amanda.

"Not at all."

"Thanks. I'll meet you in the lobby then."

Danny reached out to shake Jack's hand. "Captain. Thanks for coming by.

And for finding me up in that hellhole."

"You've got Tessa to thank for that," Jack said. "And this lady too, from what I understand."

"That's right," Danny said, smiling at Amanda.

"Lauren Cooper's gonna be calling you. She wants to get a statement from you about Katie."

"Did she and the team find anything else up there?"

"Not that I've heard. But the FBI's getting involved now since this goes across state lines. I imagine they'll have people up in Coldfoot for quite a while." Jack grinned. "Lucky sons of bitches."

Danny chuckled. "I'm sure the agents fought over who got that assignment."

Jack patted Danny on the shoulder. "Take care of yourself, Fitzpatrick. And I don't want to see you back at work before the end of the week. This time, I hope you'll listen."

"I will, trust me. All I want to do is go home and sleep."

CHAPTER 71

Danny followed the signs leading from the ER to the hospital elevators, and made his way up to the intensive care unit on the sixth floor. He introduced himself to the floor nurses and was immediately led to Maria's room. He wasn't surprised to see Nate Clancy waiting outside in the hallway.

"Mr. Clancy," Danny said. "Good to see you."

Nate rose quickly from his chair. "Detective! You're the one it's good to see. Thank you for finding Maria."

"My pleasure. I'm just glad we got her in time."

"I can't believe it was that damn Snow Creek place. I told you I hated it there."

Danny smiled. "Looks like you have good instincts."

"The nurse is in with Maria now," Nate said. "Her parents are on their way here, should be here any minute I think. They had some trouble getting a flight right away but they should be here soon. We're going to have a New Year's party here in the hospital."

Nate was babbling like a man overcome with both shock and emotion. As the nurse exited Maria's room and gave them the all clear, Danny held Nate back as he started to go back inside.

"Do you mind if I talk to Maria for a minute alone?" he asked. "I just want to clear a few things up for our investigation. I won't tire her out, I promise."

"No problem, no problem at all," Nate said. "I think I'm going to run over to the cafeteria and get some coffee."

"Sounds like a good idea."

Danny walked into the room and stood at Maria's bedside, ignoring the beeps of the various machines attached to her body. Maria's body was gaunt under the blankets, but her cheeks now had the faintest hint of color.

"Ms. Treibel," he said. "You look a hell of a lot better than the last time I saw you."

"I'm sorry, I…"

"I'm Danny Fitzpatrick," Danny said, holding up his hand to stop her. "I'm the cop who came to Snow Creek."

"You saved my life."

"Me and several others. Actually, they all saved my life, too."

Maria swallowed, a gesture that was obviously painful. Danny took in the bruises around her neck and on her face, and felt a rush of rage.

"I heard he got away," Maria said.

"He did. I'm sorry."

Danny sat down gently on the side of Maria's bed.

"Maria," he said. "I know Aleksei told you about the other women, the ones he killed."

Maria nodded, a look of fear crossing her face.

"Did he also tell you what he is? Did he show you anything odd about himself?"

Maria thought back to the fangs Aleksei had bared at her and his ability to whoosh across the room at speeds far beyond human capabilities. She shuddered involuntarily, causing Danny to pull her blankets closer around her frail body. Tears sprung from the corners of her eyes.

"I don't know anything," Maria whispered. "I don't understand what you mean."

Danny looked down at her, certain she was lying, but also certain it didn't matter. There was only so much evil any person could face. If Maria needed to forget the truth about Aleksei, Danny wasn't going to be the one to stand in her way.

He patted her arm and stood up from the bed. "Just checking to make sure we have everything covered," he said.

Danny walked to the doorway and turned back to see Maria's eyes were already closed, and her body moved in rhythm with sounds of the oxygen machine next to her bed.

"You take care, Maria."

Danny saw Nate Clancy walking down the hall on his way back from the cafeteria and quickly turned the other way to avoid him. He didn't want to do any more talking. He headed back towards the elevators and pushed the down arrow. Grateful to see an empty car when the elevator doors opened, he got inside and hit the button for the lobby. As the car descended, it dawned on him that Nate had mentioned a New Year's party. So was it New Year's Day? It must be. Danny knew exactly how he was going to celebrate the beginning of 2013. He couldn't wait to get home and go to sleep.

EPILOGUE

THREE MONTHS LATER

Danny walked up the sidewalk to his apartment on Slater Street, having just returned from his long-planned jog in Griffin Park. Tessa's Siberian Husky Maya had accompanied him to the park and the two had spent the afternoon enjoying the first taste of spring. Danny had spent the night at Tessa's the night before to look after Maya while Tessa and Amanda worked on Danny's apartment. Now, Maya pulled ahead of him, anxious to get inside and find her mother. Danny was equally anxious, as he wanted to see what Maya's mother and Amanda had done to his living room.

The two women had insisted on renovating his apartment from top to bottom and, having no interest in doing the work himself, Danny had given them carte blanche to do what they thought was best. His only requirement had been that he didn't end up living in a "girlie" apartment. He didn't want to see a shred of pink. Tessa had raised an eyebrow at this, wondering when she had ever given him the impression she was a fan of pink.

Amanda and Tessa had started their work yesterday afternoon and now Danny was returning home to see his new living room, the first room they were tackling. He took off Maya's leash and let her run inside ahead of him as he checked his mailbox. Danny grabbed a stack of mail and followed the dog

312

inside.

He found Tessa and Amanda standing in the middle of the room, with Maya wiggling excitedly and running in circles around their legs.

"What do you think?" Amanda asked, her hands outstretched.

Danny's first thought was that he had entered the wrong apartment. Gone were the white walls with their chipped paint and scuff marks. Gone was the tattered brown sofa and nicked coffee table. Instead, the room was awash with gray, white, and black. A black and white rug lined the floor, and a gray sofa matched the freshly painted wall it was up against. A flat-screen TV hung on the wall across from the sofa, and two white armchairs were arranged on its side. A black coffee table decorated with white candles and a stack of books sat between them. A black glass-front cabinet lined the opposite wall next to the windows, which were now framed with long white curtains.

"It's amazing," Danny said.

"Masculine enough for you?" Tessa asked.

Danny chuckled and decided to test what he considered the most important part of the room, the sofa. He sat down on the gray cushions and immediately gave the couch a thumbs-up.

"It's comfortable, that's what I care about. And, there's no pink."

Maya jumped onto the sofa beside Danny and began to lick his face. He leaned back into the cushions as the dog climbed into his lap.

"Maya get down from there," Tessa said. "You're not a lap dog. And we don't need you tearing up the new couch."

"It's fine," Danny said, scratching the dog's ears. "I don't mind."

The dog nuzzled Danny's face and began to lick his hair.

"Alright, alright, that's enough," he said. "I don't need you washing my hair."

He pushed Maya off the couch and tried in vain to smooth his unruly hair back into place.

Amanda sat down next to him. "So you do like the room?"

"Yeah, it looks great. Love it."

"It was fun to do."

"For you two. For me it would have been hell."

"Well, as soon as we get your credit card again we'll start on the bedroom," Tessa said.

Danny chuckled. "Let me pay for this first, okay?" He patted the couch, gesturing for Maya to come back over to him. "You know, I was thinking while Maya and I were walking, maybe I'll get a dog."

"Really?" Tessa asked.

"Yeah. I've always liked dogs. Caroline and I were going to get a dog before.." Danny paused and cleared his throat. "Before she died," he said, forcing himself to say the words.

"I think it's a great idea," Amanda said. "You should go to the animal shelter. Get a rescue dog."

"I think I'd like to get a mutt."

"That would suit you," Tessa said.

Danny grinned. "I think so too." He got up from the couch and walked across the room to the TV. "Can I buy you ladies dinner after all this work you did for me?"

"That's okay," Amanda said. "I actually have to get going. I'm covering for my boss tonight."

"And I need to go too. I have a date," Tessa said.

"A date?" Danny asked. "I thought you'd sworn off men."

"Maybe I changed my mind. And besides, it's just dinner. And I'll take a rain check on your offer."

"Fair enough."

Danny walked Tessa and Amanda to his front door. "Thanks again, ladies. I'll let you know when I can afford your services again."

"Don't wait too long. That bedroom of yours is depressing as hell," Tessa said.

Danny chuckled and closed the door behind him, giving Maya one last pet before he did. He walked back to the sofa and sunk down on it, marveling in how much the room had changed in just 24 hours. He couldn't deny it actually felt like a home now. It was a room Caroline would have approved of.

Danny glanced at the coffee table, remembering the stack of mail he had tossed onto it when he and Maya had first returned home. He picked up the stack and leafed through it, finding the usual assortment of catalogs, bills, and credit card offers.

At the bottom of the stack, a post card caught his attention. And sent a chill down his spine.

It was a photo of a snow covered square in St. Petersburg, Russia. Danny flipped it over, noticing the postmark was several weeks old. A message was written in blue ink, with a clear and precise hand. There was no salutation.

"I was so glad to read in the Daily News Miner that you had escaped from your predicament at Snow Creek. Did you ever think more about the ending of the movie I mentioned to you?"

Danny stopped reading and looked up, searching his memory before it came to him. The Silence of the Lambs.

"Doctor Lector told Agent Starling that he wouldn't bother her, as the world was more interesting with her in it. I understand now what he meant. I wish you well, Detective. And Katerina sends her regards."

Danny put down the postcard, his friends and his newly decorated room now forgotten. He leaned back on the couch and looked outside as if in a fog. He stared out through the white curtains that now adorned his windows and saw large white flakes falling from the sky.

An early spring snow had started to fall.

Julie A. Flanders

Polar Night

CPSIA information can be obtained at www.ICGtesting.com
Printed in the USA
LVOW130039180413

329509LV00001B/94/P